Editor: Caroline Palmier—Love & Edits

Cover Designer: Melissa Doughty—Mel D. Designs

Formatting: Cathryn Carter—Format by CC

———

Copyright © 2024 by Erin Mackenzie

All rights reserved.

No part of this book may be reproduced in any form or by any electronic or mechanical means, including information storage and retrieval systems, without written permission from the author, except for the use of brief quotations in a book review.

This novel is entirely a work of fiction. The names, characters, and incidents portrayed in it are the work of the author's imagination. Any resemblance to actual persons, living or dead, events or localities is entirely coincidental.

the PLAYBOOK

BOOK THREE OF THE

OUT OF BOUNDS

SERIES

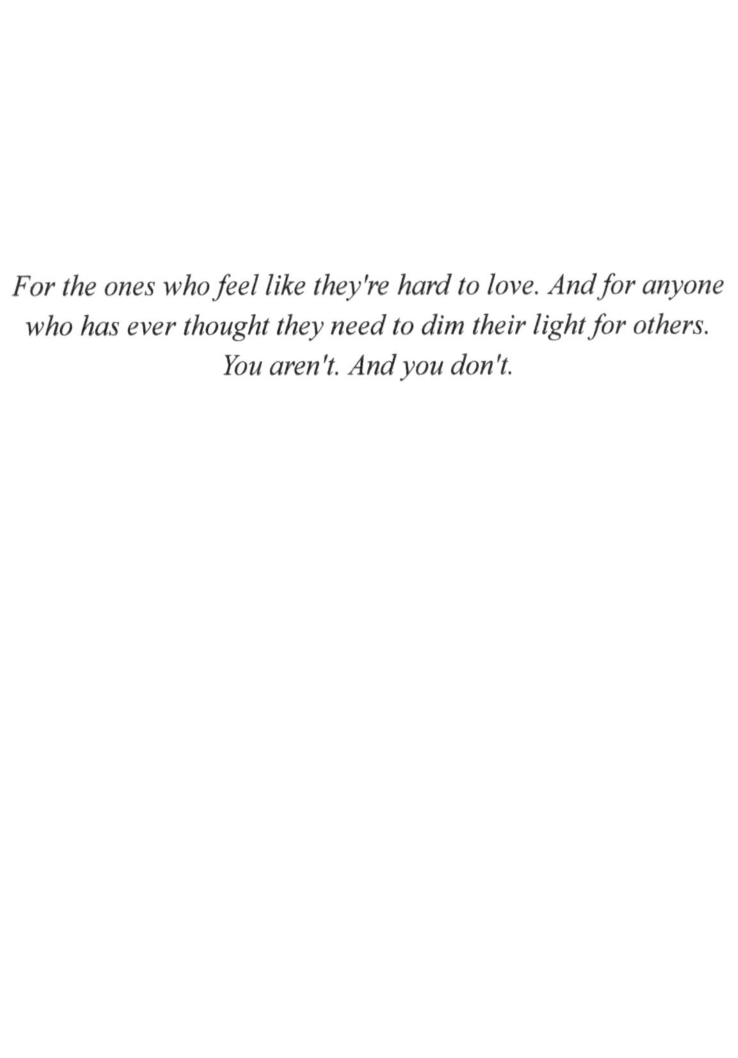

For the ones who feel like they're hard to love. And for anyone who has ever thought they need to dim their light for others. You aren't. And you don't.

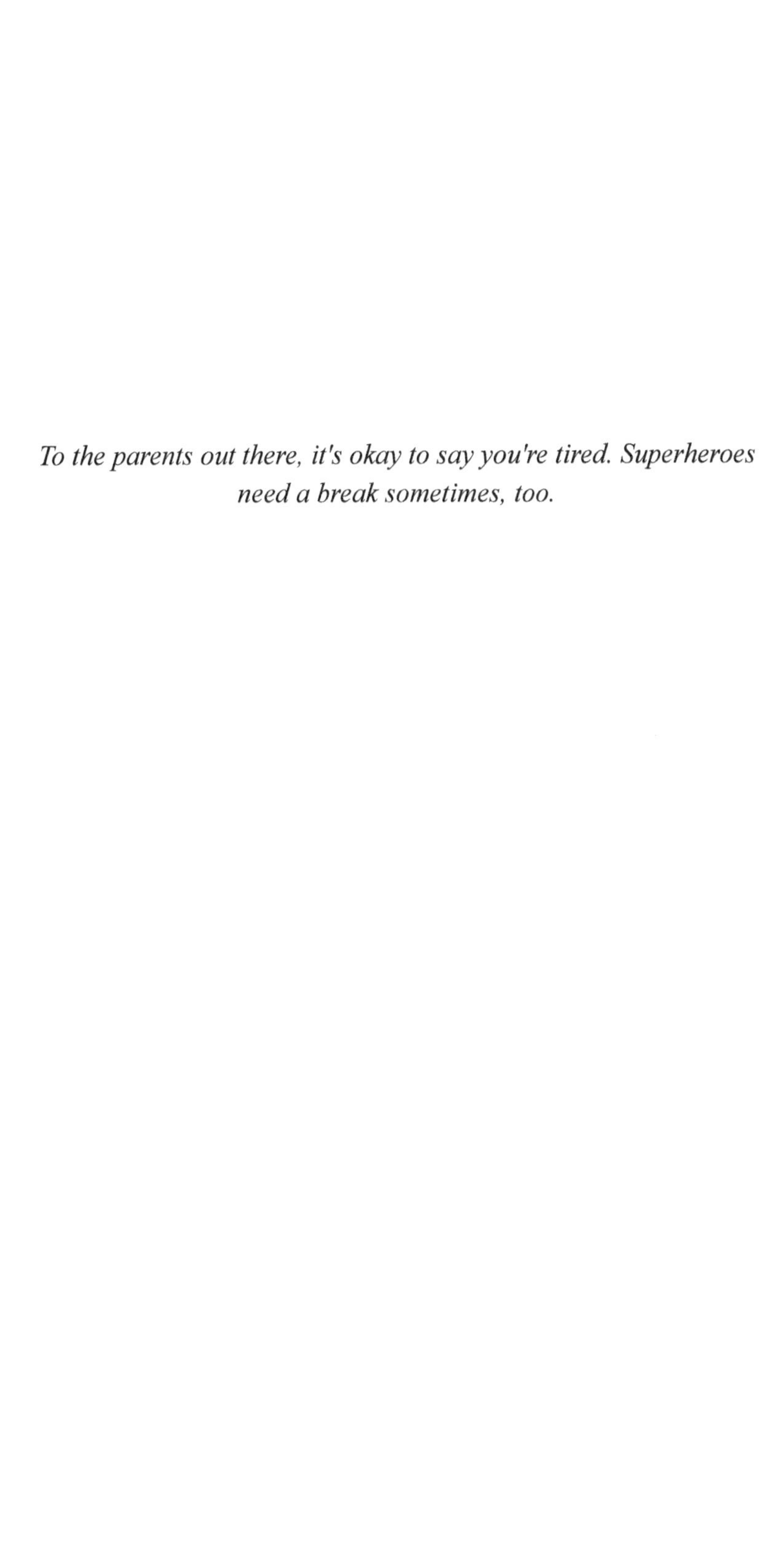

To the parents out there, it's okay to say you're tired. Superheroes need a break sometimes, too.

A NOTE FROM THE AUTHOR

Please note *The Playbook* does discuss the issues of infertility and death of a parent. Readers who find these topics sensitive should be advised.

CHAPTER ONE

CHASE

"Shit!"

There's a loud crack outside of the training facility that makes my body coil together. I've been able to hear the rain for hours, but the addition of booming thunder is new and jolts me out of my daze as I'm taking a knee on the sidelines.

Practicing indoors is never something I enjoy, I always prefer our outdoor field since it helps prepare me for the most realistic conditions during an actual game. But with the way the rain has been coming down all day, there was really no other option but to bring it inside.

The thunder cracks again as I pick my helmet up from the ground and stand. My knees ache with each step I take. Some days, my body makes me think I'm getting too old for this game, but my mind swiftly tells the achy joints to suck it up.

I feel lucky that in all my years playing football—college and high school included—I've never had an injury so bad that it took me out for multiple games. Sure, I've experienced bumps and bruises, a pulled muscle or two. Hell, if you're not getting beat up on the field, you're probably not doing your job. And doing our job is the one thing that Coach Aarons drills into us each day. In the last couple of years—he's become less tolerant of bullshit and a lot more business-minded. I get it, at the end of the day this is a business, it's just a shift from previous years where he seemed to be more lenient.

A quiet groan leaves my chest when I look ahead, noticing two of the interns at the double doors that lead out of the indoor facility and into the main building. They both stand there, eagerly waiting for each of us to walk by, holding their tiny microphone right outside the doors. Another day, another ridiculous question they poll us on for the Knights social media page.

I understand a social media presence is important for a team, but the media side is the one thing about this life I can't fucking stand. I'm not showy and I have zero interest in making myself into some internet click bait story. It's nothing against the girls who make the posts, I'm sure they're all nice enough, it's merely a me thing. Sometimes, I can skirt by them and get in unnoticed. When we're outside it's so much easier, but these doors are the only way in and way out.

"What have you got for us today?" Liam Evans, our quarterback, asks, smiling at the two wide eyed interns, and they blush at the sound of his voice.

One of the girls clears her throat before she speaks, but her voice cracks a bit and she giggles before starting over. It takes everything in me not to roll my eyes.

Women are constantly tongue-tied around Liam Evans. He's a handsome guy, tall and a great athlete, so I suppose I get it. He's the kind of guy who likes to take up space, he enjoys being the one people talk about. Going out and being in the spotlight is something he thrives off of, the exact opposite of myself. He doesn't even have to say much; his game can speak for itself, honestly. It amazes me sometimes that we're actually friends— good friends—because half the time when he talks I want to knock his teeth in. He reminds me of the little brother I never had.

"Who on the team would you let date your sister?" the short redhead asks when she regains her composure. She then points the microphone at me and Liam awaiting our reply. My head shakes back and forth just as Ford, my brother-in-law and teammate, walks up behind me.

"Yeah, Hunt, who on the team would you let date your sister?" Ford gives me a shove before he walks by, able to bypass the question himself.

"I have no sisters, but if I did, there's not a guy on this team I'd let near her," Liam says, cocking an eyebrow.

"My sister is married to Anderson, so I'd have to go with him. Although, *let* is kind of a loose term. I mostly tolerate it." I nod my head toward the doors Ford just walked through, giving him an amused smirk.

When I found out my sister was seeing Ford, I definitely could have reacted better. It was a combination of shock and anger that came out in giving both of them the cold shoulder for weeks. I was pissed Abby would go behind my back and I was pissed Ford was hooking up with my little sister. It wasn't my finest moment, but I see now what they have. What they've had for years. He protects her, he loves her, and he's completely committed to her. She's happy and that's all that I can ask for.

Both girls gawk at me as if I've just given them the juiciest news they've heard all day. It's no secret my sister is married to my teammate, but clearly it still carries a shock factor. I nod at the girls and pivot past them. I can hear their voices whispering as I open the doors, but I can't make out their words. Not that I have any interest in what they're saying anyway.

"You just gave them something to talk about for the rest of the day," Liam says with a husky whisper as we walk down the hall.

The walls on the way to the locker room are filled with newspaper articles and photos of all our team's success over the last couple of years. A constant reminder of the greatness that we should be seeing this season, only we aren't. This season has been tough. We haven't been playing our best, making bullshit mistakes and too many guys are getting hurt, causing backups to fill in who are inexperienced when it comes to live game play.

The Halloween decorations that were up just a week ago are coming down to make room for the Christmas ones that will take their place. It's hard to believe it's already the first week of November and that only adds pressure to the season, knowing it's almost over and we're not in a position we want to be in. We're nowhere near the position we *should* be in. Aside from guys getting hurt—which, in most cases, is beyond our control—it's all things we can work on. We all have shit we're dealing with outside of the field. We all have a home life and personal things that are important, but we're on this team to do a job and some days it feels like no one wants to do it.

Once I'm showered and changed from practice, I immediately feel ready to get home. My knees are still giving me trouble and I'm fucking gassed from a tough day of practice.

"Can I convince you to come to the hockey game tonight? Dunn gave us these." Nate Campbell—one of my closest friends and our running back on the team—waves four tickets in my face. He puts them back into his jeans pocket before pulling his hair back with a blue scrunchie, no doubt belonging to his wife, tying it in a low bun. In all the years I've known Nate, he's had short hair, so this is a new look for him.

"Can't." I brace for the follow up questions that are sure to come.

"We haven't been to a hockey game in years, come on," Nate urges.

I shake my head at Nate and quickly finish putting my clothes in my bag before he can say anything else to try and sway me.

"Not going to happen." My mouth forms a firm line and I grab my duffel bag, hauling it on my shoulder.

"I'm afraid you're going to forget what it feels like to be around a woman other than your sister and this guy's wife." Liam jerks his thumb in Nate's direction. "We can even go to a bar afterward."

"Funny," I answer flatly, tossing a towel into the laundry bin nearby.

"Hey." Liam walks up closer to me just as I'm about to leave, practically cornering me. "I'm just fucking with you, but it wouldn't hurt to make some time for yourself, man. I know I don't know the first thing about being a dad. All we're saying is, we know it's been a while since you've let yourself have some fun."

My definition of fun has drastically changed in the last few years. Fun for me now is defined by early bedtimes and documentaries. It's finding out that my three-year-old did not, in fact, eat the last Fudgsicle and I can enjoy it while learning about different whale species on a Saturday night.

"You guys go have fun," I say as I walk out, not acknowledging the first half of Liam's comment.

It's more of a hassle than anything to even attempt a night out anyway. I'm not interested in trying to make extra arrangements for someone to watch CeCe when I'm already away from her all day long, just for me to have beers and watch hockey. I can do that on my couch after I've tucked my daughter into bed.

My friends understand my situation, but it doesn't stop them from trying to get me to go out with them whenever the occasion arises. They knew me "pre-dad" and have seen it all unfold over the last few years. From the moment I found out I was going to be a dad, to now, and everything in between. It isn't that I don't want to go out and have some time to myself, I just can't. The guilt creeps in any time I even think about doing something.

I'm the only parent CeCe has around, and I refuse to spend extra time away from her for things that aren't important. When Kristen left shortly after CeCe was born three years ago, I made a promise to myself. A vow to keep my vision on track and keep my family at the forefront of what's important. CeCe would never have to wonder about me or my priorities because she *is* my priority. I know my friends understand that.

I may be a single man, but I don't have the luxury of a single life anymore. My responsibilities are all waiting for me at home. I'd be lying if I said I didn't miss the company of a woman at times, but I don't even allow my mind to wander long enough to those thoughts to let them have any control over me. I'm a different man now. Some people choose to use words like uptight or overprotective, I've even been told I'm downright rude once or twice. But I had to grow up. I had to take on the role of two parents for my child and I'm doing it the best way I know how.

Adding responsibilities to my plate isn't something new to me—I became the man of my house when my father died years ago, constantly making sure my mother and sister were taken care of. And once I had CeCe, my role as a provider only intensified.

I choose to be direct and upfront with people about what's important in my life. I look at CeCe and there hasn't been a single moment that I regret anything, not a single moment that I haven't wanted exactly this. CeCe is the very best part of me.

I won't be another person who fails her.

I never expected to be doing this parenting thing on my own. None of this is how I expected it to be. I always assumed one day I'd get married and children would follow, not a casual hookup buddy turned into a half ass relationship, followed by becoming a single dad. In the end, Kristen didn't want to be with me and that's fine. But the fact that she doesn't want *her*? It's a cruel reality I'll never understand.

———

When I get home, before the door is even closed behind me, I can hear the pitter patter of little feet running toward me. The screams of excitement and the happy laughter get closer, a warning that CeCe is about to barrel right into me. Just as I put my bag down, the sight of a blue princess dress comes into view.

"Daddy!"

"Hey, Peanut," I say as she flies into my leg, gripping it tightly. I bend down to pick her up, kissing her head before pulling back and smiling. She smells like cinnamon, a clear indication that she's been doing something in the kitchen with my sister. CeCe's honey colored hair sticks to my beard and I wipe some kind of batter off of her cheek.

"What's going on here?" I ask Abby as I walk us both into the kitchen.

"We made snickerdoodle cookies." My sister smiles, wiping her hands with a dish towel. "Well, I made them, CeCe was more of a... taste tester, if you will." She laughs and places the towel on the counter.

It ended up being a blessing in disguise that my sister moved here a few years ago. And an added blessing that she has so much flexibility in her schedule to help me with CeCe as often as she does. She recently stopped teaching kindergarten to focus more on the downtown Recreation Center that she and Ford invest so much of their time and funds into. Our mom doesn't live nearby so Abby has really stepped into the role of being my primary helper for CeCe. I've had a few teammates suggest hiring a nanny, but I've heard fucking horror stories about stolen items, them not showing up, and even the occasional one who tries to make a move on an unsuspecting single dad. No fucking thank you. Those are all things I'm not interested in dealing with. Abby's been a lifesaver and CeCe loves spending time with her.

CeCe wiggles out of my arms and runs down the hallway toward her bedroom, closing her door only to whip it open not a minute later and come running back with a piece of paper in her hand.

"For you," she says sweetly, giving me the smile that's had me wrapped around her finger since the moment she was born. One little dimple and squinty eyes as she beams up at me.

"Wow. What is this right here?" I ask, pointing to a giant blob of pink, purple and sparkly blue crayon.

"It's a unicorn!" CeCe shouts, as if it's obvious.

"Oh, right, okay, I see it now. Great job! But hey, we need to leave for gymnastics soon, go get your leotard out. I'll be right there to help you."

"Yeah, Chase, that's a unicorn," Abby teases, pointing at the drawing.

I smile at my sister and lean against the counter while she cleans up.

"Thanks for today." I finally let an exhausted yawn leave my chest.

"No problem. Also, she mentioned her ear hurt. No fever or anything, I checked. She's acting totally normal."

I always feel a rush of panic whenever CeCe says something hurts or she doesn't feel good. It makes me question everything we did the previous day, things she ate, who she saw. All trying to jog my brain and figure out what could be wrong.

"Okay, I'll keep an eye on it. Thanks. What would we do without you?" I cross my arms over my chest.

"Who knows?" she jokes. "I'm sure one of these days you'll have to figure it out."

The smallest hint of annoyance creeps up my neck thinking of a day where someone other than my sister or mother watches my daughter, but I quickly remind myself Abby has her own life and her own responsibilities. The fact that she's helped me as much as she has already is more than I could have ever expected.

My thoughts are put on hold when I hear myself being summoned from the back bedroom.

"Daddy!"

I move to make my way down the hall only to see CeCe walk out of her room before I get there with her leotard on wearing a proud smile.

"I did it!"

One of the shoulder straps on the pink and orange leotard is slightly falling, but CeCe pulls it back up and gives me a thumbs up. When I smile, she does a twirl and nearly loses her footing but catches herself on the wall before she bursts out in a fit of laughter. She runs past me and back toward Abby, lunging into her arms.

"Should we fix your hair before you leave?" Abby reaches for the small hair tie on the counter and splashes a bit of water on her hand before she smooths out the wild strands of CeCe's hair. All the while, CeCe's brown eyes are focused on the coloring book she swiped from the counter, flipping through the pages to seemingly admire her own work.

The other day, CeCe asked me to braid her hair. A question I should have expected, but was dreading all the same. Another little girl in her class had her hair braided and CeCe couldn't wait to get home and ask me for one. It felt like a punch in the gut when I had to tell her I wasn't sure how to do one and she looked at me with the saddest eyes before telling me, "it's okay." I assured her that I'd learn, though; so every night before I've gone to sleep, tutorial videos have been my best friend. I grabbed one of her dolls to test it out on, but turns out it's just as confusing as I thought it would be. I'll get the hang of it, but fuck, if it isn't one of the more confusing things I've had to learn.

"I'm going to take some of these cookies home for Ford, but there are some already in the blue jar. You can save the rest in the freezer so they don't go bad," Abby says, gathering cookies from the sheet and placing them into a Ziploc bag.

"Okay, thanks. CeCe, what do we say to Aunt Abby before she leaves?"

CeCe thanks my sister and gives her a giant hug and kiss before she goes back in her bedroom to get her shoes and we head out ourselves.

A few months ago, I wanted to get CeCe signed up for some kind of sport or activity since she isn't in school just yet and figured it would be good for her. As I expected, gymnastics is a huge hit. She gets excited to try new things and I love that I can sit and watch her learn. It's mostly the moms there and I know CeCe notices that. For being only three years old, she's incredibly perceptive. Some days, the things her imagination comes up with or the questions her little brain decides to ask, floor me.

As I'm watching her from the window at gymnastics, I see her eyes searching for me from the gym floor. When she finds me, her thumb, index, and pinky finger go up. I bring my fingers up in front of the glass mimicking the gesture for her to see and her face lights up.

It's a relief to me that she's so outgoing. She loves being around people. She loves talking and singing and dancing. She enjoys making friends and being social. A massive contrast from me.

I'll be the first to admit I can be untrusting, even dull at times, but every decision I have made in the last three years has been for the benefit of my daughter. I shed so much of the person I used to be, I don't even recall much about that man. The only thing that matters right now is CeCe.

CHAPTER TWO

SUMMER

"So, what are you getting at?" My eyes narrow as my boyfriend gets out of my bed.

He leans forward and runs his hand under my chin, a gesture that I think he believes to be sweet or romantic, but I actually find it incredibly uncomfortable. Like he's purposely pointing out my double chin when he does it.

Drew starts pulling his scrubs over his shoulders while I sit on my bed covered by a sheet as the rain falls outside my window. It feels every bit like I'm in some early 2000's pop music video.

The two of us hadn't spent the night together in weeks and last night really was no different. It felt platonic… at best. We cuddled and I made it very clear I wanted more, *needed* more, but he wouldn't budge. I would never force it. I've always been the one with the bigger appetite in our relationship, but aside from that, something felt off. And not just last night or this morning, but for weeks. Not feeling desired or wanted in a relationship feels every bit as crappy as one would assume.

On paper, Drew and I make sense. He's about to officially

become a doctor and I'm currently a pediatric nurse. We both work at the same hospital and have nearly identical shifts. We care deeply about our jobs and we're both good at what we do. But outside of the fluorescent lights and sterile gloves, we couldn't be more different.

He's Dockers and cufflinks, weekends spent at conferences and constantly being *on*. While I live in the moment more, and I don't feel like being a nurse defines every part of me. That's my job, yes, but it's not who I am.

To his credit, when we first started dating, I do think I fit his picture of what he wanted in a partner. I was eager to begin working in the hospital and I let that excitement consume me at first, which is probably what he liked. It's almost as if the more he got to know me, the less he liked me.

"I've got to be at the hospital in thirty minutes, I don't think we have time to dive into everything right now." Drew pulls the drawstring on his pants, tightening them as he walks toward the bathroom.

I can hear the water running and the sound of him brushing his teeth. What the hell does he mean we don't have time to dive into everything? How much could there possibly be to discuss?

Swinging my legs over the side of the bed, I toss a tank top over my bare chest and throw some shorts over my underwear before getting up. A quick chill runs down my spine when he reenters the bedroom.

"You just told me things between us have changed and I agree things do feel different. But shouldn't you elaborate? Shouldn't we discuss this?"

My fingernails feel like they're digging into my hips while I stand there in front of him. I'm no idiot, I can see where the conversation is going and I don't have any objections as to how it ends, but be a fucking man and spit it out.

"Why don't we have lunch together later and we can discuss it then?"

"No. We need to talk and I think we should do it now. I think I know what you're going to say and I… I agree with you. Things are different and it's not fair to either of us."

His head lowers slightly, reaching for my hand and like a complete fool I let him take it.

"I just don't want to waste time anymore. I'm about to really settle into my career and I'm looking for someone serious. I'm ready for a wife, Summer. I hope you don't take this the wrong way, but I just need someone who is ready for those things."

My mind is saying a thousand words, but none seem to leave my lips as I stand there.

"You've been a lot of fun, but I can't do this anymore. It's too hard to change who you are and I need someone serious, someone who wants the same things I do. And I think we both know you aren't ready for marriage, you have a lot of growing up to do."

I was fine with everything he said up until the last part. I understand that he's ready for a wife. I'm not there yet. I understand that's why we've been so distant lately, he checked out. I can respect that.

But the last part? *It's too hard to change me? I have a lot of growing up to do?* I don't want to be with someone who wants to change me or make me feel like I'm hard to love. I've been down that road. I've heard the "you're a lot to handle" comments plenty of times and not once have they made me consider changing. I sure as hell won't make the exception today. I would've been fine ending this amicably, I didn't realize we were throwing punches.

"Excuse me?"

"Oh, come on. This can't be a shock."

I pull my hand from his grasp.

"Ending our relationship isn't a shock, no. We should've done it a while ago, honestly. And I'm fine with going our separate ways. But telling me that it's too hard to change me and that

I have a lot of growing up to do is a low blow. Especially for you. I won't change who I am to fit the idea of who you think I should be."

"All you're doing right now is proving my point. You're lashing out and taking this personally." Drew shakes his head as he sits down to get his shoes on.

I haven't moved from the spot in my bedroom, my body literally feels frozen. How else would he like me to take it? He insulted me and I'm supposed to just roll over and take it? Before I can say anything, he lets out a sigh and continues to run his mouth.

"You aren't mature enough for a serious relationship, let alone a marriage. The other day, you asked me to have sex in a damn on-call room, Summer. While we were at work. Are you fucking kidding me?"

I scoff, rolling my eyes at his example.

"First of all, I said I was kidding… and second of all, does the thought of having sex with your girlfriend really disgust you that much? You've barely touched me in weeks."

He stands, rubbing his hands on his blue scrubs as he does. His dark hair is perfectly styled with the most obnoxious comb-over that makes him look ten years older than he actually is. I can't even believe I'm letting myself sit here and get annoyed by this man.

"I'm sorry if I've hurt your feelings, but this"—he gestures between us—"we're over."

Drew pulls his phone from the charger and slides it in the pocket of his white coat he just slid his arms into.

"I look forward to us still having a working relationship, though."

"Oh, lucky me." I lock my eyes on him.

"You're a good nurse, Summer."

"Believe me, I know."

His lips press together, as if forcing them closed not to say anything more before turning his back to me and leaving my bedroom.

My bare feet shuffle across the cool wood floor as I follow him.

I hear the doorknob turn without a word from him and before he officially leaves my apartment, I call his name.

He stops and looks down at me. I let myself study his face for a moment. The face of a cowardly man who was trying to prolong the inevitable today.

"If your *wife* doesn't ask you to have sex in an on-call room, joke or not, your relationship is boring and I stand by that. Have the day you deserve, Dr. McCall," I say quietly, closing the door in his face.

After a break up, I'd normally feel some sadness, regret even or a longing to have them back. Not today, though. I feel relieved. Like a huge weight has been lifted from my shoulders that I didn't actually realize needed to be lifted until thirty minutes ago.

Thank God I don't have to go to the hospital today and see him all over again.

Sundays are for football.

————

"You promised me sunshine and tequila when I said yes to moving here, yet lately, I'm seeing no sunshine and very little tequila." The umbrella pops open in front of me as I'm standing under the covered walkway, ready to trek back through the stadium.

It's now pouring rain and we're trying to make our way back to the family suite. I'm just glad Mia decided to bring the kids to this game, otherwise Abby and Mia would want to be out in this awful rain, sitting in the stands wearing their ponchos like all of the other fans.

"Weather is a fickle little bitch, isn't it?" Abby snarks as she rushes past me. Having her as my best friend for the last twenty years really has been the highlight of my life. And I take comfort in the fact that we are completely filterless with one another.

Her long brown hair is up in a high ponytail and the windbreaker she's wearing bears her last name, Anderson, in big bold letters. She and Ford have been married for just over a year now, but I'm not sure I'll ever get over the fact that she's married to an NFL player.

"I'm going to bust out of these jeans, who let me have so many waffles before we even left the house?" Mia holds her stomach that sports a tiny baby bump. It'll be her and Nate's third, since they already have twin boys, and I think she's already booked Nate's vasectomy.

"Who wears jeans while pregnant?" I ask, as I'm trying to keep pace with two of the fastest women alive. "And why are we running?" I pant out.

"Well, who wears jeans at all these days?" Abby chimes in, pulling the hood over her head as she rushes toward an awning.

"I'm just trying to get out of the rain. Plus, Hannah is with my boys and CeCe in the suite, so I want to get back before they make her pull her hair out." Mia rushes ahead.

Once we're back in Ford and Abby's family suite, I take my coat off and place it on the chair next to the sweetest three-year-old I know. Abby's niece CeCe sits on the big red chair with a large bucket of soft pretzels and a box of apple juice on the tray in front of her. Her hair is up in pigtails with custom made bows, one with the number nine and the other with a seven. She has on the cutest white t-shirt that says, "*Go Daddy!*" on the front with the number ninety-seven on the back.

"Hey, my girl!" I say as I take a seat next to her. I've known

CeCe since she was born and feel an overwhelming sense of protection over her. She's always just been *my girl*.

"Hi!" CeCe smiles, offering me a pretzel as the kickoff happens and we both get settled in for the game.

Watching them play in the rain makes it look ten times more dangerous than it does on your average Sunday. The field is slick and you can tell it's affecting how the game is going. As the day progresses, CeCe and I continue to sit together, cheering for each positive play and yelling at the referees on the bad calls. She huffs and puffs when she hears a penalty called on Chase and her tiny arms cross over her chest.

"Those guys don't know what they're talking about," I whisper, giving her a wink and she smiles at me again.

"Booooo!" CeCe yells, following the crowd as another call doesn't go our way. I always enjoy watching the games with her. I think she understands more than we probably give her credit for. I've always been a football fan, even before my life was so intertwined in it. So, it's fun to see it through her eyes now.

I hear Mia tell the boys for the sixth time to "*sit down and watch Daddy*" but they just turned one and I can't blame them for having no interest in sitting still to watch a game. It amazes me how much energy they have for such little people. I had them sitting on my lap at some point to take some of the chasing off of Mia, but that was short lived.

"Okay. I'm throwing in the towel. I made it to halftime," Mia says, with her hands rifling through the diaper bag. She pulls out two tablets and turns them on. "Don't judge me. I need ten minutes." She sighs heavily.

"Are you kidding? I'm never judging you." I laugh. "I'm in awe of you. You're a superhuman."

I can't help but think of this morning. I have yet to tell the girls what happened, but I already know they'll both be out for blood once I do. It still annoys me to even think about what he said. Although, I am glad we broke up, because I know I didn't picture anything like kids or marriage with him. Even though those are definitely things I want one day, he just wasn't right for me. I'm worth more than just a fun time. With the right person, just as I am, I'll be exactly what someone needs and I'll be good at it.

CHAPTER THREE

SUMMER

Another long shift, another day of actively avoiding seeing my ex. I was doing really well until I needed a consult on one of my pediatric patients and I let my chatty mouth keep me in the room too long.

"Okay, I'll just get going and let Dr. McCall answer anything else. Feel better, Simone," I say, waving to the eight-year-old with a broken arm. Broken bones are a common occurrence for kids, especially those that like to live on the edge a little and give their parents minor heart attacks daily.

As I'm walking out of the room, I walk right into Damien, one of my colleagues and quite frankly, the only person who helps keep me sane most days. This morning, I told him Drew and I broke up simply so he'd help me in avoiding having to be around him much today. I'll be fine as the days go on, but one day apart wasn't enough and I'm already annoyed at his crooked eyebrows and mediocre smile.

"Were you able to avoid the snake today?" Damien asks as we walk together down the hall. Both of our shifts are coming to an end and I couldn't be more thankful for a Monday that flew by like today.

"Mostly. Of course, he had to slither in for the last patient of the day," I say.

"You know you're too good for him, right? Break up or not, I've always thought that. He just has really great hair, that's it. And that's what got you hooked to begin with, wasn't it? The dark locks of glory?"

I laugh at Damien's comment, feeling grateful I have him around to lighten the mood.

"The hair. Definitely." I slowly nod, and he leans down, giving me a hug before he leaves. Even after a twelve-hour shift he still smells utterly incredible. His boyfriend works with a fragrance company so I'm not completely shocked, but whatever he has Damien wearing is definitely long lasting. *Can withstand a twelve-hour hospital shift in the Emergency Room* would be great for marketing.

My phone dings with a text from Abby as soon as I walk in my apartment. Her and I haven't been able to spend as much time together as we'd like just due to your basic adulting, aside from Sundays at the football stadium or someone's house for an away game.

ABBY

I'm starting to think I'll never see two pink lines. Another negative

I sigh at the text message, not even knowing what to say anymore. My heart hurts for her and Ford. I wish I had the words to say that would comfort her or some kind of advice to be able to give that might help make her situation easier, but there isn't anything I can do to ease the pain she feels.

I'm sorry this has been so tough. I love you

I've learned in the last year as Abby's shared more on the ins and outs of what she and Ford are going through that she doesn't want my two cents. She doesn't want someone to sit here and tell her not to stress over it. She doesn't want to hear that everything happens for a reason, or it'll happen when it's supposed to happen. She's tired of being told to "just have a lot of sex" or the "when it's meant to be, it'll be" cliché. She doesn't need to hear that. My job is to love her and support her, no matter what. All she needs to know is that I'm here, for the good and the bad and the uncertain.

Tossing my purse on the bar stool, I turn the light in the kitchen on. I barely had time to eat today and a granola bar with a string cheese is definitely not substantial enough to last me much longer.

Although, reality sets in when I realize that I've been neglecting my apartment for the last few days and my refrigerator reminds me that it's bare when it makes a sad, creaking noise as I open it. I could be upset by this or I could look at it as an opportunity to get tacos for dinner from the food truck outside my building.

I pass it nearly every day and there's always the sweetest older man sitting at one of the picnic tables right beside it. I have no idea if he works at the truck, owns it, or if he's just a frequent visitor, but he smiles every single day, rain or shine.

Instead of waiting for the elevator, I opt for the stairs on the way down. Stairwells usually freak me out, and this one is no different. It always feels like the walls around me are closing in and like some crazy horror movie, the door I'm trying to exit will be locked and then when I go back up to the door I came from, that one will mysteriously be locked too. And then I'm trapped in a stairwell, left to fight for my life. It's incredibly far-fetched, I realize that. My mind just likes to make up bizarre scenarios that I'll most likely never be in, but somehow need to be prepared for.

"Can I please have two of the Carne Asada tacos and a side of chips and salsa?" I hand the woman my debit card and glance to my left, seeing the same old man I've noticed every day before.

She hands me back my card and receipt and I step aside to wait for my order. I'm tempted to strike up a conversation with him, but by the time I convince myself to do it the woman calls my name and my hunger beats any other desire at the moment, causing me to offer him only a smile before taking my food inside.

Again, I opt for the stairs on the way up and immediately regret the decision. I'm winded after two flights and wishing I would've been patient enough to wait for the elevator. When I reach my floor, there's an immediate sigh of relief and I make my way into my apartment and to the living room where I plan to spend the remainder of the evening before I crash out for the night, just to wake up and do it all over again tomorrow.

"If you need anything else, just hit that button and I'll pop back in." I smile as I leave the patient's room.

I don't typically work the night shift, but I'm helping out this evening for another nurse who needed a swap. While the change in pace is nice, I think I'm built for the hustle and bustle of day shift. It's probably why I liked being a bartender for so many years. The constant conversation, always staying busy and occupied. Plus, I usually love being around other people.

"Summer, someone is in the lobby asking for you," another nurse says with a tiny hint of red on her face. "It's for his daughter, but he's um… very handsome." Her eyebrows wiggle, but mine crease in worry. The only handsome man I know with a daughter who would ask for me is Chase.

I rush through the hallway, glad that it's not busy at midnight so that I can get to the lobby quickly. The fluorescent lights feel much brighter at night and I swipe my badge at the double doors seeing Chase through the window cut out with his back toward me holding CeCe in his arms.

When the wooden doors open, I call out his name and he turns around to face me. His brown eyes look heavy and riddled with worry. He's in a pair of black sweatpants and a Knights t-shirt. His hair covered by a baseball hat and a hard-set jaw directed right at me.

"What happened?" I ask, instinctively rubbing CeCe's back and taking a look at her face. She feels warm to the touch.

The instant relief that covers his face when he sees me makes my heart flutter.

"She's had a fever for hours, I can't get it down with any of the medicine I've tried. She keeps saying her ear hurts but I can't see a goddamn thing. Abby mentioned the other day she said her ear hurt, but she was acting fine then, no fever." He pauses. "I'm surprised you're even here, I didn't know if it was too late to text you. And then when I got here, I figured I was taking a chance asking for you." He blinks his eyes hard a couple times, squeezing them shut, almost to try and make himself appear more alert. "I wouldn't normally bring her in, but the fever..." He trails off, looking embarrassed, but I shake my head at him.

"No, no, it's fine to bring her in. Let's get her triaged and see what's going on." He follows me down the hall and into the pediatric department of the ER.

Chase lays CeCe down on one of the beds, and I take a seat next to her as he paces the room. His hand squeezes the back of his neck and his head falls back, almost in defeat, or exhaustion. Possibly both at this point.

"Hi, my girl. What's going on?"

She looks up at me and pulls at her ears. CeCe has soft brown eyes just like Chase's. Sometimes they look so golden and warm. God, she looks *so* much like him.

"Both of them hurt?" I ask.

She gives me a small nod as I stroke her cheek.

"Okay, we'll take a look and get you feeling better so you and Daddy can go home and back to bed, okay?"

As I stand, I see Chase is still pacing and breathing heavily around the room. It's no surprise seeing him so distraught over CeCe being here and not feeling well.

"I'm going to grab her water and we'll check her ears. It's probably an ear infection, Chase. They're really common with kids," I whisper.

"I've been giving her water all night, it's not helping." There's an edge in his voice. Frustration. But I don't take it personally.

"Okay, well, I'm going to grab her a water and get a more comfortable chair in here for you and we'll get her fever down," I say softly, realizing he hasn't looked at me the entire time I've been talking to him.

"I don't need a different chair," Chase says with clenched teeth just as I'm turning to leave the room but I ignore him. The chair is so he will sit down and relax for a few minutes so CeCe doesn't see him leaving footprints all over my ER with all of the worry pacing he's doing.

"Who is that?" Angie asks when I get back to the front desk.

I sigh at her question because there are so many ways I can answer this. The simplest and less embarrassing way is simply that I'm friends with his sister. Or, I could opt for a little more detail and say he's an old friend of mine from childhood. The third and much more complicated description would probably sound something like, he's the guy I've loved since I was a teenager and despite trying to forget about him, all I've been able to do in the last decade is find more things to love about him. I don't have the energy tonight to delve into anything specific, so option one it is.

"Oh, and you said he plays for the Knights? That's why he's so... big," Angie sighs like she has hearts in her eyes when she looks over at him and the territorial side of me wants to growl and show my teeth. I've been the President of the Chase Hunt Fan Club for years and I don't take well to others wanting my spot.

Chase "overprotective and incredibly too handsome" Hunt.

If I could remember a time I didn't have feelings for Chase, I'd lock into that moment and try to make it happen again. But I can't. Because ever since I understood the premise of having genuine, romantic feelings for someone, my sights have been set on Chase.

I met him when I was five, he was my first crush when I was ten. I first saw him as a man when I was sixteen—he was pulling his hair into a backward hat while playing beach volleyball, and that pretty much sealed the deal. I remember in the summer he would drive me and Abby around to the movies or to the beach. I remember every time he'd have a girlfriend in the passenger's seat, I'd secretly be plotting her demise. It was always one of those harmless crushes that I think everyone just assumed would go away. It was never a secret; I was always very vocal about my feelings for Chase. *Mrs. Chase Hunt* was written in probably every notebook I've ever owned. When he was leaving for his senior prom was the first time I put lipstick on, hoping in some delusional way that would make him look at me as something more than his little sister's best friend.

And now, he's a dad and he's in the NFL and he's grown up to be this really amazing man and the crush I think everyone— myself included—assumed would fade, only intensified. I still look at Chase like he's hung the moon, even after all these years. And as he stands in the doorway of my ER giving me a scolding look as he watches two men carry a bigger, more comfortable chair into his daughter's room, I wonder if that'll ever go away.

"Summer!" he says with chomped molars when I walk by, and I happily stop at the door. "I said I didn't need another chair."

"I think you mean *thank you*, and with that I'll say *you're welcome.*" I smile and walk past him to where CeCe is sitting up on the bed.

"Hey," I say softly, taking a seat next to her.

She smiles at me just as the night shift doctor comes into the room and introduces himself. I rarely work with him, since I'm on the day shift, but he's quick and professional, exactly what Chase needs right now. He pulls out his stethoscope and explains to CeCe and Chase that he'll just take a quick listen to her breathing. I give him space, but stay close by and continue smiling and nodding at her as her sweet brown eyes look to me for assurance. He then takes a look in her ears and I hear him make a humming sound as he does, causing Chase's head to pop up.

"She has a double ear infection, but this happens with kids, it's common. It's what's causing her fever. Antibiotics will help clear it up," he tells Chase before he swiftly leaves the room as if he were never there. I nod in the doctor's direction and stand to type information into her chart.

Chase sighs, still on his feet, probably making a stand against sitting in the more comfortable chair I arranged for him.

Before I walk out, I nod at him to follow me to the doorway.

"Listen, Chase. I get you're… *you.* But I'm here to help, I'm trying to help, so let me do that. Believe it or not, I'm very good at my job. Rave reviews from all the kids." I prop a hand on my hip and the smallest bit of a smile tries to creep up on his face before he quickly looks annoyed again. I get that nobody wants to spend their evening in an ER, but for what it's worth, he's making record time being in and almost out. "If you would relax for five seconds, you'd see that CeCe is okay. She's resting, in fact, and I'm going to get your discharge papers and everything settled now. Happy thoughts, Chase." I tap his forearm lightly, knowing it'll affect me far more than it annoys him.

"Are you this demanding with all of the parents who bring their kids in?" His arms cross over his chest as he stands in front of me like some kind of bouncer at a club. Although, he doesn't intimidate me.

I smirk, beginning to take a step back. "Only when they're being a pain in the ass."

CeCe sits up when I walk back into the room barely ten minutes later, poor kid still looks exhausted, but at least she's on her way to feeling better.

I wave at her when I notice that Chase is passed out in the chair I brought him. I should really take a picture to prove to him that I was right and he was wrong.

"Daddy's tired," she whispers when I sit down next to her. She stares at him for a moment before looking back at me. For a three-year-old, sometimes I think she's wise beyond her years. Her daddy *is* tired. But he'd never want her to know that.

"Maybe he just needed a quick nap, but I bet he's excited to get you home."

"Daddy," CeCe says seconds later.

When I look up, Chase's eyes are open and he stands immediately.

"Wow, really lucky you had that chair, right?" I tease before handing him the discharge paper. "She's going to be fine, Chase. You can take her home." I smile softly, letting my eyes linger on a very tired, but very good dad standing across from me.

"Thanks," he breathes out.

CHAPTER FOUR

CHASE

Last night was the longest night I've had with CeCe since she was a baby. I can't help but feel a little ridiculous taking her into the emergency room for an ear infection, but I was out of options and running on no sleep.

By the time we finally got back home and she got settled into bed, it felt useless for me to try and sleep so I stayed up watching a documentary on the animal channel about sea lions. I fully expected for it to put me to sleep, but it managed to keep my attention and I now know a ton of facts about them I'm sure I'll never need.

My sister's knock on the front door stirs me out of my thoughts as I stand against the kitchen island holding a room temperature cup of coffee.

"You look like hell… did you sleep at all?" Her steps slow with each one she takes toward me.

"Barely. I brought CeCe to the ER. She has a double ear infection so I was up all night just making sure she was okay."

"Oh no, really?" Abby reaches into the cabinet pulling out a coffee mug for herself. It's the green one with a sloth on it that I found at the dollar store. CeCe thought it was funny, so I had to buy it.

"Summer was actually there."

"Well, yeah. She works at the hospital, you knew that."

"Yeah, I just didn't expect to see her there so late." My fingers pinch the bridge of my nose as I recall our conversations last night. "She's a real piece of work," I say. "But she was helpful and I—well, CeCe, I think appreciated her help, so I'm glad she was there."

"Imagine that," Abby remarks and sets her cup down on the island.

I had half a mind to call my coach and explain the situation to him and why I needed to stay home with CeCe today. I know he'd understand if I need to stay home. Despite his all business attitude lately, he constantly preaches that our family and our kids should always be our number one priority. But I know I need this meeting and I know—and trust—that CeCe is in good hands with my sister.

"She's still asleep. With any luck, she'll rest a little longer, but then she needs antibiotics when she wakes up." I slide the bottle to the middle of the kitchen island so she sees it and doesn't forget. Although, my sister's never forgotten anything when it comes to CeCe.

Abby nods and begins to make another pot of coffee so I head down the hall to take a quick shower before I leave. Steam fills the bathroom as I let the hot water run for a few minutes before I get in. Hopefully this will pop some life into me before I have to get going, but I'm not counting on it. A couple of years ago, I got pretty good at running on a few hours of sleep, but CeCe quickly became a great sleeper after she turned one, so my body has become accustomed to the seven hour stretches.

Abby's stirring pancake batter in a bowl when I get back into the kitchen and I grab my keys from the dish on the counter, sliding them in the pocket of my jeans.

"So the antibiotics," I say. "It says the amount on the bottle and there's a syringe in the cabinet you can use to make it easier. And—you know what? I'll just write it down."

I reach into the drawer, grabbing my planner and flipping to today's date, writing down the information I just said aloud.

"Got it," Abby says in a sing-song voice while she waits for the stove top to heat up.

"Thanks, Ab. I'll see you later."

———

"We need to get it the fuck together. I'm tired of losing, man. Three in a row is unheard of around here," Liam says while we stand outside the conference room. Liam's a competitor through and through. He might joke around off the field, but when it comes to the game, he's as serious as they come. It explains why he's been a league MVP and a Super Bowl MVP in past seasons. And unlike me, he loves the public and the media side of things. Truthfully, though, I have no business even being in the public eye. What does someone want with a thirty-two-year-old single dad who watches documentaries in his spare time?

The doors open to the conference room and we all walk in silently. Like kids who know they're about to get reamed out. The room feels like an igloo when I take a seat, causing a chill to run up my spine; although, that could just be from the eerie feeling I have for this meeting. The lights are already dimmed and I see the projector sitting front and center with nearly every single coach and assistant coach in attendance today.

"Take a seat, turn your phones off or put them on silent. Nobody say a fucking word until I'm ready to let you talk, understood?"

A hefty sigh leaves my chest as I glance his way. Coach is about to lay into us today.

I can count on one hand the amount of times over the years

I've seen him look this heated. I can't blame him, but fuck, I'm just not in the mood for it today. Running on no sleep and then being forced to sit in a dark room for a meeting is a risky combination when all I want to do is close my eyes.

Hour three ticks by and I think I've heard one guy cough the entire time. Everyone's too on edge to make a damn sound. Coach Aarons has been playing footage and stopping practically every play to tell us how the high school team down the block would be better suited to play than us right now. Offense, defense, special teams… we weren't impressive on any side of the ball on Sunday and he's making sure we know it.

Almost another hour drags by before we're finally shuffling out of the conference room and I can feel my brain processing everything we just went over. The words "do your job" ring in my ears over and over again as I enter the weight room and see Ford and Nate in the back corner.

The weight room is full this afternoon. Practically every teammate is in here, probably trying to prove to themselves or the coaches that they deserve to be here.

This whole place got a facelift during the offseason and somehow it still smells new, despite the fact that fifty guys sweat in here almost daily. The walls are painted bright red with words like *respect* and *commitment* written on them. Our Knights flags hang from rafters above and there's always some kind of music being played from the speakers. The floor is lined with different workout equipment and machines. Free weights line the west wall and there are a few stationary bikes closer to the entrance. The large garage doors are open today, letting a small breeze in. It feels good, even though I'm sure this is just the calm before the storm.

'Stay healthy' is the phrase I wrote over and over in my notebook today during the meeting. I know that coach is relying on me as a veteran and captain to set the tone for how things continue around here this season. It adds pressure—but it's something I'm trying my best to exemplify for the younger guys.

"I'm heading out," I say to Nate as we're finishing up on stationary bikes. "CeCe's been sick and Abby's been there all day, so I want to get home." Nate and I shake hands and I make my way out into the warm breeze just as it begins to drizzle.

———

The house is quiet when I walk in. Not even the television is on for any kind of background noise, but I know they're here. When I walk around the corner from the foyer and have a sight line to the living room, I can see two adult figures on the couch and then one small ponytail sticking out from one of the blankets. There are pillows all over the floor, an empty bag of popcorn on the end table next to the remote control and a half empty bottle of water. When I get closer, I see Abby's arm outstretched over CeCe, tucking her in close with the pink and white blanket draped over them. On the other end of the couch is a blonde bun nestled in the corner of the couch with a small rose tattoo behind her ear. I know that tattoo. But what is Summer doing here?

Just before I'm about to walk away to shower, Summer's eyes squint open.

"I felt you staring at me," she quips quietly. A tiny smirk peeking at the corners of her lips. I've become almost immune to Summer's comments; they've been coming at me for years.

"I wasn't staring *at* you. I was pondering… wondering what the hell you're doing on my couch," I whisper, nudging her foot under the blanket.

A breath leaves her lips as she wiggles herself out of the blanket, careful not to wake up CeCe or Abby.

"I stopped by to check on CeCe, but then she asked me to stay and watch a movie. It had princesses and talking animals, not sure what it was called. I fell asleep almost immediately."

Summer yawns, and I follow her as she walks into the kitchen as if she lives here and I'm the guest. Her black leggings have a piece of pink string—likely from the blanket, hanging off of her hip with the small of her back slightly exposed as her tank top rides up when she walks.

"Want some coffee?" she asks.

"It's five in the afternoon. If I have a coffee now, I'll be up all night and I'm not in the stage of my life anymore where I can do that two nights in a row. I'm just going to grab some water." My eyes lock with hers for the first time since we've been talking and a sting of regret kicks in.

I should've been kinder to her last night. I shouldn't have been so short tempered and overall just a dick. I'd blame it on my lack of sleep or the fact that I was worried about CeCe, but it's more than that. I've always been like this with Summer. She has this way of always getting under my skin, even when she's being helpful. I can't fucking help it. And I can't pinpoint the reason why I get like this around her.

I've known Summer practically my entire life. She's been my little sister's best friend since the moment they met, subsequently making her a constant in my life. She's loyal, almost to a fault, and one of the few people I know my sister trusts with her life. I'd be lying if I said I didn't care about Summer, because I do. I've always looked out for her, the same as I've done for Abby. But Summer is also impulsive, a little reckless sometimes even. She's challenging and there's always been something that irritates me. I know she enjoys watching me squirm. It's like I can see the devil on one of her shoulders just egging her on.

"As you wish," Summer replies, handing me a water bottle.

CHAPTER FIVE

SUMMER

Chase doesn't make eye contact with me often. In fact, I'm not sure he ever makes eye contact with anyone. But he just held my gaze for a solid five seconds, and I think my heart fell all the way down to my toes. It's hard to tell if he's completely oblivious to his effect on me, if he's ignoring it entirely, or if he actually likes seeing me drool in his presence.

When Chase walks down the hall, I can't help but follow his movements. He's built like a tree—strong and sturdy. *I haven't climbed a tree in years, but I'd make an exception for him.*

His hunter green joggers outline his thighs where I know he sports a tattoo. I've never seen the entire thing; though, I imagine it goes higher than he wants my eyes to see. His arms start to pull his white t-shirt off before he's even in his bedroom, giving me a split second where I get a glimpse of the muscle definition on his back. His broad shoulders take up nearly all the space as he walks through his doorway and I'm practically panting over my cup of coffee.

"Ahem!" Abby comes up beside me, knocking her hip into mine. "Am I interrupting?" she asks in a playful tone.

"Just admiring. The usual," I reply.

I've always appreciated that she's never been weirded out by my everlasting crush on her brother. When we were younger we'd always talk about how much fun it would be if Chase and I were married because that would make us sisters, but truth be told, Abby is already my sister. She's the closest thing I've ever had to a sibling with me being an only child. Having Abby, I never really felt like I missed out on not having a brother or sister. I went on family vacations with them often, we spent holidays together sometimes, and when my parents had to travel for work I'd stay at her house for weeks at a time. All of that time around Chase is likely part of the reason I developed feelings for him, but part of me believes it was inevitable.

"I think I'll get going. I'm sure he saw enough of me last night." I reach for my purse just when he's walking down the hall back into the living room and my thighs press together as he shakes the excess water from his hair. It's like a knee jerk reaction at this point when I see him. Stare, get turned on, leave immediately, and pretend it didn't happen.

Of course he'd come out shirtless and wearing athletic shorts that barely keep his legs contained. Tree trunks, I swear.

"I was just heading out, I'll see you later." I try to rush out but Abby grabs my attention.

"Wait, wait." She waves her hand.

"While you're both here, it's probably good to talk to you at the same time." Abby takes a seat at the kitchen island and Chase follows her lead. I eye her suspiciously before putting my purse down on the white marble counter and leaning my elbows on the cool surface.

"What's up?" Chase asks, taking a sip from his water.

"I don't want to make this into a whole thing, but my schedule is about to change a little, Chase. Although, I'm here to bring you a problem *with* a solution. I'm not totally sure if either of you will go for this. I mean, I didn't really even want to suggest it at first, but I think it's the best option. And well, the solution involves you, Summer, so that's why I need you both here." Abby twists her wedding band on her finger and sighs.

"Okay, so Ford and I were referred to a fertility clinic." She clears her throat before she goes on, and Chase leans over to check that CeCe is still asleep. "We've been trying for over a year to have a baby and it hasn't happened yet, so we're hoping that the doctors will be able to help. We're both in the beginning stages, just getting bloodwork done and I've done an ultrasound, but still need to do a handful of more tests. They're really thorough and it makes me feel hopeful. So far, everything has looked fine, but like I said, there's still a few things to test."

"Okay… and if things look normal so far, what do they think is going on?" Chase leans forward.

Abby sucks in a deep breath before exhaling. "It could mean a number of things. I mean, just because things so far look okay doesn't mean the next test will say the same. I guess right now we still just don't have a reason as to why we aren't getting pregnant. I'm almost wanting something to come back that will give us a reason, you know? Being told it's just unexplained infertility might be harder to wrap my head around. But we'll see with all the testing and then of course, they will have some suggestions either way."

Abby seems optimistic. Even though I know deep down she's anxious about it. I can't even imagine how she's feeling.

"What are their suggestions? If they've told you," I ask.

"There are a number of things we can try, anything from different medications all the way to IUI or IVF. Ford and I both really like the team of doctors we've been seeing, so we feel comfortable and confident in their advice. This office is highly rated and recommended by so many people." The green in Abby's eyes deepen as she looks to her brother. I suspected that she might be seeking out a specialist, but I know this is all new information to Chase.

"I didn't know…" Chase says, almost in a whisper. His

brows crease as he looks up at her and she tilts her head slightly, her lips curving into a small smile. "I'm sorry. I didn't know," he repeats, and it's not lost on me that Abby's eyes are tearing up.

Knowing Abby, telling Chase was probably hard for her. She looks at him and sees her dad. He's a direct reflection of him and I think in some ways sharing that with Chase feels like she's telling him.

"No, it's all right. How could you?" She laughs lightly. "We didn't want to share anything until we had more of an idea on what was going on. But pivoting to my reason for telling you both together... With more testing and the possibility of procedures taking place, I just wanted to make sure you weren't completely blindsided. I know how... *particular* you are, Chase, about who is with CeCe."

I snicker at her word choice, glancing in Chase's direction and he immediately gives me a side eye.

"I'm suggesting that you let Summer help you. She isn't a stranger, she's in the medical field, you know she's good with CeCe." Abby folds her hands in front of her like she's a mediator.

"Summer?" he gapes, jerking his head in my direction, and I can't stop the eye roll from happening. I expected as much.

Abby gives him an encouraging nod.

"I don't know. I can probably figure something else out for the days you aren't free, Ab. No offense, Kincaid," he says, one hand running through his damp hair.

"Your call." I shrug. "But you can trust me, you know. I love CeCe, and if you need the help..." I trail off, watching the wheels internally spin in his head as he thinks about this.

He scoffs, but Abby jumps in.

"He does need the help," she says firmly through a smile.

There's a stress line already forming at the corners of his eyes and a vein in his forehead that might explode if he actually has to agree. And as I'm staring at him, I know he's trying to come to terms with the fact that I'm his best option. He doesn't trust easily—or at all, actually. He has a good reason for it, so I don't blame him. But one of these days, that'll have to change.

"Well, you think about it then," I casually say, grabbing my purse. "I'm a nurse, so I know all the things. Well, not *all* the things, but you know… I know things."

His eyes narrow and I know my poorly worded sentence doesn't give him a whole lot of confidence.

"Let me rephrase that so I sound like a competent adult who is able to watch your child… I'm happy to help. And we both know that this is important for Abby. Don't be stubborn right now."

He knows I'm right. I wouldn't be this pushy with just anyone, but I love Abby and I know how badly she wants this. Helping him out is also in a way helping her. She doesn't need the added stress of trying to cater to her brother's needs all the time.

Both hands skim his hair for the third time and he leans back in the stool as he sighs, nodding his head at Abby and then looking at me.

"So, you'd be like a nanny?" He cringes at the word, and I nearly do the same, shaking my head back and forth.

"No, oh God, no. I have a job that I love and I don't want your money. You let me know when you need help and I'll help. Just like Abby does. I usually know the days I work pretty far in advance, so we'll work it out from there." Feeling Chase's glare nearly burning through me, I risk looking directly at him.

I understand this isn't ideal for him, but he had to know that Abby wasn't a long term solution. Plus, her reason for being unavailable isn't something she can really control. His reservations are warranted, but whatever I need to do to earn his trust, I'll do it. And I really enjoy being with CeCe. She's fun and silly and she's creative and it makes me feel like I can be those things too, even though I'm twenty-eight and should probably be opening up an IRA… or at the very least, figuring out what that is and why I need it.

No one has said a word in what feels like the longest thirty seconds ever and the house is quiet as we're all gathered around the island. Both of us glancing at Abby as if we're waiting for her to say something, anything.

Chase's body is stiff, giving away his reluctance, but this actually might be good for him. It might help him loosen up a little bit and learn to let himself lean on someone else for help every now and then. It might backfire for me, of course. Spending more time around him with my track record will probably only make me fall even more in love with him. But I've grown used to admiring from afar, so what's another decade of being in love with someone I can never have?

"Fine," he says with a sigh. "We'll try it out."

"Great, my next appointment is Wednesday afternoon, so I can be here in the morning and then Summer, if you can take over?" Abby perks up with our verbal agreement in place.

"I'm already off on Wednesday, so… I guess I'll see you then, boss."

"Don't call me that." Chase's head spins so fast to scold me and a feeling of excitement spurs at the edge in his voice.

CHAPTER SIX

SUMMER

I'd love to say I'm excited to clean out my closet this morning, but I'm not. I feel an overwhelming sense of dread knowing that I have to sift through items and decide if I want to save them or donate them. I've been putting this off for weeks, but finally decided today is the day.

Growing up, I've always loved clothes and fashion. I'd spend weekends at the mall and in different boutiques, always looking for something that was a standout piece. My closet and dresser are packed to the brim—explaining why I'm dreading having to sort through everything. My love for clothes hasn't changed with age, but my body has. I'm not ashamed I'm not the same size as I was back in high school; hell, I shouldn't still look like I'm eighteen when I'm closer to thirty.

Having thighs and hips, a bigger bust and maybe a little extra around the edges has never felt like an issue for me. And confidence isn't something I generally lack. I've always embraced the body I was given. Sure, I'm not as thin as Abby or as tiny as Mia, but I've never been those things. I've always been a little taller and curvier, but it wasn't until recently that I started to wonder if maybe that wasn't actually as great as I used to think.

Drew basically stopped touching me toward the end of our relationship and I'd be lying if I said it didn't cross my mind that maybe my body was no longer desirable for him. But I refuse to let the opinion of one very small-minded man dictate how I view my body. If I workout, it's because I like the feeling of it, the high afterward, and the strength I feel. And it will have nothing to do with trying to make someone like him want me.

I've spent all morning tucked away in my closet, barely making a dent, but now that it's nearly two o'clock, I have to get myself ready to head over to Chase's. I've been living in this oversized t-shirt all day and while I wish it were acceptable to walk the streets in this and nothing more, I don't have *that* level of confidence. But as I stand here looking at thousands of dollars' worth of clothing, all I can think of is, wow I have *nothing* to wear.

Sighing, I grab a pair of distressed denim overalls, pulling them up over my thighs before grabbing a yellow tank top and tossing that on as well.

Overalls, I say to myself with a laugh. When was the last time anyone saw me in these?

———

CeCe and I have spent the last hour coloring pictures out of this giant coloring book. When she brought the book out to the living room it was nearly as tall as her. She's so into arts and crafts, which I love. Her creativity is nonstop and her imagination is limitless. I've been around kids so much in the last few years with my job and then between CeCe and Mia's boys, it's given me such an appreciation for how their minds work. I joke that even though I'm the adult in the situation, I always feel like I'm the one who is learning. I think there's something to be said about how filterless kids are. Sure, sometimes it's absolutely hilarious to hear what they think about things, but a lot of the time it's actually pretty thought provoking. Being asked "why" a bunch of times eventually makes you think about a question more thoroughly.

There's an ungodly amount of crayons spilling out of her crayon box on the floor as we finish up and even some markers and colored pencils. Chase really doesn't hold back when it comes to enabling her artsy side, it's like he bought out an entire store here. Some of the crayons have glitter and sparkles and some are even ombré colored. There are a handful of markers that are supposed to be scented; although, they all just smell like regular markers to me. I had high hopes for the one called strawberry shortcake, but it didn't live up to my expectations.

"How'd I do?" I ask, holding up my picture just as I hear a door close and then heavy footsteps coming from behind me. CeCe takes off running toward the kitchen.

The low rasp of Chase's voice breaks the silence as he greets her and she immediately starts telling him all about her day. I stand to my feet, placing the picture I colored on the end table near the couch and walk over to the island where Chase is now standing holding CeCe. My heart starts to race and my stomach does somersaults as I watch him interact with her. This always happens when I see him in dad mode, it's one of the few times he looks genuinely happy and it's intoxicating to watch him light up like he does around her. His usual face is so stoic and a little... sad looking sometimes, but when he's around her, he shines.

Growing up, Chase was pretty outgoing and he was social— or at least more than he is now. Kristen hardened him. She hurt not just him, but the most important person in his life and sometimes I think he still isn't over it. Over *her*, yes, but the situation —what she did and how she did it—no. She took his ability to see the good in people and I don't know when he'll get that back.

"Did everything go okay? She seems to be feeling much better." His face becomes indifferent when he looks my way.

"Yeah, everything was great. She seems to be in much better spirits, so I'm sure those antibiotics are doing their job. We actually spent the majority of the time coloring. My masterpiece is on the end table if you'd like to hang it on the fridge." I smile, and he cracks the tiniest smirk as he nods, pulling his feet out of his shoes and placing his phone and keys on the island.

A small breath of relief leaves his chest now that he's home and sees CeCe is, in fact, alive and well. I don't take his lack of trust or conversation personally. It's who he's become in the last few years. Except around CeCe, of course. He's tired, you can tell. Doing everything on his own takes a toll on him, but he'd never actually admit it to anyone.

"Why don't you go get cleaned up for dinner?" Chase ruffles CeCe's hair before she skips down the hall and he turns on the sink.

"How was practice?" I ask, tapping my fingers together in front of me. A weird nervous habit I developed around Chase when I was younger. My eyes follow the way his hands move under the faucet as he washes them. I could watch this man be still for a painting and my insides would still overheat.

"Another day in paradise." He swats his hand at the faucet, turning it off and grabbing the towel.

His jaw clenches and he spreads his hands out on the marble countertop, flexing his fingers while his brown hair curls just slightly atop his ears. God, I love when he lets it grow a little like this. A little messy and a little unruly… it's sexy.

"That bad, huh?" I ask, knowing that their coach has been on their asses. "I'm telling you, move Frank to left guard and it'll help. Who do I have to call?" I ask, playfully, getting another small smirk out of him as he dries his hands.

"Summer Kincaid with all the answers." He smirks again. If small smirks and half smiles are all he'll give right now, I'll take it and count it in the win column. I want him to trust me and feel comfortable with me being here more now. The fact that we've known each other as long as we have doesn't seem to matter when it comes to CeCe. He's still on edge and overprotective, almost to a fault.

There are moments when I look at Chase and think, *get over him.* And then there are others, many others, when I'm around him watching him do the most normal, everyday tasks, like filling a pot with water to boil, and my heart just *pounds.* Something embedded within my DNA is just so hopelessly in love with him. I can't shake him. You'd think after years, literal years, of nothing happening and him never reciprocating the feelings, that it would be easy to let it go. But I just can't.

"Do you want help?" The offer falls from my lips before I can register what I'm asking, knowing he's likely going to turn me down. I can't imagine he wants two favors from me in one day.

"With?" He doesn't turn around to face me, just reaches for a box of macaroni and cheese from the pantry.

"Dinner. I can help if you want."

"Cooking wasn't part of our agreement, I've got it."

I sigh, rolling my eyes as I walk around the island.

"You're acting like this is some kind of business deal with a stranger from Craigslist. We're friends, I can help you as a friend. Plus, you look exhausted. I can throw macaroni and cheese together for CeCe while you relax for fifteen minutes." I pull open one of the drawers and grab a spoon and make my best attempt to *scoot* this wall of a man out of my way.

"What was that?" he asks with a low chuckle.

"My shitty attempt to move you out of the way, obviously. Just go relax. You don't have to do everything yourself. I'm here, let me help."

I can tell he wants to tell me to kick rocks. Chase has these tells I've learned over the years and it's so easy for me to see when I'm being too much for him. His nostrils are flaring and his breath begins to deepen. But then the soft smirk from his chuckle falls into a stare and he looks down at me, letting our gazes interlock for a brief moment until his eyes flick to my mouth and back up. Within seconds, a door opens down the hall and CeCe runs toward him calling his name.

"Go," I whisper.

CHAPTER SEVEN

CHASE

"Watch this!" CeCe says, tiptoeing across her balance beam in the living room as I kick my feet up on the ottoman.

I can't remember the last time I just sat after practice and it makes me feel restless, even though I should be feeling grateful for Summer's help. The sound of metal clanging against a pot, tied with some country song coming from the kitchen almost has me on my feet to see what she's doing, but if I'm going to accept her help, I have to try to relinquish a little bit of control.

God, help me with that.

A timer goes off and Summer pops up in the living room, holding a pink bowl full of macaroni and cheese with a spoon sticking out the top for CeCe.

"All right. Come eat," she says, running her free hand over CeCe's head as they walk together back to the dining room. Summer's blonde hair is cascading down her back in big loose curls against a pair of denim overalls. *Overalls.* Who would've thought?

My hand runs through my hair and I let my head rest against the couch cushion for a few moments, closing my eyes in an attempt to relax.

"Yours is almost done," Summer says.

I squint open one eye, but she's already gone back into the kitchen before I've had the chance to say anything.

She can't make me dinner. Doing it for CeCe is one thing, but me? I can't allow it. Somehow, it feels like crossing a line in this arrangement we have, and I don't need her to start getting overly comfortable in my kitchen.

Sighing, I get up from the couch to head into the kitchen. There's an old country song playing on Alexa, and Summer's back is to me as she stands over the stove. She sways a little to the slow rhythm of the song and I catch myself staring for just the briefest moment. It's been years since I've had a woman in this kitchen. Well, aside from my mother or my sister. I shouldn't be staring at her. Under any other circumstance, I wouldn't be. But Summer's always so… happy. I can't decide if I find it irritating or something I'm actually envious of. She's always been this way—bubbly and friendly—but a shark when she needs to be.

My mind flashes to three years ago when Summer found out that Kristen left. She was so angry and protective that day. I think if I would've given her the green light, she probably would've hunted her down that night. Something was different about Summer at that moment. I saw a side of her that was full of more than just jokes and positivity. She was sincere and thoughtful, earnest and strong. She spoke like she was making a speech in front of a room full of people, but it was just me and her. She was a friend in a moment where I needed one.

I shake my head, snapping myself out of wherever I was going with that memory.

"Thanks for making CeCe's, but don't worry about mine."

"Well, it's already done," she says, spinning around with a pan of chicken, carrots, and roasted potatoes in her hand.

"What is that?" I ask, practically salivating as the smell drifts my way. It's been so long since someone has cooked for me, and while it's not something I expect to happen again, it's nice.

"Parmesan chicken with roasted carrots and potatoes. I have no idea how long these carrots were in there, but you've got a drawer full of veggies that probably need to be used." She cocks an eyebrow at me in warning.

I swallow, staring at the plate as she places the food on it like she's trying to earn a Michelin star. Carefully centering the chicken and adding the carrots and potatoes around it.

"Yeah." I chuckle, pinching the bridge of my nose. "I actually suck at making vegetables. I never know how to season them."

Summer doesn't miss a beat when she hands me the plate. "You don't suck at anything, Chase. But I can teach you how to season vegetables, it's easy."

I barely wait ten seconds before I start digging in, noticing CeCe smiling at me as I sit across from her while she scoops another spoonful of macaroni in her mouth. Instead of Summer joining us at the table, I hear the sink running in the kitchen and the sound of pots and pans clanging together. I've been so busy daydreaming of the past, or brainstorming how to make sure she doesn't do this whole dinner thing again, that I forgot to be a decent fucking human and offer the woman who just watched my child a seat at the table.

The chair legs scrape against the floor as I pull my seat back and walk into the kitchen.

"You didn't make any for yourself?"

"No. I figured I'd get out of your hair and not overstay my welcome. I know there's only so much Summer you can handle, Chase." She smiles, but somehow that makes me feel like shit.

She turns on the disposal and adds the soap to the dishwasher while I stand there feeling like a moron. Most of the time Summer and I have spent together, there has always been a third person, my sister or one of our friends. It's rare that she and I are ever alone together, and this moment reminds me of why. We are so different in every way I can think of. She's carefree and goes with the flow, I need plans and a nine o'clock bedtime. I never mind being around Summer, she's always been a good person in my life, but she's right about one thing—there's only so much of her I can take.

"Right, okay." I definitely feel like I owe her more than I'm giving her at this moment. But at the end of the day, she took care of CeCe when I needed her to and that's what we agreed to. Anything more is just… unnecessary.

"I can come by tomorrow afternoon too. That is, if you haven't already decided to fire me." She points the dirty spatula at me before quickly adding it to the dishwasher and closing it.

I bite my lip slightly to stifle a smirk at her sarcastic comment.

"You aren't my employee, Kincaid. I can't fire you. I… I guess I need you," I say, tipping my head at her before I walk back to the dining room table as she softly laughs.

"Have a good night, Chase." The sound of her laugh carries into the next room. "And you have a good night too." She blows a kiss at CeCe.

"Yeah. Tell Drew I said hey," I reply.

At the mention of his name I see the smile fade from her face. And the light in her bright blue eyes dull as her shoulders fall the slightest bit. She doesn't answer, she just nods and pulls her purse over her shoulder. I want to ask her why her lip just quivered and why her body tensed when I said his name. But that's not my business and I don't need to know about Summer's love life. I've never given it a second thought before.

"Hey, Kincaid," I say before she can walk out the door.

"Yeah?" She turns, her dark eyelashes fanning her cheeks when she looks my way.

"Thanks for dinner."

CHAPTER EIGHT

SUMMER

Avoiding Chase's mention of Drew last night seemed like a good idea at the time, but now I can't help but wonder if I should've just casually told him we aren't together anymore. That he and the rest of the guys can stop pretending to like him, because I know they couldn't stand him.

When I walk into Chase's apartment this afternoon, I expect to see Abby greeting me with homemade cookies and telling me all about the most recent thing she has going on with the Rec Center. But instead, I'm met with her sleepy gaze as she lies on the couch. CeCe perks up from her coloring book, giving me a big smile and a wave.

"Um, hi. When you texted me saying to just walk in the door I thought maybe your hands were full of dough or something. I didn't expect to see you all cocooned up." I wave my hand around as I stand over her.

"Sorry. I've been so exhausted."

"Why didn't you have me come over earlier? I was off all day, I could have helped," I say, scolding her for her stubbornness. Two peas in a pod, Abby and that brother of hers, I swear.

"I felt bad doing that last minute." She shrugs, getting up from the couch.

"Well, go home. Now," I say, grabbing her purse and cell phone for her, practically pushing her out the door.

Abby never leaves her brother's home in any kind of disarray. I imagine that's because he's pretty tidy and has a place for everything. Down to the way the coaster sits on the coffee table. But right now, looking at this place, it's a giant shit storm.

CeCe is still seated comfortably at the table coloring, so I don't bother her aside from refilling her water and placing some snacks on the table next to her.

The Alexa on the counter has Chase's calendar on the home screen and looking at today's date, it seems he'll be home in just over an hour. That gives me enough time to try and clean up the kitchen and living room at the very least.

I take ten minutes to create a playlist on the device, naming it *Summer's Cleaning Jams* and set it to a moderate volume before I get started. The nice thing about Chase being so particular about his house is that everything is where you'd assume it would be. Dish soap under the sink, the broom in the laundry room closet—nothing is randomly placed.

Before I know it, I've got his kitchen smelling like a freshly squeezed lemon, nice and squeaky clean with the dishwasher running and clean water for the flowers on his counter. I will say, the flowers—well, it was a little bit of a shock to see fresh flowers, but my guess is CeCe suckered him into buying them.

"Can we go outside?" CeCe asks the minute I sit down after I just speed cleaned. I get it now when parents say the moment they relax their kids immediately need something.

"I can't bring you to the park or anything downstairs, but we can sit on the balcony if you want to. We can people watch."

"What's people watch?"

I forget that a three-year-old doesn't understand the allure of this yet. Maybe this means I'm getting older if people watching is an activity I offer a child.

"People watch. It's just like… Well, we'll just watch the people downtown walk around. Is that weird?" I ask, laughing while I pull a bag of popcorn from the box for myself.

CeCe shrugs and stands beside me, and I can't help but feel like I'm about to really age this sweet girl with my people watching tendencies.

"Four dogs, she must be a professional dog walker," I say, motioning to the young girl on the sidewalk across the street.

There hasn't been as much activity as I was hoping for, creating a pretty boring experience for the last twenty minutes. And I'm pretty sure CeCe has lost all interest, but at least she's occupied with the Swedish Fish candies I let her have.

The sliding glass door opens and I turn around to see both Chase and Liam walk through. Chase smiles when he sees CeCe and then glances over at me, but I stay seated on the couch that I moved closer to the side so it was easier for CeCe to see.

"What are you girls doing?" Liam asks, holding his fist out to me for a fist bump.

"Watching people," CeCe proudly declares.

Chase's brow creases and he directs his attention toward me.

"What?" he asks.

"We were just eating and people watching… you know," I say, casually shaking my head as Liam laughs.

"Teaching her how to judge people so soon, Summer? Shouldn't you wait until she's at least, I don't know, five?"

I stand up, shoving Liam's arm as I walk over to where Chase is standing. "We weren't judging anyone. In fact, I was pointing out cute dogs." My arms cross over my chest and both of them scoff, walking inside after me.

"Abby's a clean freak like you, isn't she?" Liam comments, running a finger over the counter I just cleaned.

"Why would you assume that Abby cleaned?" I butt in.

"You cleaned?" Chase asks, stopping mid stride as he hands CeCe a box of apple juice.

"Well, yeah. I mean I did a little cleaning. Abby was exhausted when I got here, so I just picked up a few things." I shrug my shoulders and lean against the kitchen counter across from Liam. I watch the corner of Liam's lips curve into a devilish smirk as he stares at me.

"And you're not even paying her?"

"I don't work for him," I say in response to Liam.

"You don't have to clean, Kincaid." Chase sighs, flipping his baseball hat backward, and I instantly can't focus on what he just said. My eyes stay glued to the bicep muscle that flexes with that simple movement.

"It was just a few things," I finally spit out.

Liam walks over to the living room and sits on the couch with CeCe just as Chase walks up closer to me. His scent engulfs me, nearly paralyzing me from any movement. My feet want to take a step to my right, but my brain won't connect with my body to force any readjustment.

"Thank you," Chase whispers in a low voice, letting his brown eyes connect with mine for a millisecond.

I finally swallow the lump in my throat when he brushes past me to the pantry and invites me to stay and watch a hockey game with him and Liam. I'm sure it's just him being polite, I can't see him actually wanting me to stick around.

"I work tomorrow and have a few errands to run before I get home, so thanks, but not tonight."

"Okay," he says, standing still with both hands shoved in the pockets of his jeans.

"Bye, Evans," I say as I'm hugging CeCe. I offer a smile in Chase's direction before I head out the door.

CHAPTER NINE

CHASE

It's been nearly two hours since Summer left and CeCe has brought her up every chance she's had. Her vocabulary isn't that expanded, but she's found a ton of different ways to essentially tell me that Summer's her best friend. I've got to admit, part of me wanted to laugh when she said they were people watching earlier. The fact that Summer chose to just sit and do that with her isn't surprising in the least.

She's only babysat CeCe for me a couple of times, but so far, I can agree that having Summer around has been helpful. It doesn't come without its challenges in some ways and she's definitely more of a texter than my sister is when it comes to updates.

Abby would usually only text me if she wanted me to grab something on my way home, but Summer seems to think that everything CeCe does deserves a picture. Can't argue with her on that, I appreciate seeing CeCe's face on my phone when I'm not around.

I did feel cornered at first in having to agree to accept her help, but I didn't actually have any other options unless I wanted to go down the nanny route. It crossed my mind for a split second, thinking maybe the cons of a nanny wouldn't be that bad. But I know myself. It would last an hour before I was driving home from practice, firing whatever stranger was probably snooping in my bedroom. At least with Summer, I know she's snooping—I don't have to wonder.

The idea of relying on anyone else to care for CeCe has always been something I've struggled with. Even trusting Abby to watch her at first was huge for me. Letting CeCe out of my sight those first few months after Kristen left felt physically impossible.

Liam and I have been watching the hockey game while CeCe has been busy setting up her dolls at the table for an ice cream party. One I promised her she could have if she ate the beans on her plate. She didn't eat them all, barely half, but I fold for her pleading eyes every time.

"So… earlier, what was that?" Liam pops the top on a cold beer.

"What are you talking about?"

He lowers his voice, making sure CeCe isn't within earshot. "Don't bullshit me, Hunt. Something going on with you and Summer?"

"Something as in she's helping watch CeCe for me, but that's about it." I can feel my jaw tick slightly.

"Bullshit," Liam says, my reply seeming to amuse him.

"Believe me. Summer Kincaid is the last person I'd have something going on with."

The grin that spreads on his face has me already rolling my eyes, knowing some stupid fucking remark is about to follow. "Do you ever think your irritation for her is actually just attraction?"

I choose the wrong time to take a sip of water as it doesn't make it past the back of my throat before I'm coughing it up with a hearty laugh.

"Oh, that's a good one." I pound my chest with my fist to clear my throat.

"Come on, you're not fooling me," he scoffs.

"There's nothing going on. I don't look at her like that."

"You say that, but your face tells a different story, man."

"What's my face saying?" I challenge him.

Liam leans back against the couch, placing one arm behind his head as he looks me dead in the eye.

I've got a couple years on Liam, and a lot more life experience. And right now, I'm thinking a solid fifty pounds if I needed to level him. Not that I would, but the knowledge of knowing I can is all I need right now.

"That you like her attitude. She fires you up and you want to look annoyed, but I think deep down you actually like it. You enjoy that kind of back and forth repartee the two of you do. I've thought it for years. Ever since the first night I met her back at Louie's. I saw it. I have eyes."

"Well, get them checked, because you're fucking nuts."

"You know she's into you, right? That's not something you're learning right this moment."

I nod with a heavy sigh. "I've known."

"Well, either way… I'm just glad to see you're spending time with women other than the ones you're related to." Liam winks.

"We aren't spending time together. You're reading way too much into this. She helps with CeCe, that's it."

He doesn't grace me with another comment or even a look, he simply nods and smiles and the rest of the time is spent talking about the game.

———

"Nine seven, nine seven!" I hear my number from the opposing side of the field. The quarterback sees me on the edge completely unblocked and alerts his team of my looming presence.

Once he spikes the ball, he immediately scrambles to his right, causing me to follow. Instead of moving east and west on the field, he moves up and down. He's back at least fifteen yards now from the line of scrimmage and he's looking everywhere trying to find an open receiver. I can feel my knees aching as I follow his quick movements, until finally I'm able to sack him. I pin my body against his, hearing the collision of our pads and helmets, hoping the ball was also knocked out, but no such luck. He's gripping it like his life depends on it, and I stand, offering my hand to help him to his feet since it's just the two of us this far back into the field.

"Fucking got me." The quarterback smiles, spitting out blood as he lifts his helmet.

"I'm coming again," I taunt, clapping my hands as I turn to jog back down the field.

I've always loved being a defensive player. Back in college, they'd use me as an offensive tackle every now and then, which I didn't hate, but there's nothing like running toward your opponent like you're ready to snap their neck.

A few more downs and we're off the field, securing a win and a nice break for a bye week coming up that my body desperately needs. I've been slacking on my recovery this season, but trying to find extra time has been hard when my only option is really just asking Summer to stay later.

I head into the locker room to get showered and changed, and Coach Aarons gives us his post-game speech, handing me the game ball. I don't get nostalgic often, but there are still small things that happen at this level that bring me back to being younger. Getting a game ball is one of them.

The game became my obsession when I really started treating it like a job back in high school. My dad would run drills with me every chance he had, my parents bought me all the shit I needed in order to practice at home when I wasn't practicing at school. Simply put, it became the love of my life. I'd have some of the most ridiculous superstitions before games, some I still do now. Always using a certain coffee mug on game days, not wearing any eye black under my eyes, same socks every game. When I was in college, I remember having a giant bowl of ramen noodles the night before every game. I'd combine three packages and just inhale it.

My dad would tell me how bad they were for me all the time. Fuck, he'd tell me how bad most of the food I ate was. Meat and vegetables were in every single meal he ate, and eventually, I started listening to him and eating better. I dropped weight in college, gained muscle and ultimately worked my ass off to make sure I got drafted. It was as much his dream as it was mine, but I always knew if I wanted to step away he wouldn't question it.

I often think of what he'd say about my situation now. A single dad wasn't exactly what he would've expected, but I like to think he'd be proud of me for the way things have turned out.

He's everything I strive to be as a father. He was patient, kind, loving, and supportive. But also strong and hardworking. There wasn't a thing my dad couldn't fix. From scraped knees all the way to rebuilding decks and making a home where nothing but dirt once sat.

You don't think about all of the things that go into being a parent until you become one. And we often don't truly appreciate the sacrifices of our own until we're in their shoes. I'm humbled as a parent. As a man. When I was a kid, I'd look at my dad and see Superman. How the hell could he do it all and still sleep? Still eat? Still have time for himself? I realize now that he simply chose to make me and my sister the priority.

Thinking about it now, I know he was tired. He'd pull into the driveway close to six at night, after working since seven in the morning and he'd still get me to my football games on time.

He'd stay up late fixing a screen I broke when I was being a damn idiot with my friends. There's just so much we don't truly see as kids. It wasn't until I had CeCe that I understood what unconditional love was.

He wasn't even someone who dropped that word often now that I think of it. But he said it every day.

"Here's twenty, put gas in your tank."

"Let me know when you get to that party."

"Your tire looks low, son. Fill 'er up."

"Are you feeling okay?"

He said it the only way he knew how.

CHAPTER TEN

SUMMER

Hey, I'm sorry for asking you this last minute when I just told you I wouldn't need help for a week, but any chance you can watch CeCe today?

An impromptu text from Chase comes through, surprising me to say the least. We spoke briefly after his game the other day and he was very adamant that he would see me *after* the bye week. I laughed, knowing that lately we've been seeing more of each other than normal, and it's clear that my presence is starting to take its toll on him.

If you miss me, just say that

I don't.

I won't tell anyone

Kincaid.

What time should I be there?

It's a far cry to assume he asked me instead of his sister, but Abby's been so caught up in what she has going on, I've barely seen her. I'm just glad she's doing what she feels is best for her and Ford.

When I was at the store the other day, I found myself meandering around the craft aisle. It's not exactly a place I'd usually find myself, but something caught my eye that made me think of CeCe. The aisle was lined with different markers, crayons, colored pencils, and sidewalk chalk. The marker package that caught my eye said scented markers.

I remember flipping open the package and grabbing the blue marker that read blueberry, holding it up to my nose. To my surprise, it actually smelled like blueberries, giving me hope that the rest of the package would also ring true to their descriptions, so of course I had to buy them.

Tossing the pack of markers into my purse, I reach for a jacket since it's already drizzling outside. I don't know exactly why Chase needs my help this afternoon, but whatever the reason, I don't mind. I had no plans aside from watching whatever documentary I could find.

"Again, sorry this was last minute," Chase apologizes the moment I walk through the door. He's already dressed and ready to go, backward hat and a pair of jeans with a dark green t-shirt.

Simple. Mouthwatering.

"You don't need to apologize, I'm happy to help." I wave him off, walking past him.

CeCe is eating a bowl of strawberries at the kitchen island when I place my things down beside her and casually toss the markers in her direction, giving her a smile and a wink.

"*These* are real scented markers," I say, giving her shoulder a little squeeze as I pass by.

Chase follows me back into the kitchen as I'm tossing my phone in my purse. His boots sound like they're scraping up his wood floors, but he continues to drag his feet across the kitchen, heading toward a drawer at the end. He pulls out a small note-book, maybe it's a planner? It's a little bit bigger than an address book.

"Oh, is that your little black book full of phone numbers?" I tease, biting the strawberry I snatched from CeCe's bowl.

His brows crease and the veins on his forearms protrude as he flexes holding the paper.

"Hilarious." He doesn't look up as he sifts through a couple pages before stopping on one, folding the notebook and turning it toward me.

"This has every important number you might need while I'm gone. I know Abby gave you a run down, but I've been meaning to show you this." He clears his throat before he continues. "It's got, uh, her doctor, my coach, some of the guys on the defense with me, my mom is in here… um, oh, my publicist. The doorman downstairs is in here too if you need anything, his name is Dave. Obviously, you know 911." His finger trails down the page like he's going through a checklist with me.

"Hold on. Who is 911?"

His eyes shoot to mine, clearly not fond of my joke as they sear into me.

"Kincaid," he says through clenched teeth.

"I'm kidding, just a joke. Clearly an ill-timed joke. Every-thing will be fine. This isn't my first rodeo, but I promise I'll refer to the notebook if there are any issues," I assure him, patting his shoulder as I walk toward the living room.

He sighs and leans over, kissing CeCe on top of the head.

"She has ten more minutes of that iPad and then it goes off."

I give him a double thumbs up and grab the blanket from the ottoman, tossing it over me as I sink into his couch. I just want to become one with this sofa, I could melt right into it.

"Where are you going anyway?" I ask, wondering if it's even my business, but curious minds and all of that.

"Apparently"—he sighs heavily—"I agreed to do a radio ad.

They must've caught me in a good mood because I hate this shit."

"You're doing *media?*" I emphasize. "So, like, did they ask you on Christmas?"

"I think it was the other night when you finally left my house. I was relieved and I guess I would've said yes to anything."

My eyes widen as I look back at him, almost with pride at his quick witted response.

"I'm sorry, was that a joke?" I can't help but smile at his attempt.

"I've got to get going," he says, completely ignoring me.

"Did you just joke with me? Where's my phone? Do it again so I can record you."

"Kincaid." The roughness in his voice causes me to blush at the simple use of my name.

"Use that growly voice in your ad. It'll catch people's attention when they're listening."

"What? I don't have a *growly* voice," he says, very clearly trying to soften his words.

"You most definitely do." I laugh, clearing my throat ready to imitate him. "*Kincaid,*" I say as low as my voice will allow.

He always sounds husky, like he needs to clear his throat or take a sip of water.

"You say my name with that kind of rough voice all the time. It's obviously deeper than what I just did, but you get the idea. It's like a warning tone. Although, I'll be honest, it's kind of hot, Chase, so I don't know, I think it's having the opposite effect than you're intending." I smirk, grabbing the TV remote.

"I'll let you know when I'm on my way home," he grunts out with a sigh.

I'm easily responsible for every exasperated sigh this man has made in the last few weeks since I've been helping him out.

"All right, let's see what we've got." I open the pantry with CeCe at my side.

Chase didn't seem to love me cooking for him—*although, he devoured the plate*—but he's good with me cooking for CeCe.

Looking in the pantry, I notice how perfectly placed every single item is in here. The boxes are lined up from tallest to shortest and the cans are neatly stacked and displayed showing the labels for each. My eyes scan the shelves, taking in every organized detail of this pantry, knowing if Chase ever saw the clutter of mine, he'd probably pass out. His organization seems to have gotten more… *intense* with age. I know he's always been very particular and simplistic, his house is still very minimally decorated, except for CeCe's room which looks like a unicorn threw up all over it.

"Can I have noodles?" CeCe climbs on the stool as I'm carefully picking through the boxes to find what she's asking for.

"Of course."

Once I find the box of "spinny noodles"—also known as Cavatappi—she asked for, I get a pot of water boiling. While I'm standing near the stove, I can't help but notice the mess we've made this afternoon. Countless coloring book pages all over the place, empty juice containers… I know the last time I cleaned, Chase looked at me like I committed a crime, but I'm not leaving this stuff all over the house. I don't even have to ask and CeCe is already helping clean up, putting away some of her toys that made their way from her bedroom into the living room.

There's a strike of lightning that illuminates practically the entire apartment when I stand from the floor. I was hoping that Chase would be home before the storm rolled in this afternoon, but that doesn't seem likely now. It's unseasonably late to have a storm hit in November, but technically, hurricane season runs through the end of the month.

The only time I actually care about the news is when it's regarding the weather. I feel like, in another life, I could've been a storm chaser because I'm weirdly interested in weather. But they said this would be making landfall tonight, not at four in the afternoon.

Chase's chair slides across the balcony and all I can do is watch as plants fall over and a cushion gets carried away.

I grab the remote and switch the television from the rolling credits of the latest movie we watched to the news channel. Hurricane season is like the Super Bowl for meteorologists, you can see how excited they get to talk about storms.

My phone dings with a simple "OMW" abbreviation from Chase at the same time another lightning bolt strikes, causing an even louder crack and CeCe to run from the hallway into my thigh. Her little fingers dig in tightly as she grabs my leg.

"Hey, it's okay. It's outside. You're safe," I say, stroking her cheek before I bend down to pick her up. "Does Daddy let you eat on the couch?" My instincts tell me no, but how big of a mess can noodles make?

She shrugs her shoulders as her eyes focus on the sliding glass door and the havoc on the other side. The rain is beating down now, and it feels like midnight with how dark it looks already.

Once CeCe's dinner is finished cooking, I bring her plain noodles into the living room and decide to set up a comfortable little place for her to eat. I grab the blanket from the arm of the couch and spread it across the cushions, telling CeCe to have a seat and then grab another blanket to cover her with. Blankets are easier to wash than a whole couch, so this should cover it. I'm not going to have her sit at the table next to a raging thunderstorm outside when she can cuddle up with me on a perfectly cozy couch and watch the weather channel.

"What's that?" CeCe asks as the weatherman circles a big orange blob on the screen.

"So, that's the storm. The one that's outside right now. The weatherman is showing us how fast it's moving and where it's moving to, how strong it is, things like that."

"Hm." Her little chin tilts up like she's actually interested in what he's got to say. "Is it fast?"

I stare at the screen, listening to the update coming from the television and concluding that this damn storm isn't going anywhere soon. Sometimes, these things barrel through and leave as fast as they show up and others they just take their sweet ass time seeing themselves out.

"Sadly, no. Looks like it's moving really slow… like a snail," I say, wiggling my fingers at her.

"Ew!" she squeals.

The two of us continue to watch the weather update and the warnings flash on the bottom of the screen with different alerts.

When she finishes eating, she puts her bowl down beside her and reaches for the remote, turning the volume up higher. I can hear it clearly all the way from the kitchen as I'm getting myself a quick snack.

The front door swings open and then closes abruptly, startling me out of the daze I was in watching the number tick on the microwave.

"Loud enough?" Chase tosses his keys on the counter and makes his way into the living room where CeCe is.

"I think she's trying to drown out the noise of the storm," I say with a laugh, coming to her defense.

His massive hand covers the top of her head and he ruffles her already frizzy hair. His attention shifts back to me when he realizes that she's completely enthralled by the ongoing storm coverage.

"Trying to scare my kid by making her watch hurricane footage?"

"This is nothing, you just missed the Great White Shark

video I showed her. Very bloody, gory, full of nightmare inducing stuff."

He shakes his head and then wags his finger in front of me, but it's almost… playful? "You're lucky you're joking. That one is prone to nightmares."

I shove a handful of popcorn in my mouth and take a seat at the island while Chase chugs two full water bottles in record time, and I add extra melted butter to the popcorn.

"More butter, huh?" He raises his eyebrows at me.

"The butter is what makes it delicious," I say, licking my fingers.

He laughs and places the water bottles in the recycle bin.

"How was the radio ad? What was it for?"

"Well." He licks his lips before speaking, and I have to remind myself to breathe like a normal human. It should be studied how easily he affects me. I really hope I was never this obvious when I was around him with a boyfriend, how shitty. "Hated every second. It was for a car dealership the team has a partnership with or something. Thanks for watching her, by the way. I should have led with that when I got home."

I shrug, shaking my head and inhaling this bowl of butter riddled popcorn, "I know you're thankful for me. No need to say it *over and over.*" My eyes roll in dramatic form, and he scoffs before pushing himself from the counter and walking down the hall to his bedroom.

Despite the weatherman's prediction of heavy rain and storms all night, I'm still somehow hoping there will be a small break for me to leave without risking being swept up into a tornado. Sadly, it's not looking good. I don't live far, and technically, my car is in the parking garage, so it's really just managing the quick drive home.

I've learned that one of the worst parts about living in Tampa is when it rains, especially when the weather is so intense, the streets flood. And it's not worth risking a puddle when you don't actually know how deep it goes. Even though I know my route and it's pretty straight forward, I've witnessed one too many people get stuck because they think they can drive through flooded streets. I can't afford to make that kind of mistake, but I can't possibly invade Chase's space for much longer.

"Fucking wind," he mumbles as he stares through his back door, seeing the way things have moved around. "I thought I'd have time before this happened to bring everything inside."

"It came pretty quick, otherwise I would've tried to grab some things… but by the time I noticed, it was already crazy."

He waves me off when he turns back to face me. "No, no, that's not your responsibility anyway."

I hear the loud beeping noise on the TV indicating another type of severe weather warning is about to be announced. Both Chase and I glance at the screen as a red alert displays across the bottom.

Tornado warnings in effect until midnight. Tropical storm warning in effect until 4 a.m.

Damn it.

"I should go now so I can get home before this gets insane," I say, reaching for my purse.

"You wouldn't call this insane?" he asks, jerking his thumb behind him as the palms are literally flying off trees with the wind.

I sigh, letting my head fall back slightly, annoyed at this situation.

"It's not safe. Stay here and see if it dies down a little first."

More time ticks by, and I've already colored, done a puzzle, and put on a puppet show with CeCe while Chase braves the balcony trying to secure what he can. The weather isn't slowing down and it's only getting later and darker.

Chase hurries back in, slamming the door shut and pulling the hoodie off over his head. "I'll go grab a comforter and some pillows. You can have my room for the night."

"What? No. I can't stay here overnight." My mouth instantly becomes dry. I have *nothing* here except for the clothes on my back and a half eaten protein bar in my purse.

"Did you think that was a question? You're not driving in this weather."

He doesn't wait for another reply from me, he just walks down the hall and opens the closet.

CHAPTER ELEVEN

SUMMER

This can't be happening.

I've never slept here without Abby and I've definitely *never* slept in Chase's bed.

The thunder, lightning, and rain continue as I sit on the stool in the kitchen, eating a plate of leftover tortellini Chase said I could warm up for something to eat. We've officially changed the weather channel to something more kid friendly for CeCe to watch for the last hour or so before she has to go to bed, and I no longer have a buffer in this situation I've found myself in.

In any other circumstance, I probably would jump at the suggestion of sleeping in Chase's bed. Although, in most—well, all—of those scenarios he'd ideally be sleeping *with* me in it. I can't be mad at him wanting to make sure I'm safe, but to be honest, it's probably just because he is fresh out of babysitters and if something were to happen to me he'd probably force himself into an early retirement.

"All right, teeth, pajamas… let's go."

Chase grabs CeCe from the couch and tosses her in the air. She screams and then laughs, her honey blonde hair falling into her face as she lands safely back into his arms. I can't help but smile as I watch them together. It's pure joy, happiness. It's like CeCe knows she's the safest she could ever be in his arms.

I can hear them down the hall in the bathroom, she's singing the ABC's; although, it sounds gurgled through brushing her teeth and he keeps reminding her to get the teeth in the back.

I haven't seen him in this setting in so long. Abby, Mia, and I would come here some nights when CeCe was a baby. He was so overwhelmed and would never admit it, but in the haze of trying to take care of a baby, he let us help. He eventually found his footing and somehow that meant he didn't need help anymore and so he stopped accepting it.

My guess, though? He wanted to prove he could do it on his own. Prove that Kristen leaving wasn't the end of the world like he originally thought. It's why I don't take a lot of his remarks or quirks personally.

I think when you're hurt the way he was, and you finally dust yourself off and get back up… there's something in you that vows to never let it happen again. So, you put up walls and barriers. You make routines and rules and set different parameters in place to make sure you don't let anyone hurt you like that again.

Once I'm done eating, I busy myself in the kitchen, cleaning up my plate and moving the dishes from the sink into the dishwasher. The weather still hasn't let up, even though I keep checking the news app on my phone to see if I can find even a sliver of calm to drive home. It feels wrong that I'm still here, like I'm invading his alone time, his quiet time. My plan for the evening is to make myself scarce, hopefully not bother him too much and just get through the night and duck out first thing in the morning.

"Future music hall of famer you've got there," I say, smiling when Chase walks out of CeCe's room carrying a dinosaur stuffed animal.

"She asked for you."

"Really?"

He shrugs, probably just as confused as I am. "Really."

Grabbing the towel on the counter, I dry off my hands and walk down the hall toward her bedroom. His white hallway walls feel like they're almost closing in around me and I glance quickly into his bedroom as I approach hers. I barely know what his bedroom actually looks like, and a peek is no help with how dark it is right now.

"Hey, my girl, ready for bed?"

Her sound machine is ridiculously loud and I have no clue how she finds this helpful to sleep. It would absolutely keep me awake. I'd have to assume he turned it up to try and drown out the noise of the weather outside.

CeCe reaches her hand out to me as she lays there, one arm tucked in the blanket with a puppy stuffed animal secured under her arm. But her outstretched arm isn't empty. She hands me a small penguin stuffed animal and smiles.

"Here. If you get scared."

My shoulders sink and I smile back at her.

"Thank you," I whisper, squeezing her hand and kissing the top of her head.

It's the sweetest gesture anyone's ever done for me and it came from a three-year-old.

"For your fears?" Chase's voice catches me off guard when I come back into the kitchen holding the penguin. He holds up the dinosaur in his hand.

"Yeah." I laugh, running a hand through my hair and placing the stuffed animal on the counter next to me. "She's the sweetest, Chase. You're doing a great job with her."

His brown eyes soften and his body relaxes when he hears those words. I'm not sure how often people tell him that, but by the looks of it, he should hear it more than he does.

His head bobs up and down before he starts the dishwasher and dims the kitchen light. His apartment feels so peaceful right now, so homey. Even with the bare minimum decorations and the storm still swirling outside, it's cozy in here. The fireplace in the living room is on and he's got the TV guide up when he finally takes a seat on the couch. He must've changed his clothes while I was in CeCe's room because he looks a lot more comfortable in a pair of joggers and the faded t-shirt on his back.

"So, I think I'll probably just go to sleep then." My fingers fidget with the hem of my t-shirt.

"It's seven thirty…" He looks at me, eyeing me suspiciously.

"Yeah, well beauty sleep and all that… you understand."

He chuckles lightly, a sound that's so few and far between. "Kincaid," he says while scrolling through the guide.

"I don't want to interfere with your night, Chase. It's enough that I'm having to stay here longer than you originally planned, the least I can do is give you your space."

I turn and walk down the hall, but I hear footsteps behind me and his dreamy woodland scent drifts into my nose. Would it be rude to just plug my nose every time he gets close? It's going to be heaven and hell sleeping in his bed tonight.

"I know where your room is, I don't need an escort."

"Do you want something more comfortable to sleep in or are jean shorts and that shirt good enough for you?" His eyebrows raise as he stares at me when we both enter his room, and I sigh.

The walls are a crisp white, but he actually has decorations in here. There are many photos of CeCe; although, that comes as no surprise. But he has an entire corner of his very large master bedroom more decorated than the rest of his house.

"Wow," I whisper as I take it all in.

He walks into his closet, flips on the light and grabs a t-shirt, pulling it from the hanger. Oh God, a shirt that will undoubtedly smell like him. What is he doing to me?

"Wow what?" He tosses the shirt my way. It's black with the Knights logo on the front and a schedule on the back from a few years ago.

"Just your bedroom… it's not what I would have pictured."

I don't have much time to look around the room before another thunder crack makes both of us jump. I'm surprised CeCe slept through that one.

There's an old whiskey barrel in the corner that I'd have to assume is from a distillery. I know when he was in his early twenties, before his dad passed away, they would go to different tastings all the time. There are shelves above it, one with a picture of him and Jack, his dad, next to a bottle of unopened Jack Daniels. There's something on the other side of the barrel, but I don't have a good enough view to see exactly what it is.

"Oh," he says. "You can wear these too." He pulls out a pair of shorts from his drawer. Red with a white drawstring.

"I don't have to wear your clothes, Chase. It's… I'll be fine." I gesture to what I'm wearing. He places both hands on his hips and his head falls back with a loud sigh.

"Don't be so difficult." He rolls his eyes as he walks toward me. "I promise you can wash my stench off of you in the morning."

Wash it off? God, I want to live in it.

Chase swiftly exits his room, giving me privacy to change into his clothes. For as confident as I feel like I am most days, there are still moments where Chase Hunt makes me feel like a shy school girl. And standing in his bedroom about to change into his clothes is one of those moments. Clothes are reserved for significant others and maybe the occasional family member who spilled salsa on their shirt and needs a clean one to wear.

His shirt is loose on me and the shorts are roomy and comfortable as I tie the drawstring to keep them in place. When I would try to wear Drew's clothes they didn't hang off my body in the cute and sexy way I always hoped they would. They *fit* me. I hated it. It's why I never grabbed anything from his closet when we were dating and why I had exactly three things to give back to him when we broke up. A phone charger, his old stethoscope he left in my car, and a laptop bag he was letting me use that I no longer wanted to have.

After I toss my hair into a bun, I open his door quietly and head back toward the living room. I can hear the TV still on and the voice coming from it sounds weirdly familiar. I'd recognize David Attenborough's voice anywhere.

Rain pounds the pavement outside when I pass by the sliding glass door. I can see the street lights in between the water splashing. I'm sure no one is out in this weather, if nothing else it's just miserable to be out and about in the rain.

"Are you watching a bird documentary?" My question startles Chase, like he forgot I was even in the house to begin with. His shoulders rise and fall quickly and he places his glass down on the coaster next to him. Of course he's using a coaster.

"Yeah, we can change it, though." He reaches for the remote and I walk into the living room, taking a seat on the loveseat.

"No, no. I actually planned to watch this one too. I've been waiting for it."

"You watch animal documentaries?"

"*You* watch animal documentaries?" I ask him the same question.

His lips pull together like he's just been caught doing something he isn't supposed to be doing, but little does he know he's just adding little stupid things to love about him.

"Guilty." He raises the glass to his lips and I watch as he takes a sip and then lets his tongue dart out between his lips before he places the glass back down.

I settle in on the couch and pull the blanket over me while the documentary continues to play.

"Damn," he breathes out when they say how wide the wingspan of an Albatross is.

"A ten-foot wingspan… that's crazy. I need to see that in person one day," I say, eyes wide still focused on the screen where they're listing a bunch of facts.

"I don't think I'd ever want to own a bird, but they're pretty cool to learn about. I watched a whole show on sea lions the other night… It was interesting." Chase's face lights up like a kid —so excited about learning something new. It's so dorky and endearing, and I find myself wishing he hates the things I love.

When it ends, we both sit there and watch the credits roll. It's just past ten and I wish I could say I felt exhausted, but I feel awake and alert. It could be the fact that the storm outside is just as strong as it was hours ago which is keeping me alert or the fact that I am acutely aware of where I am.

At home, Chase is the same Chase I've known for years. He's gotten a little rougher around the edges, but he's still thoughtful and kind, funny, and makes me feel safe. Even though sometimes I'm sure he wishes he could staple my mouth shut. It's kind of interesting to watch, actually. He's so much more guarded when he's out, even around his friends, it's like he's constantly on watch. He tries to hide this part of him, the tender pieces. It just makes me wonder if it's some kind of defense mechanism.

He glances at the time on his phone and then turns to me. "Can I ask you something?"

"Of course," I whisper into the dark.

His head is leaning back on the couch cushion and aside from the rain still beating away outside, there's nothing but stillness, quiet.

"When I mentioned Drew the first night you were here, why didn't you tell me you broke up?"

"I didn't see a reason to, it doesn't matter. I'm guessing Abby told you."

"It matters if you're upset. Are you okay?"

He sits up, giving me his full attention, keeping his golden brown eyes trained on me.

The TV has gone into sleep mode, making the screen black

and leaving the only light in the living room being the fireplace and the pieces of lightning that set the sky ablaze every so often.

"I'm okay, believe me." I laugh. "Why?"

"I'm not heartless. We're still friends, even when you're being a menace."

My lips press together to stop a smile from escaping.

"Can't have your sole babysitter become a pathetic blubbering mess, is that it?"

A groan rumbles from his chest as he sits there, arms hanging on either side with his massive hands carefully placed on the couch for a beat before he speaks again.

"Yeah, that's it."

CHAPTER TWELVE

CHASE

Summer has a knack for making everything seem more difficult. Even in the moments when she's actually being helpful, she can't stop herself from side comments and challenging me. Pardon me for wanting to protect her from getting swept up in a tornado or stranded in flooded water. Is it that hard for her to accept my help now?

Wow, if that's not the pot calling the kettle black.

I'm not surprised at the liking CeCe has taken to having Summer around more, though. She loved being around my sister all the time and Summer is just like another version of that, only with even less rules probably. When she wanted her to stop in her bedroom before bed, I knew she was probably going to give her a stuffed animal to sleep with. What I didn't expect was for Summer to come out of the room and compliment me—or my parenting. It's not that I've never been told I'm doing a good job and it's not like I need to hear it around the clock, but every time I do, I have to allow myself to believe it. I have to take a minute and let it sink in. Because for so long, *so fucking long*, I didn't know if I was doing a good job or if I was screwing her up.

I give Summer a lot of shit—in some ways, it's just how our

dynamic has always worked. She bothers me, I complain she's annoying me, rinse and repeat. But I can't help but wonder if in some really twisted way, Liam isn't completely off base. Maybe I do enjoy it.

It startled me when she walked out of my bedroom wearing my t-shirt and shorts. Not because I forgot she was here, but because seeing Summer lately has been throwing my normal annoyance with her for a loop. I've never looked twice at Summer and I've never thought about her after she's left a room.

Am I just lonely? Is it because she's been spending so much time around lately and being so helpful with CeCe that it's forcing me to see her as more than the kid with a crush?

Her face was bare of any make up and the way she seemed to just float across the room like she belonged there made the hair on my arms stand up. Seeing her watch the documentary was thrilling, somehow. She smiled when they talked about baby birds and covered her eyes when an inevitable circle of life moment came on and one bird wasn't so lucky against a bigger animal. Alarm bells were ringing in my ears, telling me to get a fucking grip and not let my mind wander, but for some reason in the last week, Summer's gotten under my skin and not in the way she usually does.

Hearing her and Dr. Know-It-All broke up was actually a relief. And that's simply because the guy thought he knew more about the game of football than anyone else and would constantly comment on what he'd change about our team. A passionate fan is one thing, but I wouldn't even call him a fan, more like a giant pain in the ass who just liked to hear himself talk.

"Do you want a drink?" I ask, instantly wondering if I'm stepping into dangerous territory here.

"Um… just water, thanks." Her voice goes up as she looks up from her phone.

I get up from the couch and walk into the kitchen to grab two water bottles, handing her one before sitting back down. The moment I do, there's more thunder and another earth-shattering crack of lightning, causing the lights to flicker and power to go out immediately. I see the moment it happens downtown as the lights in buildings across from me all disappear at the same moment.

"I'll be right back," I say, walking down the hall to check on CeCe.

When I peek my head into CeCe's room, she's still fast asleep. The power loss made her sound machine turn off, but at least it somehow didn't wake her up. Her stuffed animal is still tightly tucked under her arm when I briefly flash the light on my phone into her room to get a better look. I quietly close the door and walk back over to the living room. I don't see Summer when I walk down the hall and it has me wondering if maybe she decided to call it a night. I guess I wouldn't blame her.

But then I hear a faint noise in the kitchen followed by "shit" and figure I've found her.

"What are you doing?"

"I was looking for candles and a lighter." She reaches down, fixing the t-shirt that's riding up. "I just can't reach up there so I'm not sure if there's anything we can use."

"Let me," I say, moving to where she is.

Her breath snags as I stand with my chest to hers, involuntarily pinning her against the counter, and her palms press against the countertop.

My ears suddenly become in tune with hearing Summer's breathing, as if the storm outside is no longer there and I can hear her taking slow, steady breaths. I can hear her heart pounding as we both stand here in the darkness.

When I back away from her I watch her exhale a deep breath, and her shoulders slowly fall and relax.

"Is CeCe okay?"

"Still out like a light." I pull a glass candle down from the top cabinet. Who knows how long this has been up there, but it'll do in a pinch like this.

"Can I ask you a question now? It's kind of personal, but I'm just curious," Summer says once she lights the candle and we settle back into the living room. She brings her legs up, crossing them at her ankles and propping a pillow behind her head.

"All right."

"Do you hate Kristen?"

Her question stuns me. I wouldn't have expected Summer to bring her up. I know she was never her biggest fan.

"Where'd that come from?" I ask, pulling one arm behind my head as I lean back.

In the darkness it's hard to see much with just the candle, but her eyes light up. It's almost as if the flame itself ignites them even brighter.

"It's just something I've wondered about. If you don't want to talk about it I respect that, though. Just say the word and I'll —" She runs her finger across her lips like she's zipping them up.

"No." My answer comes without hesitation, nearly cutting her off.

How could I hate the woman who gave me the greatest gift I could ever ask for? I may not like her a lot of the time, we may be at odds and she has definitely done things that I can't even begin to understand, but do I hate her? No. I can't.

"I was mad at her at first. I didn't understand. I couldn't wrap my head around her decision. I spent months thinking of every vile thing I could say to her if she ever responded to any of my messages or showed up again. All that time and energy… I can't get those months back. The moments I sat idly in this living room staring at the wall with rage, letting CeCe play on the floor in front of me or the moments she would be screaming at night, crying herself to sleep. I did what I could to console her. I tried fucking everything I could think of. I called my mom and my sister for help. Shit, I know everyone tried to help. I missed practices and meetings. I let myself be angry with Kristen for a long time, too long." I sigh, letting that time race through my mind. It's foggy, yet I can see it like it was yesterday. I can't explain it.

"Now, I'm disappointed in her more than anything. God, what a fucking dad thing to say, huh?" Summer softly smiles. "I still tell her when we're doing parties for CeCe. I've told her to stop by. But she never even replies."

I shrug, looking everywhere but at Summer. I know her expression will show pity, sadness, all things I don't want to be faced with because I've moved on from those feelings.

"I don't hate her. I don't think I even dislike her. I just feel indifferent about her. She's still the mother of my child, I'll never belittle her, especially not in front of CeCe. I just wish she would've stuck around for her."

"You're a better man than most." Her voice is just a whisper.

I scoff, shaking my head. "Am I? Because there are days where I feel like I should hate her. Even though I can't bring myself to it. There are days where I'm watching CeCe play or I'm watching as she's learning something new and in those small instances, I want to hate her for missing it. I want to track her down and bring her back here to see this amazing kid she left."

"CeCe is amazing because of you," Summer says quietly, and my head jerks in her direction, noticing a small piece of blonde hair falling into her face. "You have handled every single tough day you've had. Was it always pretty? Of course not, but CeCe looks at you and she sees a superhero. *Her* superhero. That's what you are to her. You've dealt with emotions and demons that we probably have no idea about, Chase. I honestly can't even imagine how you were feeling when everything was so fresh. I know you weren't in love with Kristen, but she still broke your heart."

I'm not sure what prompted Summer to ask about Kristen tonight, but there's a small part of me that's glad she did. I think most people just assume I hate her. It's refreshing to see that Summer isn't most people.

"Well, you saw me in the days after... I was a fucking disaster. Didn't know up from down, could barely console my own child. It was chaos. It's why... I don't know, I guess it's why now I make everything as routine as I can." Summer and I both laugh as I remember life three years ago.

"Yeah, you're definitely very particular. But look at you now." She smiles. "It's nice, you know? Despite all of the things you were dealing with back then, you turned that pain into growth. You healed so you could be everything you are for CeCe. You did that for her. She's amazing because of you."

I have to give credit where it's due and sometimes Summer surprises me.

"So, I guess you're not all sarcasm and jokes... you can be serious too."

A low rumble fills my chest as I look at her.

She nods slowly. "I'm often serious, but you just... I don't know, believe it or not, you make me nervous sometimes, Chase."

"I make you nervous? I can't picture you being nervous about anything, Kincaid."

She tilts her head with a smile. "Oh, so you picture me?"

"It's a new development." My tongue swipes my bottom lip and her eyes dart nervously back and forth between my mouth and my eyes.

I wasn't expecting to give into the small urge to let my guard down tonight, but this side of me has been slowly trying to seep out all evening.

After trying to hide it, her lips finally give out and curve into a smirk. "I've been casually flirting with you for a decade, are you telling me... Is Chase actually flirting back? Someone must alert the press."

"Kincaid," I warn, sitting myself up with my elbows planted on my knees to lean forward.

She matches my body language, moving her legs off of the couch and in front of her. The curve of her thighs peeking out as the side of the shorts ride up just a little.

"Yeah, boss?" Her head tilts to the side as her fingers interlock in front of her.

She's testing me. She knows it, too.

I never expected to welcome flirtatious conversation with Summer, but I just feel tired of keeping my walls so high all the time. Tired in general.

And Summer is making me feel a little carefree tonight.

CHAPTER THIRTEEN

SUMMER

The empty bottle makes a loud thumping noise as it falls from my grip. Did I really hear what I think I just heard? Kristen left?

"She what?" I ask, eyes wide with confusion as I stand in the kitchen.

Chase takes CeCe from Abby and walks her down the hall toward the spare bedroom where he has her diaper bag and I'm practically running after him.

"Chase, what the hell did you just say?"

"I think you heard me loud and clear." His brows crease together as he lays CeCe on the bed to change her diaper. Her cries start to calm down when he looks at her and her tiny hand wraps itself around his index finger as he smiles at her.

"Well where did she go?" My question seems to only add to his frustration as he gets CeCe changed. Her cries turn into coos as he softly talks to her and smiles. His hands look gigantic next to her little body and he scoops her up so effortlessly, holding her like a football and she relaxes into his arms.

"Do we have to talk about this now?" He sighs as he rubs

her back, and I take a seat on the bed, feeling confused and upset, as if I'm the one Kristen left. But Chase and CeCe are family to me, and Kristen—hell, anyone—doing anything to hurt them makes some kind of protective lioness instinct come out of me.

"No, of course not. You don't have to talk to me about it." My head shakes back and forth, realizing this isn't really my business. Plus, I'm aware I wouldn't be his first choice as someone to confide in.

He moves restlessly around the room. "I didn't mean it like that. I just feel so tired of talking. I couldn't change her mind. It's all just so fucked up." I've never seen Chase look so... lost. The dark circles under his eyes and the extra scruff lining his jaw give it away so clearly. He looks exhausted and defeated.

"I understand." I get up and walk a few steps closer to him. "I'm around if you need anything."

He nods at me and instincts tell me he's about to walk out the door, so I move first, giving him space. But he doesn't move. He stands there, still as can be. It looks like maybe this is the first time he's had some silence in a while and he wants to just relish in it for a moment.

CeCe twitches a little against his arm, I can see she's fighting a nap she desperately needs based on her tired eyes too.

"Here, let me," I say, grabbing CeCe's pacifier from the bed and pulling her into my chest. Chase doesn't resist and lets me take her, bringing her to the other side of the room. Abby showed me a while ago how to swaddle her for naps, so I jog my memory to get CeCe nice and snug before placing her in the small bassinet Abby has set up in here. The shades are closed and this room is far enough away from the kitchen so any noise from the group shouldn't carry over here to wake her up.

When I give her the pacifier she squirms a little bit, making a few small noises before she soothes herself and settles into a comfortable position, closing her eyes again and seemingly drifting off.

A deep sigh from Chase on the other side of the room makes me turn my head and he slowly takes a seat on the bed.

"Do you want a nap too? I could try to swaddle you," I say, giving his shoulder a playful shove.

"I'll pass on the swaddle, but I will probably just rest my eyes a little in here." His legs swing onto the bed and he lets his head fall back against the headboard, eyes closing before he's even fully settled.

"I just can't believe this is my life," he mumbles before I'm out the door, causing me to stop my feet and turn to face him.

"You'll be okay, Chase."

He scoffs, shaking his head. "Yeah? How do you suppose that?"

I pull the door completely closed and walk to the side of the bed where he's lying. His eyes are closed and his breathing has evened out. For all I know, he could've fallen asleep in the last ten seconds.

"Because I know you," I whisper. "And I know that you feel really alone right now, but you aren't. She left and that sucks. Becoming a single parent probably feels like you're now carrying the weight of the world on your shoulders. But I promise you can do this. I'm here for whatever you might need, we all are."

Without saying anything else I take a few more steps toward the door before Chase whispers when I turn the doorknob.

"Thanks, Kincaid."

I want to say more. I want to tell him I'd do anything for him. For CeCe. I want to confront Kristen, ask her what the hell she's thinking. He looks so hurt, so confused, and just helpless. I know he's hurting more for CeCe than himself, though. Instead of saying anything more, I simply nod my head, smile, and quietly exit the bedroom.

I've never been Kristen's biggest fan. And it has nothing to do with my personal feelings toward Chase and everything to do with how I've seen her treat him in general. She always gave the impression that she felt she was too good for him. Like his fame and money were appealing, but Chase personally wasn't someone she wanted to be with. When Chase told us he was having a baby and Kristen was the mother, I instantly felt sorry for him. I didn't feel excitement like a normal friend should have, and at first, that made me feel bad. And the more I got to know her, the clearer things became to me. I never voiced my opinion to him directly, I think it would've been perceived as jealousy. But I always had my doubts about her intentions. I always wondered if she would walk out on him when she got bored or maybe he lost his appeal.

It's heartbreaking to see that regardless of whatever her feelings were toward Chase, an innocent baby still wasn't enough for her.

I played nice, for the most part. I knew they had their ups and downs, but I never expected him to drop the bomb one day that she just up and left. I could see the two of them breaking up, but leaving CeCe?

My heart hurts as I walk back down the hall and leave him in the room. Maybe one day, he'll want to tell me what happened, but until then I'll keep showing up for him. He's been in my life for decades, he's kind and thoughtful and he doesn't deserve to be hurt like this.

———

PRESENT

I feel like I've entered the twilight zone. Chase is being playful and fun tonight, like he's high school Chase all over again and instead of watching him be this way with another girl, I'm the one on the receiving end and I'm chomping at the bit to have more of it.

I meant every word I said, though. Chase has done a great job raising a kid on his own. It wasn't his choice to do it this way, but he's built a life for CeCe where she knows she's loved and cared for. He's a better man than he gives himself credit for. He doesn't have to live so on edge, so terrified that he's doing things wrong or so specific that he thinks if he does one thing off plan the world will end.

My feet run through the rug on the floor of his living room, feeling the pieces of carpet between my toes, forcing myself to think of how that feels instead of focusing on the way Chase is looking at me. The corner of his lip curves up, followed by a rumble of his chest. He stands from the couch and pulls both arms behind his back, making his chest stretch against the fabric, ready to cause a rip right through the center and my eyes are glued to the motion.

"I need some more water," he abruptly states.

His arms go above his head briefly and the candlelight casts a perfect glow on his stomach, giving a small glimpse of the way his abs look beneath his shirt as it rises and then falls with his movement. An involuntary sigh leaves my lips, and I know he catches it by the head shake that follows.

"What's your workout routine like?"

Nice one, Summer.

"My workout routine?" He stops walking and turns around with a throaty chuckle. "You're interested in my workout routine?"

No, I'm interested in being *your workout routine, but I can't exactly say that… can I?*

"Sure. Your physique is… notable so I'm just curious."

"My physique is notable?"

"Okay, are you just going to repeat everything I'm saying?" I stand, popping a hand on my hip.

His hand pulls at the back of his neck.

"That depends, are you going to continue asking questions you know the answer to?"

My nose scrunches up as I walk past him and attempt to force away the warm, blushing feeling from my cheeks.

"Well, this has been fun. I'm going to bed."

This time he laughs. Not a small chuckle, or a subtle smirk, no. Chase laughs.

"You can dish out the smart remarks, but can't take them? That doesn't seem like you."

My teeth clamp down on my bottom lip as I stand in the darkness of the kitchen. Chase doesn't talk to me like this, he doesn't joke with me and he *definitely* doesn't flirt with me.

I open my mouth to challenge him but the kitchen light flickers on and the TV screen comes back into view. The power returning seems to have snapped us both back into reality and Chase quickly looks anywhere but at me, finally focusing on the hallway where CeCe's bedroom door slowly pulls open.

"Hey, Peanut, it was just the lights coming back on." He begins walking toward her and ushers her back into her bedroom, closing the door behind the both of them.

I lean my elbows on the counter and run both hands down my face, feeling flushed and aroused and exhausted all at once.

CHAPTER FOURTEEN

CHASE

"We should probably get some sleep." I exhale a heavy breath when I walk back into the kitchen, grabbing my unopened water bottle from the counter, taking a sip.

I can feel Summer's eyes on me. She's focused on my throat as I swallow another sip and watch her pull her chin down before she looks away.

"Yeah, that sounds good. Thanks for letting me stay here." Summer walks by me slowly, bumping her elbow into my side as she passes.

The only thing that feels appropriate right now is a firm nod before I exit the kitchen and walk to the living room to get my bed for the night situated.

Summer disappears down the hall and I hear a click as my bedroom door closes. I can't for the life of me explain the way I've acted over the last few hours. I haven't let myself flirt with a woman in years, and never in a million years would I have thought the first woman I let my guard down for would be Summer fucking Kincaid. But I can't deny it's easy to be a little carefree with her. It's easy to not take things so seriously because that's how she lives.

Her little comments and jokes didn't annoy me tonight like they so often do. In fact, I welcomed them, I *wanted* them. I wanted for a moment to feel like I could be a little like my old self, and Summer made it feel so simple to do. I question if it's because we've known each other so long that there's just this familiar comfort.

Or maybe, I'd like to blame it on the atmosphere, the dimmed lights and the rain outside. The candle burning on the coffee table between us that lit up her presence. Maybe my loneliness officially got the best of me, and Summer just happened to be the woman I was trapped with tonight. Although, it didn't feel like I was "trapped"—I felt comfortable, and dare I say, I enjoyed her company.

I've known for years she has a thing for me, but she's also always dated others, so her crush always felt juvenile. Like it didn't actually mean anything in the grand scheme of things. She makes her comments and does her flirting, but I've grown to take that just as who Summer is. She's flirty, and friendly, and bubbly with pretty much anyone. I know she cares for me and CeCe, that isn't even a question, but tonight I just felt *something*. And I don't know what the fuck to do with it.

Much to my surprise, I'm having a harder time falling asleep than I thought I would. I'm physically exhausted, my body doesn't want to get up from this couch, but my mind won't stop racing and I can't turn my thoughts off no matter how hard I'm fucking trying.

I groan again, yanking the blanket off my legs and pulling my shirt off over my head, letting the cool air hit my skin now that the air conditioning is back on and running to get the apartment temperature back down. Everything in me feels heightened, and despite my best efforts, there's a pair of blue eyes I can't escape from. When I close my eyes, I see Summer sitting on the couch across from me, narrowing her stare and looking at me with a challenging smirk, and blood pumps through my veins almost forcing me into picturing something I shouldn't be.

When I left for college, I remember saying goodbye to Summer. I don't know why it's stuck with me, but it has. Naturally, she made some joke about not missing her too much, but then we hugged. And it didn't mean anything to me then, I still don't know if it does, but I just remember the hug. It wasn't one of those halfway hugs where you just use one arm, or a quick awkward one. Her arms pulled my sides closer to her and I remember wrapping her up against my chest and holding onto her for a moment. I don't remember hugs often; in fact, I don't hug people often to begin with. But Summer's hugs are always meaningful. She pulls you into her personal space and squeezes tight. It's right on the line of being too much, but it's not. It's completely all consuming, but in a good way. In the way that makes you feel important, cherished. It's like a warm hug, a familiar sweater, it's a feeling of complete comfort.

A similar memory of the Super Bowl win a few seasons ago flashes in my mind when she hugged me on the field, and another when I remember a night in the aftermath of Kristen leaving. I was having a bad day; fuck, they were all bad days for a while. But she dropped off a can of formula for CeCe so I wouldn't have to make a trip to the store the next morning. She hugged me in my doorway for longer than necessary, but I must've needed it. I wonder if she even knows she hugs like that.

I've spent the last couple of hours in and out of small bouts of sleep. The rain is still coming down outside, but it's nothing like it was hours ago. It's calmer, almost a drizzle, but enough to hear it gently hitting the patio floor. It's soothing and should help me fall back asleep as I turn over once more with my face toward the hallway.

The lightest sound causes me to peek one eye open as I see a shadow coming down the hall. Too tall to be CeCe, so I know it's Summer and a weird ache in my gut occurs at the thought of her sneaking out in the middle of the night. But when she finally comes into view, I pull the blanket up a little higher to hide my face as I watch her move. I shouldn't want to watch her move around my apartment, but I'm glued to her silhouette in the light coming through the back door. The shirt I gave her hits just at her upper thigh and it appears she must've been warm too as the shorts I gave her to wear are nowhere in sight, causing my mouth to become dry. Her hair is loose, no longer pulled up on top of her head and she slowly opens the cabinet next to the pantry, pulling out a glass before she grabs the milk from the refrigerator.

My body moves without consulting my brain first and before I can turn back around, it's too late. And I'm standing near the kitchen island, Summer's back to me as she pours a little more milk in the cup and takes another hefty sip. I'm finding it hard at this moment to find reasons to convince myself to go lie back down, when every thread of my being just wants to…

"Chase!" she whispers when she finally turns and sees me, jumbling my thoughts. "Gosh." Her hand flies to her chest as she puts the milk away.

"Didn't mean to scare you."

"No, it's okay. Sorry for waking you up. Sometimes, when I can't sleep I chug milk." She raises the glass to me and takes another sip, and all I can do is stare.

I feel like giving into the single side of me for just a moment. Giving into the small part of myself that I keep hidden away in a corner. Because for some fucking reason tonight, I can't stop thinking about Summer.

"You didn't wake me," I say, slowly shuffling my feet closer.

I can see her fingers grip the glass a little harder as I inch toward her, like she's bracing for something she feels coming. Her back leans against the counter as I make my way toward her, settling barely two feet in front of her.

"If you're not comfortable out here, we can switch. I'm sure you'd prefer your bed."

I don't answer and as expected she takes my silence as a reason to keep talking.

"Plus, you really don't fit on that couch."

My chest feels tight as I watch her mouth move. "Kincaid… please, stop talking," I say, breathing heavily and taking one more step toward her.

The pad of my thumb skims the fabric of my shirt on her body as I trace down her arm and I feel oddly territorial. An emotion I never expected to feel when it came to Summer, but tonight something has shifted between us. Her attitude doesn't irritate me, it excites me. Her constant rambling doesn't make me tune her out, it engages me. Her flirting isn't something I want to ignore, instead it makes me want more.

"Chase… what are you doing?" Summer's chest pumps up and down rapidly and her eyes flash to my hand once my thumb hits her bare skin on her arm. She watches my fingers move and then brings her gaze up to me.

She really is beautiful. How have I never noticed?

With her fingers still clutching the glass of milk, I stare down at her, not moving my eyes from hers, and I gently take the glass from her hand, placing it on the counter.

"What are you doing?" she asks again, but this time with a hesitancy in her voice. Her bottom lip quivers slightly.

"What I should have done earlier… years earlier, I'm starting to think." I breathe against her ear as I lean down. I can practically hear her heartbeat jumping from her chest.

"Chase," she breathes out heavily just seconds before I capture her lips with mine.

CHAPTER FIFTEEN

SUMMER

I can't explain what's happening, but Chase is kissing me and I feel like I've just been swept into a dream. A really magical fucking dream I never want to wake up from.

His hand immediately grips the back of my neck, pulling me closer to him as I stand here in his kitchen, very aware of the fact that I'm not wearing shorts under this t-shirt. His free hand roams my back, as if he's exploring a place he's never been before, and I whimper every time he digs his fingers in. His tongue collides with mine in what feels like the most natural movement ever. Like kissing Chase is something I do every night without practice or rehearsal, it just feels easy and expected.

We break apart briefly, and I inhale a deep breath, feeling sated and yet needy for more as our foreheads rest against one another. Both of our breaths are heavy as our eyes lock and a sense of realization over what just happened begins to set in. His skin is hot to the touch and I can feel mine ready to burst into flames.

The need to have just one more taste of him overcomes me. I grip his neck, pulling his lips back to mine and he comes without any resistance. My hands entangle in his hair, running my finger nails down toward the nape of his neck. He groans into my mouth and as if I'm weightless, Chase picks me up and sets me onto the counter. My thighs welcome the cold surface of the countertop and he pushes his body against me.

He lets his fingers graze my thighs and all I can do is moan at the touch. His hands rest on the top of my legs and he squeezes firmly, causing me to grind myself against the counter in a way I never thought I would. I need pressure and friction in places I can't ask him for. Because no matter how badly I want him in that way, I know that's not what this is. I know this is just a moment in time for each of us. A small blip that will be avoided in the morning, but right now, in the dimming moonlight, I'm accepting whatever he wants to give me.

My hips move slowly back and forth as he continues leaning into me, letting the kiss mature from hungry and chaotic to something slower, a more relaxed and comfortable rhythm.

It's the way his lips feel against mine, like they own me and I'm simply following his lead. And the minty taste that somehow still lingers even though it had been hours since he brushed his teeth. Kissing Chase is something I've only dreamed of until now and I'm happy to report that the reality far outweighs anything my mind could have imagined. Our lips stay interlocked for much longer than I would have expected, but we both feel so caught up in the moment, so completely consumed by what's happening.

When he finally pulls away slowly, my eyes stay closed for just a moment after we break the kiss. My fingers skim my bottom lip and I calm my breathing, letting myself relish in the brief moment we just shared.

And when I open my eyes, I can see he's fighting it. The urge to go further, even though we both know it won't. His eyes are a dark shade of brown, nearly black as he stands here. But it's his breathing that's the most telling. It's heavy and deep, like a wild animal foaming at the mouth for one more bite, a small taste. I know in the light of day, there's a good chance he'll look at this as a mistake, something he regrets doing. A moment of loneliness that got the best of him, but right now he looks like he's in pain over not being able to go any further. And I'll admit, I kind of like seeing him tormented over me.

Even if it is temporary.

"Kincaid, I—"

I hold my hand up and shake my head before he can go further.

"We can talk in the morning," I say, knowing he's going to hit me with an apology he doesn't owe me.

He nods his head, helping me down from the countertop, and I put my glass in the sink. I can still feel his eyes on me and I want nothing more than to keep kissing him, keep touching him and keep this moment lasting a little longer. But I know better. My smile softens and I force myself to walk past him back to the bedroom.

———

The fact that I thought I could just go back to sleep after that is laughable. Especially when I had to come back to Chase's bed and once again be wrapped up in his bedsheets that smell like him.

After finally giving up on trying to fall back asleep, I sit up and pull out my phone. The battery is probably going to die any minute now, but mindless scrolling should keep my mind off of the kiss I just shared with Chase, right?

As if the universe is out to torture me, the first post I see is from the Knights social media page. It's a post from a charity event the team participated in the other day. As I scroll through the photos, there's one of Chase next to Alex Farr. He's one of the newer guys on the team but you'd never really know it. He's disciplined, fast, and a great athlete. Not so bad to look at either, except even with Alex's pretty boy smile trying to distract me, the brick wall with a smirk next to him has my full attention. My thighs press together remembering his lips on mine only hours ago and how badly I wanted more, *needed* more.

I guess I could be angry with Chase for kissing me. After all, he knows how I feel about him, how I've felt for years. I could look at it as some form of a mind game, but I'm not that sixteen-year-old girl anymore who was ruled by emotions. I can recognize a kiss for what it is and sometimes a kiss is just giving in to a momentary impulse, and I think I'd rather have that—even if it never happens again, rather than never having it at all.

I double tap the photo before closing the app and roll out of his bed. Six in the morning seems reasonable to try and leave. I quickly get changed out of the clothing Chase gave me and place them in his hamper before putting my own clothes back on.

The bathroom light in the hallway is on when I walk by and I hear the sink running, but I don't linger to see who comes out. The couch where Chase was last night is empty, the blankets all perfectly back in place and the pillows look fluffed as if they'd never been used.

I pull my hair into a low ponytail and slip into my sandals near the front door, unlocking it and slowly turning the handle in hopes to get out unnoticed. But lady luck isn't in my corner today and Chase emerges from the bathroom as I'm halfway out the door. Our eyes briefly meet so I stop, taking in how he looks in the early morning hours. I dip my head slowly, smiling softly as his eyes sear into me like there are a million things he wants to say, but can't.

He nods just as I finally encourage my feet to move out of the doorway and walk out. Leaving the memory of last night on the other side of the door.

CHAPTER SIXTEEN

CHASE

How fucking stupid could I be? Kissing Summer like that last night. The hot water burns my back as I stand here letting it brand my skin as it rolls down. God, I fucking kissed her and then I laid on the couch for hours after wondering when I could do it again.

I want to kiss her again. Even though I know it's wrong and I know I shouldn't, because I have no intention of this becoming anything. But how the hell could I do that to her? How could be that guy who kisses someone out of my own selfish need? I know what something like that might mean to Summer, and I can't believe I let my urges win last night. But fuck, it felt good.

The taste of Summer's bottom lip as I sucked on it flashes as I close my eyes and my hand slams against the shower wall. I can't allow myself to go there with her. Which means I can't be around her right now. I've never been more thankful for a bye week in my life.

"Morning, Sunshine," Abby says when she walks into my apartment. Days like this I regret giving my sister a key. I could've used a moment to prepare for her entrance. The pot of coffee I made not even an hour ago is practically empty as I'm pouring my third cup and getting things out to make another pot.

"Morning," I say, tipping the cup in her direction.

Abby puts her purse down on the stool before noticing the mess out back.

"You should have brought that stuff in..." She trails off, pointing to the balcony.

"I got some of it, I would've been able to get more if I was home."

Her brows crease in confusion. Shit. I never told her Summer was here with CeCe.

"I had something come up last minute, and by the time I got home the storm was already crazy." I down the rest of the coffee in my mug and place it near the coffee pot when I'm inevitably going to be ready for a fourth. Abby glances at the brewing coffee pot and then back to me.

"She'll probably be up any minute," I say, referring to CeCe and grabbing my phone off of the charger in the kitchen. It's barely half way charged, but it'll have to do for now.

When I leave my apartment, it feels like I'm stepping into an entirely new reality. A reality where I kissed Summer and now have to live with that and hope she doesn't hate me for it.

———

It's been three days since I've seen Summer. But even though my mind has often been reeling over what happened between us, I've stayed busy with CeCe. Having a bye week right now has really worked in my favor and I've been able to get a lot of one on one time with CeCe, which is so rare during the season. We were able to spend a day at the zoo—which she loved—and spent another day at the Children's Museum downtown. It's full of different activities for kids and it wore her out as I expected it would.

"Hold still." I run the comb through CeCe's hair, getting her ready for gymnastics tonight.

She asked for a braid, so I've been sitting with her for the last fifteen minutes with a tutorial up on my phone trying to figure it out. I understand the basic logistics of it, but the twisting of all the pieces is a fucking nightmare. How are my fingers supposed to tie her hair together when it's so fine and slipping through my hands? I let out a frustrated sigh when I have to rewind the video for the third time to watch a certain part again, and CeCe notices.

"It's okay," she says, pulling her head forward and almost completely out of my grip.

"Sorry, Peanut. I'm almost done." I look at the twisted pieces of hair and consider just tying it up as it is and calling it a day. It's kind of braided, if you don't look too closely.

CeCe stands up straight again on the foot stool as she watches me in the mirror and I'm trying my best not to look as frustrated as I feel. It's so close to perfect and I want it to be that way for her.

"Cross the right strand over to the middle and then cross the left strand into the middle. Repeat these basic steps all the way down until you've reached the desired length and fasten with a hair tie."

I pause the video on the image of the completed braid and try to study the way it looks. How can I read a bunch of football plays, but can't follow two simple steps for a damn braid?

When she winces after I pull one of the strands through, I realize I must've tangled one of the pieces.

"Oh, sorry." I kiss her head and gently take the left strand to cross over the middle, like the video says.

By the time I'm finished, it doesn't look like the finished product in the video, but it looks better than the first time I tried, and I think the progress is good for today. Plus, we've run out of time to keep trying.

"Thanks, Daddy!" CeCe shouts when she reaches behind her head to feel the braid. I know she can't see it, but I want it to be perfect for her next time.

———

At the gym, I stand against the glass as I look down and watch her do a bunch of forward rolls in a row. I'd be dizzy after one, let alone four. There's another mom down at the very end, but rather than watching she's on her phone. The door squeaks open when someone else walks in and I don't bother to look and see who it is, but the slam when it closes followed by a quiet "sorry" does grab my attention.

My head tilts in confusion as I stare at Summer walking toward me. Blue crewneck sweater over a pair of bike shorts and her hair pulled back in a clip. She mouths sorry again as she gets closer to me and all I can do is stare at the way her lips look. They're full with a shade of light pink gloss on top, but I remember how they taste. I wasn't expecting to see her today. In fact, I wasn't expecting to see her for at least another week due to my schedule.

"What are you doing here?"

She scoffs and takes a seat on the chair next to me. "It's so nice to see you too."

Pulling the chair out a bit, I take a seat next to her with the intention of starting our conversation over, but she starts waving excitedly out the window and blows a kiss down below. When I glance out, I notice CeCe jumping up and down, waving up here. Summer smiles at CeCe and then points down to where the coach is explaining something to the girls, attempting to refocus CeCe on her class.

"She asked me to come last time I was over... I didn't think it would be a problem."

It isn't a problem. It shouldn't be at least.

"No, it isn't. Sorry. I just wasn't expecting you, that's all."

She nods her head slowly and smiles, crossing her right leg over her left knee, getting comfortable in the chair as she settles in to watch my daughter. The only other person who's come to this has been my sister and honestly, it's only been when she had to bring her.

"Nice job," she says, tapping my boot with her sandal.

My cocked eyebrow no doubt gives away my confusion.

"The braid. A few more tries and you'll be a natural."

I chuckle at her observation. Of course, she would notice the braid. "It's harder than it looks." I cross my arms over my chest as I defend myself.

Summer tries to cover a laugh with her hands before removing the clip and fluffing her blonde sea of hair in my direction.

"You can practice on mine if you want. I won't even get upset if you pull it." Her eyes narrow and she grins playfully.

I sigh, shaking my head at her.

I guess we aren't addressing the elephant in the room and just diverting back to our regularly scheduled programming. Maybe it's just better this way. If she can so easily fall back into our normal pattern, then I should be able to as well. I have to say, though, I am a little surprised she's acting like nothing happened. Who the hell knows? Maybe to her, it was nothing. But it sure as shit didn't feel like nothing, and it didn't sound like nothing with her whimpers and moans, and the way her body rocked back and forth on the counter didn't look like nothing.

But maybe this is just how Summer is. She's spontaneous and reckless, maybe that's what the other night was for her and nothing more.

"I'm kidding. If you pull my hair, I might yell a little." She scrunches her nose with a smile before spending the rest of the time focused on watching CeCe.

I cherish the nights I'm able to watch CeCe do something she loves. It's become routine after gymnastics to get ice cream on the way home and it's the one time I tend to be okay with dessert before dinner. We both look forward to the extra quality time together.

Summer stands slightly behind me as we're waiting for the kids to come out of the class. CeCe shouts my name, running into my leg before she notices Summer and a squeal leaves her mouth as if she didn't see her in the viewing room earlier and she's surprised to see her.

"Summer!" she yells, flying into her arms as she's bent down to hug her.

There's a real joy on CeCe's face when I see them interact. Summer immediately tells her how great she did and how brave she was for flipping over the bar. It's obvious to me how quickly the two of them have formed a bond in the last few weeks. Summer's always been in CeCe's life, but never as constant as recently and I'm starting to wonder if I should've had her around more. Having positive, reliable women in CeCe's life is something she needs, and I'm finding myself relieved that Summer is one of those women for her.

When we're walking out, I overhear CeCe behind me asking Summer to come with us for ice cream. There's a part of me that wants Summer to say yes. A small part that feels like Summer's presence is good, for both of us.

"I can't today, but why don't we plan for another time?"

"Yay!" I hear CeCe skipping behind me.

"Where'd you park?" I look back and ask.

"I'm just over there." She points and hits the button on her key fob, so the lights blink.

"Come on." I gesture toward CeCe and have her hop on my shoulders to cross the parking lot quicker.

"What are you doing? You're right here." Summer points to my truck sitting three feet away.

"Yes, and you're over there. Let's go."

"Quite the gentleman," she whispers as she nudges my arm and walks beside me.

Yeah. Except, I've been thinking of her in the most ungentlemanly way since I kissed her.

CHAPTER SEVENTEEN

SUMMER

"There's an EMS on the way. Engine nine just called it in." Damien swipes his badge and we walk outside the double doors.

When the ambulance pulls up, the first paramedic to hop out of the truck is Landyn Evans. He happens to be Liam's brother and someone I see often as our jobs overlap quite a bit.

We're the closest hospital for his station and the biggest in the area, so many patients prefer to come here for treatment.

"Pediatric?" I ask when he looks up at me.

"Yeah, twelve-year-old girl." Landyn nods at me and then helps his partner get her out.

"Got it," I say.

I pull my hair into a scrunchie to make sure it's completely out of my face as they bring her out of the ambulance. She's awake, but looks exhausted. Still in a soccer uniform, shin guards and cleats included. Nothing looks broken from my vantage point and I don't see any blood, so I wait for the para-medics to give Damien a run down.

"Tiffany Smith, twelve years old. Fainted on the soccer field, but was alert by the time we got there." Landyn pulls his hat over his head as he speaks.

"Thanks, Lan," I say, walking up beside her and helping guide her into a room.

Damien goes through a bunch of questions with the paramedics and two other nurses get her vitals once we have her in the room.

"Hi, I'm Summer," I say, offering a soft smile to the girl's mom as she's standing there.

"Eileen, thank you." She briefly makes eye contact and nods her head before she looks back to her daughter. I can see the concern on her face.

"Hi, Tiffany. I'm Summer." I shift my attention to the girl next to me. Her soccer uniform is covered in grass stains, which tells me she's probably a tough competitor.

Her eyes look like they're sunken in and her lips appear dry and cracked, both clear signs of dehydration. She musters up a smile for me and then lets her head fall against the pillow.

"I feel much better now," she states, eyes darting to her mom in the corner.

"I'm glad, but we want to get some fluids in you and monitor things for a little while, okay?"

Her mom steps closer to the bed, nodding and answering for her. "Yes, anything."

Another nurse is already setting up an IV for some fluids, so I finish my notes and leave the room to go find Damien.

When I spot him, he's still talking with Landyn and one of the other paramedics.

"Hey, Summer," Landyn says when I approach the three of them.

"My favorite Evans brother," I jest.

"I know you don't mean that, but I appreciate the ego boost." His brown eyes look nearly black and the thickness of his eyebrows is almost distracting. He and Liam don't look too much alike, but when they open their mouths you know they're related. They both have that charm and charisma that's hard to ignore.

"All right, we'll see you guys later, thanks so much." Damien nods at us both.

"I'll see you at the Andersons' tomorrow, right?" Landyn asks before we go our separate ways.

I almost forgot that Ford and Abby are having a barbeque this weekend, my mind has been so clouded with work and then trying *not* to think about the fact that me and Chase kissed.

"Yeah, I'll see you there!" I answer, smiling in his direction as he walks toward the doors and back to the rescue.

Once I finish making my rounds for the last time this afternoon, I stop back in the room where Tiffany is. I've been peeking in for the last hour or so, each time she's been doing well, and taking the fluids easily. This time, her head is perched on a couple of pillows as she's resting, but she has the IV out and it looks like she's about to be discharged.

"Feeling better?" I ask, peeking my head in.

"Yeah, I feel fine."

Her mom stands from the chair to thank me for my help just as the doctor comes in with the discharge papers.

"And thank you, Dr. McCall," Eileen says, causing me to turn around and be face to face with Drew for the first time since we broke up.

"Take it easy, all right? Drink water. Rest." He points to Tiffany playfully and hands the papers to Eileen.

Drew and I both exit the room at the same time and I quickly try to head down the hall, but he calls my name loud enough to where it would look rude if I ignored him.

"Yes, Dr. McCall?"

"Okay, enough with the pleasantries. No patients are around, you can call me Drew," he says, his eyes giving me a once over.

"What do you need, Drew?"

"I just wanted to see how you were doing?"

See how I'm doing? Laughable.

"I'm great, thank you." My feet begin to move to take me far away from this conversation, but he stops me again.

"Listen, I feel like we ended things on a bad note, and I'd like to try and fix it. I don't want you to hate me." The arrogance in his words is enough to make me want to vomit all over his pretty white coat.

"Hating you would require caring."

"Wow," he scoffs with a head shake.

I sigh, knowing that I do have to work with him often and I'd rather not have things be awkward. "I just mean… I don't hate you. I don't have any feelings about any of it. I'm really over it and I'm okay. Believe me," I say, trying to find a peaceful way to end this conversation.

If Chase can go on not hating Kristen for the awful things she's done, then surely I can find it in me to not hate Drew. I can simply move on from it and feel indifferent.

He gives a curt nod, and this time I'm able to walk away without him calling me back.

———

With the guys having a bye week, I haven't seen Chase since I shocked him by showing up at CeCe's gymnastics practice. His eyebrows shot up in surprise when he saw it was me who walked through the door. I probably should have given him a heads up text, especially considering we both avoided the giant elephant in the room like the plague with my surprise visit.

Ford and Abby's pool is full of kids when I walk out back, noticing a few other guys from the team and their families are here as well. I spot Chase right away, standing next to the grill with Liam and Ford, holding a glass I'm certain has whiskey in it as they talk while watching the game that's playing.

"San Francisco by ten," I say as I walk up to them, smirking in Chase's direction.

"I'll take that bet." Liam points his finger at me and smiles.

"Dipshit, you can't bet on the game." Chase turns to face Liam with a dumbfounded look on his face.

Chase seems to have finally cleaned up the scruff he had going on for the last few weeks as he's now simply left with his five o'clock shadow. I've got to say, the unruly beard he was sporting was kind of a turn on, but now I can see the piercing shape of his jaw and his Adam's apple stands out like he did this just to entice me. Every part of his back is covered in muscle as he stands there shirtless next to Ford who seems to be adding a new tattoo every time I see him.

"I saw your brother yesterday at work," I say, nudging Liam's arm.

He looks down, focusing his hazel eyes on me and puts his arm around my shoulder, pulling me close. On instinct, my eyes swoop up and I notice a flare in Chase's nostrils. His body becomes rigid as he stands there now, when he looked relaxed just moments ago.

"Yeah? He should be here soon." Liam keeps his arm around me, hanging his forearm off my shoulder. Liam's contact isn't new, he's always been affectionate, but in a respectful way, never anything more. It's causing my curiosity to tailspin when Chase seems affected by it.

It's mid-November, but that doesn't apply in Florida when speaking in terms of weather. It's still warm enough to have a pool day and it's rare that any of my friends miss an opportunity to get together.

Abby has the entire kitchen island covered in different appetizers and finger foods. I can't fill my plate fast enough when I finally make it back inside to eat something. Chase grabs a plate next to me and starts adding a few pieces of chicken, cubes of cheese and some fruit.

"Here," I say, adding a few extra strawberries to the plate. "Don't make it harder on yourself, she'll finish those in five seconds and ask for more. Just give her more now."

"Good thinking," he replies, taking the strawberries from my hand and placing them on the plate. Instead of reaching for the napkin that's literally right in front of him, he does something that makes my chest pound and my thighs scream as I squeeze them together. His tongue skims his index finger and thumb, causing my lower lip to drop slightly as I watch the movement. He did that shit on purpose.

I've spent most of this afternoon watching the football games and eating a bunch of food that I definitely don't need, but can't say no to. Bacon wrapped jalapenos are a staple football food, it'd simply be rude to not eat them.

"Hey." Chase's voice pulls me from the trays I've been staring at for the last two minutes, debating if I really need more buffalo chicken dip or should opt for some celery sticks instead.

"Hi." I smile at him as he comes up beside me.

"Can we talk?"

I feel the lump in my throat build at those three words and just nod my head and follow him down the hall. I wipe my greasy fingers on the swimsuit cover up I'm wearing, even though it's useless with this kind of sheer material.

He opens the door to the spare bedroom down the hall and I walk in first with him just behind me. Before he begins talking, he pulls the baseball hat from his head and turns it backward after running his hand in his hair. My breathing picks up when he takes a step in my direction, but I don't move. My feet somehow feel like bricks and I can't pick them up.

"Okay." He begins on a heavy exhale. "You've been avoiding it. I've been avoiding it. And we just can't anymore.

Especially because you're helping with CeCe so much, I can't have anything become weird between us." He stops talking and looks at me with those golden brown eyes. "I'm sorry I kissed you."

I'd like to be surprised by his apology, but I'm not. I knew the moment it was happening that Chase would feel guilty about it. He'd never want to lead me on, I know that wholeheartedly.

"Chase, stop. Don't apologize. It didn't mean anything to you, I knew that and I was okay with it. We both got caught up in the moment. And I think we can admit it was just nice having company for the night and we've always got along well, we're friends... I know it meant nothing. It's okay."

I've spent my entire teenage years and adult life lusting after Chase. I won't be stupid enough to think that one random kiss meant anything to him.

When he doesn't say anything more, I walk around him to exit the bedroom but his arm shoots out, blocking me.

"Don't say that. It didn't mean *nothing*, Summer."

Summer. He never calls me by my first name.

"But... I can't let it happen again."

"What does that mean?" I ask, confused by the conflict in his voice.

He lowers his arm, his body edging closer to mine.

The dynamic we've always had made my feelings for him somehow seem manageable. I like him, he doesn't like me, we go back and forth with our jabs sometimes and voila. Easy for me. Things were never reciprocated and in some way that made it easier for me to be so confident and playful with him.

"What do you mean, '*it didn't mean nothing*'?" My tone becoming more demanding.

He looks tormented when his eyes meet mine, confused even. Like words are on the tip of his tongue and he's debating whether or not he can say them.

But when he doesn't say anything I move around him and

this time he doesn't block me. Though, his voice stops me before I can leave the room.

"It means… I haven't stopped thinking about that goddamn kiss in a week, Kincaid. And I *shouldn't* be thinking about it. I shouldn't be thinking about *you*. But all that clouds my mind lately is how badly I want to fucking do it again."

Shock runs through my body.

I'm sorry, *what?*

CHAPTER EIGHTEEN

CHASE

How the fuck did I just let that slip out?

"Let me get this straight…" Summer takes a step back, which only puts her right up against the door she was just planning to exit. One hand goes up and she looks genuinely confused as I stand there in front of her.

I guess I can't blame her, up until seven seconds ago she thought her very existence irritated me beyond belief.

"You… you don't regret kissing me?" Her hip pops out and she places her other hand on it firmly. The gold rings on her fingers stand out against the black sheer fabric she's wearing to cover up her bathing suit underneath. She has yet to even take this cover up off, even when she was sitting with her legs in the pool.

Suddenly, I'm paying attention to the way her body looks and the clothes that have been covering it. The overalls, the big over-sized t-shirts. In all the time I've known Summer, her wardrobe has been her own. She wears brighter colors and usually things that hug her frame, but I see now how much of her body she's trying to cover.

"Why are you wearing this?" I ask, pulling at the fabric near her shoulder.

"I—What? That has nothing to do with what I just asked you."

"You haven't taken this off the entire time you've been here. And you wear overalls now, and shirts that hang to your knees. Why?"

She scoffs and rolls her eyes. "So, you've taken an interest in my clothing choices. Nice, Chase."

"You're not answering my question," I retort.

"*You're* not answering mine. I asked first, and frankly, my question is a hell of a lot more important than why I'm wearing overalls."

"God, you're difficult." A defeated sigh leaves my chest as her eyes widen, waiting for me to answer.

"That kiss…" I start. "I don't know what came over me. Dare I say, I liked being around you and fuck… I don't know. But I shouldn't *want* to kiss you. And lately, it's all I can fucking think about and it's messing with my head." Her eyes bore into mine. Bright blue and pleading for more.

A hint of a smile crosses her lips. "Careful, Chase. This might go to my head."

I tilt my head and blink my eyes slowly at her attempt to be funny when I'm trying to be serious. "It can't happen again. There's too much at stake to let it happen again. I never want to hurt you or ruin any kind of friendship we have, as dysfunctional as it may be."

I can barely believe I'm even admitting any of this shit out loud right now. If I wasn't going to see her so often, I probably would've just kept it to myself, but knowing she's going to be around more, the right thing to do was get it out.

"We are pretty dysfunctional." She laughs. "But you don't owe me an apology."

Both of us are silent for a moment before she asks, "Out of curiosity, though, why exactly can't it happen again?"

"Because it can't. For lack of a better term, you're my babysitter. A babysitter who CeCe loves and I can't screw that up for her."

She scoffs at my reasoning. I know she's thinking it's a pathetic excuse. Maybe she's right, but it's also more than that. It's the fact that I've known her for over twenty years, the fact that she's my sister's best friend, things could get messy with Summer and I don't want the mess. I've done messy and it's fucking hell.

"So, you enjoyed my company and you want to kiss me… but you don't want yourself to kiss me, so you're just simply… not going to kiss me again? Do I have that right?"

I nod.

"That easy?" Her voice lowers.

"That easy," I say firmly, hoping to convince both her and myself.

The glimmer in Summer's eye has me questioning everything I just laid out between us. But facts are facts, and I let myself get caught up in a moment and kissed the one person I shouldn't. It doesn't matter that it was the best fucking kiss I've ever had or the most relaxed I'd felt in a conversation in forever. It *can't* happen again.

"I respect it, but a piece of advice, Chase. It doesn't hurt to give in to the things you want sometimes." She shrugs as she walks past me and out the door.

Summer likes to question me and make me think twice about everything. To her, nothing is black and white, she lives in the gray areas. She's so comfortable in the unknown and the possibility of what could be. She's always open to new ideas and ways of thinking, whereas I feel like I live by a fucking right and wrong list most of the time. A golden rule book that lays things out clearly. To me things are cut and dry—have a problem?

Here's the obvious solution. But Summer thrives in the gray and looks at things differently.

————

I'm not sure what to expect as I wait for Summer to get here this morning. I haven't seen her since the barbeque; although, I've thought about her every damn day.

As far as I'm concerned, I just need to go back to how things were before we kissed and focus on how many of her quirks bother me versus intrigue me.

There are a few taps at the door and CeCe goes flying into the foyer.

"Hey, we don't open the door without a grown up," I say as I'm walking to keep up with her strides.

Summer floats in once the door is opened, blonde hair pulled away from her face with a headband and a pair of leggings with a t-shirt hanging down to the middle of her thighs. I stop myself from doing a full scan of her body as she stands in front of me, a boastful smile already on her face as she catches me stopping myself.

"Good morning." She beams, walking past me and following CeCe into the kitchen.

My temples are already throbbing, along with another part of my body that I don't appreciate right now.

"Morning," I call after she's long gone, but her coconut scent seems to have lingered and is infiltrating my senses.

"Smells good in here," she says once I'm in the kitchen.

The coffee maker is brewing another pot, and I notice Summer pulls a protein bar from her purse.

"There's food here, you can make yourself whatever you'd like." I gesture to the pantry.

"Oh, I know. But I like these bars. Plus, I'm sure we'll make some grilled cheese within the hour." She covers her lips before continuing. "A brunch, if you will."

"I love brunch!" CeCe says from the opposite side of the table.

"Oh, do you now?" My eyes go wide.

"Summer always makes brunch," CeCe reveals, and my eyes dart to Summer standing against the counter, half eaten protein bar in her hand.

"What does she make for brunch?" My question is directed at CeCe, but I stare at Summer.

"A little of this, a little of that, bottomless mimosas, naturally."

Summer's smile broadens as I shake my head at her with a hearty laugh.

"Well, I'll be back after my meeting. It shouldn't be more than a couple of hours," I say to Summer while I put my phone in the pocket of my shorts.

Her eyes linger on my face for a moment before she replies. "Okay, we'll be here."

She lightly tugs on CeCe's ponytail before she runs off to her bedroom, I'm sure to grab whatever toy she has in mind to start their day with.

While I'm reaching for my car keys, Summer comes around the island and I feel her fingers on my arm. The tips of them are warm and soft, sending a small reprieve of comfort through me.

"This always drives me nuts," she says as she fixes the sleeve on my shirt where the hem was inside out.

She moves slowly, working her way around the entire width of the sleeve to make sure it's all to her liking before she looks back up at me. Her lips are pressed together and perfect cheekbones tilted up to meet my gaze.

God, her eyes… they're so fucking blue.

Bright and crystal clear, like some remote tropical waters out in the Caribbean. They're *impossibly* blue—so much so that someone could assume they're contacts. But I know better, that's all Summer.

Both of us seemingly lost in a very brief moment are brought back to reality by the giggle of a three-year-old at the other end of the table, holding a bunch of paint brushes and her small easel.

"You can paint too? You're a woman of many talents, Cecelia Hunt," Summer says, shifting all attention from me to my daughter.

An interruption I'm glad to have had, because one more moment getting lost in her looking at me might've had me breaking my own damn rules.

I quickly redirect my focus to leaving—kissing CeCe on the cheek and heading out the door with no more than a nod to Summer.

———

"What the hell has got you so wound up today, Hunt?"

I lift the weights one more time for a hammer curl and a grunt leaves my chest when I place them back on the rack. I didn't plan on doing a workout today, but the meeting ended early and I felt like I needed something to release some of this pent up energy.

"What do you mean?" I ask Nate, wiping my brow. "I'm fine."

"You seem more… tense than normal, which is actually saying a lot. I didn't think it'd be possible. Everything okay with CeCe?"

"She's good." I grab a towel from the clean stack in the weight room and swipe it across the back of my neck.

"Did something happen with Summer?"

"No," I reply instantly, and Nate begins a low chuckle just as Ford approaches us.

Great. Someone else has entered the conversation.

"What's so funny?" Ford asks.

"I don't know for sure, but I think…" Nate starts, but before his imagination can get too carried away, I just fess up.

"Summer and I kissed. I kissed her. It shouldn't have happened and won't happen again."

"Is it my turn now to get pissed at you for kissing my wife's best friend?" Ford jokes.

"Believe me, I'm pissed enough at myself for the both of us."

"So, is something going on with you two then?"

"No," I quickly answer Nate's question. "It can't happen again. It won't."

"Just make sure she isn't upset or anything, man. You know how she feels about you… don't fuck with her."

"You don't think I've already been beating myself up over that part?" My eyes narrow at Ford. It's thoughtful of him to want to look out for Summer, even if it is simply for the sake of Abby.

"When did this even happen?"

I can feel a headache coming on already and I'm second guessing if mentioning anything to them was the right thing to do, but eventually this would've come up.

"The night that storm came through… the streets were flooded, there was no way I could let her drive home in that. My sister would've killed me if something happened to her best friend because I sent her out in a storm. So, she stayed and we talked and then it just got late. I don't fucking know what happened. I let my old self get the best of me apparently." My eyes squeeze together and I take a sip from my water. "It was a good fucking kiss, but I can't do that again. I told her it can't happen again," I add.

"Oh, you're a fucking idiot, Hunt." Nate laughs.

"Why? We talked about it and she was fine, I think."

"You kiss her, you like it and then think you can just be

around her so often and it won't happen again because you *say* it won't? Idiot." Nate's index finger rams into my shoulder like a kid proving a point.

"I've been successfully not kissing Summer for the last twenty years of my life. I think I can manage not doing it again."

The two exchange a glance.

"Good luck with that." Ford shakes his head at me.

My comment doesn't seem to convince Ford or Nate.

But it doesn't have to convince them. It just needs to convince *me*.

CHAPTER NINETEEN

SUMMER

I wasn't expecting CeCe to take such a long nap this afternoon. In fact, I don't even think I was expecting her to nap at all, but she fell asleep on me while we were watching a movie and I haven't had the heart to move her. Although, my arm feels like it's falling asleep and I'd like to stretch my legs just a little since they've been scrunched up for over an hour.

Lifting CeCe's arm, I move myself slowly from the couch, practically sliding my body nearly onto the floor to avoid moving her too much and waking her. My left hand plants firmly on the area rug when I hear the front door open and close and heavy footsteps making their way toward me. I look like I'm playing a damn game of Twister in this position.

Chase goes to speak, but notices CeCe asleep on the couch and simply shakes his head at me as I continue to slither out from under her surprisingly strong grasp.

"You're free," Chase says with a tight-lipped smirk when I walk into the kitchen. His hair is sweaty and the shirt he's wearing looks like it's also stained in sweat. Usually, he showers after workouts before coming home, but doesn't look like he took the time today.

"What are you feeding her? She's freakishly strong," I joke, walking past him to the chair my purse is hanging on.

"I buy strawberries in bulk," Chase replies with a chuckle.

He moves around the kitchen quietly. My pulse quickens when he takes a seat on a stool next to where I'm standing, his thighs dangerously close to touching my arm hanging beside me.

He groans as he leans back, allowing his head to fall completely back in a stretch.

"Are you okay?"

"Yeah," he says, twisting his body and I hear a few cracks from his back and wince. "I'm okay, just sore. My knees aren't what they used to be."

Both of his hands grip his knees, causing my eyes to glue themselves to his skin. He slides his hands over his quad muscles, lightly squeezing as he goes and his shorts begin moving up slightly with the gesture, causing my tongue to glide between my lips.

"Oh," I choke out. My heart turns over in response to his body being so close to me and the desire to touch him feels all consuming.

When we spoke about our kiss, he made it clear it wasn't going to happen again. A decision I've convinced myself to accept. But it doesn't change the fact that everything Chase does will always flip my world upside down.

"I'm actually going to go to Mia's gym later, I think. The one in my building is closed for renovations, so I've been using hers. It's just kind of far for me, but it is what it is."

"There's a gym here." It spills from Chase's lips before I think he even recognizes what he said. He instantly looks like it's a sentence he wants to take back, but in true gentlemanlike Chase form, he continues on.

"I just mean… if you need somewhere to workout, take my extra gym card and use the one here. There's a sauna, it's nice."

He smiles at me courteously and then looks back down at the

planner in front of him. I watch as he highlights a date on the calendar and writes "Friendsgiving" in the lined box.

"If memory serves, your gym is really difficult to find and you're not so great at giving out directions."

He mumbles under his breath and then glances up at me. I'm taken back by the glint behind his eyes.

"Something tells me you might be better at following directions than my sister is."

"That's debatable. I'm easily distracted," I quip, looking back down at his thighs.

Chase's hands both rise from the table and he holds up one finger on each. I can't help but stare at the massive state of his hands and fingers. How can a hand look so muscular?

"You can see both my fingers right?" He wiggles his index fingers at me and my toes want to curl right into the floor.

I can only nod my head up and down in response.

"Pick one and follow it."

He moves his fingers back and forth in front of me like he's giving me some kind of eye test and I'm probably going to fail out of sheer mesmerization.

My eyes follow his left finger every which way it moves. He keeps it still and moves it in circles, then goes back and forth and up and down. I desperately feel like I need a sip of water or a shot of tequila. I can feel Chase's eyes on me as I'm following his finger movements. A silly little exercise like this shouldn't have me feeling all out of sorts. I'm actually embarrassed that I'm so worked up over this.

"See?" He puts his hand down, clearing his throat and turning away from me. "You weren't even paying attention to my right hand to notice I was drawing this smiley face. I think you can remain focused long enough to follow signs that say *gym*."

I laugh nervously, feeling flushed and unsteady on my feet all of a sudden. What a risky little game he chose to play, knowing that a temptation like that would rile me up. He's the one who said we can't kiss again, not me. If anything, *I* should be the one tempting *him*.

Shaking my head, I try to regain my composure and bring myself back to the present, rather than staying lost in the size of his hands in front of my face.

"The card is in that bowl on the counter. Really, just use it. I don't usually workout down there, but I do use the sauna when I can. The whole place is usually empty, so have at it."

"Thanks," I say, finally finding my footing and grabbing my purse to leave. I hate leaving while CeCe is asleep, but if I don't get out of this apartment immediately, who knows what I might say or do after that little finger ordeal.

The gym key card is neatly placed in the stack of other belongings in the bowl, almost daring me to just take it and put it in my purse. I cave to the pressure, shoving the card in the pocket of my purse and heading for the door.

It amazes me that he can make me feel hot and flustered and then irritated all at once. Maybe this is how I make him feel? But I can't imagine I turn him on in the same way. Irritate him, though? No test needed for that.

———

"Is it your husband or your mother? No? Great, silence your phone, Abby! This is important." Mia pulls a tank top over her sports bra as Abby and I both sit on her bed waiting for her to get ready for the game.

"Ah, sorry, sorry." Abby presses the ignore button on her phone and pulls the pillow back to her chest. "Okay, you were saying…"

"Chase kissed me," I repeat, bringing both hands to my cheeks and feeling the rush of the moment all over again. "I wanted to tell you both sooner. Like the second after it happened, but wanted it to be just us in person."

"Oh my god! How was it? Perfect? Everything you ever thought it would be? Or underwhelming?" Mia asks.

"It was… *unbelievable*."

"Was it rough and hungry? I mean he hasn't kissed anyone in God knows how long, I would picture him just being so needy, so animalistic about it." Mia sits down next to Abby and me.

"I mean at first it was really intense. We both just kind of let the adrenaline take us and it felt so consuming, but then it slowed and we just kind of sunk into the rhythm of it."

"Oooo," Mia moans and closes her eyes. "Okay, so where did it happen?"

"The night we had that storm. I was with CeCe and he got home later than expected. He was insisting I didn't drive home because of the weather and we just hung out all night. Actually, it felt like that one night at the cabin trip we took years ago." I gesture to Abby. "When Chase and I were the only two left up after everyone else fell asleep in the middle of that scary movie. We didn't kiss then, obviously. But he's so much less guarded when it's just one on one. Like he lets himself *be* himself, I don't know." I shrug.

"I want all the details. I swear this pregnancy is making me feel so horny. Like where were his hands? Was it just the one kiss?" Mia holds my stare.

"In his kitchen… It started out against the counter, like he basically blocked me in, pushed me against it. But then he picked me up and put me on top of the counter."

Another moan falls from Mia—causing Abby and I both to laugh.

"His hands held my thighs, and it felt so possessive and I… ugh, I loved it."

"So you're just kissing all the time now?" Abby playfully shoves my shoulder.

"No. It's not happening again."

"What? He kissed you knowing how you feel about him without the intention of doing it again? I'm going to kill him."

"No, no. It wasn't like that," I assure Abby. "To tell you the truth, I understand where he's coming from. Of course I want to keep kissing him, but we both just got swept up in the moment, in the atmosphere of no power and the middle of the night and rain outside. It was literally the perfect recipe for a midnight one-time kiss. If this would've happened at sixteen, or twenty, even... then yeah, I would've been upset, I think. But sometimes, a kiss is just a kiss and doesn't mean there's going to be more."

"Blink twice if you're secretly hooking up."

"Mia!" Abby says through a laugh.

"What? I don't believe for one second that they're just never going to kiss again."

"We did talk about the kiss. He told me he wanted to kiss me again, but doesn't want himself to kiss me." I chuckle. "He did admit that, at least. But he laid out his reasons why he *can't*." I sigh. "I don't know, but Chase is one person I never want to force things with."

Mia scoffs and reaches for the door knob when we all leave her room. "Yeah, but... ugh, you're *supposed* to end up together."

———

There's a thrill that feels like it's running rampant through my body when I wake up this morning. My bed is cozy and warm, the blinds are closed, but a small speck of sunlight is peeking through casting just the right amount of light across my bedspread.

It's been weeks since Chase and I have kissed. Weeks since I got to experience everything I ever dreamed of since I was a teenager. A first kiss is often full of awkwardness and hesitations, too much overthinking and uncertainty. But with Chase it felt like home. His embrace felt like something I'd been wrapped up in long before our kiss. It wasn't any of those things that a first kiss can often be and I can't help but wonder if he also felt like that with me, too.

We've worked out a pretty good schedule in the last few weeks with me helping with CeCe a few times a week and then Abby helping when she's available. There's only a couple more months left in the season—if they make the playoffs, that is. Otherwise, this will be over after Christmas. I can't see that being the case, though. Despite the fact that the team isn't playing great, I don't think I've ever seen them end a season after the regular season. There's always been playoffs.

As I stand in front of the mirror in my bathroom getting ready, I take an extra second to stare at my body clothed in only a bra and underwear.

So it might look a little more pear shaped than before, and I may desperately need some sunshine to put some color on my pale skin, but there's still so much to love about what I see. The roundness of my face is where endless smiles take place for little kids who need them. My arms that feel a bit flappier have helped countless people in and out of beds and wheelchairs. My hips take up more space than I remember this time last year, but the curves on *my* body show young girls that it's okay to have them on *theirs*.

"Where are the mashed potatoes?" Liam's voice is the first thing I hear when I walk into Nate and Mia's for Friendsgiving this afternoon.

CeCe—along with Nate and Mia's twin boys—is in the living room with the television on and tons of toys scattered around the room. I can see straight through giant sliding glass doors to the deck out back and spot Ford, Chase, and Nate all seated around a table. Liam's voice still carries through from the kitchen where it sounds like he's making Abby and Mia crazy with questions and opinions on things.

"Can you just go outside?" Mia finally snaps, playfully pushing his arm out of her way.

"Hello," I say as I'm walking in and Mia's giving me a *get him out of here look* when I put my bag down.

"Add pecans on top of that." Liam points as I grab his arm, pulling him with me.

"It's Mia's first time hosting this, leave her alone and let her do it. She's excited and you're stressing her out." I open the door as Liam laughs.

"Yeah, you know. I realized I went too far when I told her the turkey needed more thyme on the top."

My eyes roll, and I practically shove Liam's giant frame through the door, closing it behind him. But before I turn back around to the kitchen, a pair of light brown eyes latch onto me.

And Chase stares at me like I'm the main course and he wants nothing more than to dive in.

CHAPTER TWENTY

CHASE

Summer's ring covered fingers toss Liam out like an old rag on the deck, and I'm glued to the light green dress shaping her figure. It loosens along her hips and flows down to just above her ankles, but the top is open exposing her collarbones as it hangs off her shoulders. Her lips part slightly when her gaze catches mine, but she quickly gives me a friendly smile before turning around and walking away. Lately, she's the one who's much more eager to break any eye contact we make, something that feels so ass backward from what I've always known.

"So that's why the whole patch of grass needs to be dug up and we'll just replace it with rubber mulch or something easy for the kids," Nate says, and I've completely forgotten what the hell we were talking about.

"Swing sets are a bitch to put together, though. Are you going to hire someone?" Ford asks.

"Yeah, all of you. Pizza and beer as the compensation." Nate tips his glass of iced tea in our direction, and Ford laughs louder than necessary.

Abby walks outside with a tray of appetizers, placing them in the center of the table as six little feet follow her outside and their grabby hands reach for the chips and cheese.

"Don't fill up on this stuff, though. Mia has made a whole spread in there, and you all *will* eat it."

Mia insisted on doing the Friendsgiving cooking this year. Nate said he tried to have everyone bring a dish, like a potluck, rather than having his pregnant wife do all of the cooking but I guess she was adamant.

"Even if something sucks, you eat it," Nate adds on to Abby's comment.

"Mia's a great cook, what are you talking about?" Ford grabs three cubes of cheese, tossing them in his mouth.

"Yeah, but she's been real emotional lately. A grocery store commercial had her sobbing yesterday. I'm not even exaggerating, there were many, many tears." Nate's eyes widen as he makes eye contact with each of us around the table.

I remember those days. At least, a little bit with Kristen. She's naturally not an emotional person, so I remember being surprised when she started crying over a show she'd seen ten times before.

Conversation between the guys picks back up and I'm floating my attention between whatever they're saying and beyond the glass window into the kitchen where my daughter sits at the counter. I assume she's helping with something, but that seems like a loose term as one strawberry goes on the dessert dish and the next two end up in her mouth. Summer's watching her the whole time, finally slicing up a small bowl just for her to snack on, and I smile to myself.

Nate and Mia's house is similar to what I envision for me and CeCe one day. A lot of land, privacy, a modest home but enough room to have our family and friends over for birthdays or holidays.

I used to do that all the time when I first moved into my apartment. I loved hosting poker nights and game nights. It stopped when Kristen became pregnant and my time with my friends was drastically cut down. I want to blame that on her, but I didn't have to go along with every ridiculous thing she asked me to. It was a choice I made. I thought I was doing the right thing at the time.

"Come eat." Summer peeks her head out the door.

All of us pile into the dining room and I notice CeCe putting small foam hearts on every chair like she's setting up a tea party for her dolls or something.

"CeCe, don't do that," I say, picking it up from the seat closest to me. When I glance at the others around the table, I notice they're all an assortment of colors. Probably something from one of her craft books that she brought with her.

"No!" CeCe shouts.

"Hey," I say. "No yelling."

"That's Summer's spot," CeCe says, brows creasing as she pouts.

"What?"

"Daddy, Auntie Abby, MiMi." CeCe walks around tapping each chair like she's assigning us all seats.

"Oh, these colors are our spots?" Abby bends down to CeCe's level and strokes her cheek.

CeCe nods, and without a second thought or question, everyone waits for instructions on where to sit. My chest swells at the patience and just overall acceptance the people in this room have for her. CeCe's never been looked at as a burden by them, they've always loved her and treated her as if she's their own and I can't think of anything better than that.

When I take a seat and look up, Summer's seated directly across from me. She tucks a piece of hair behind her ear and waves her pink foam heart in the air—the same color as the one I got—and looks up at me through dark lashes. The corners of her lips turn up into a smile and I'm locked in on her gaze. I didn't anticipate her to demand so much of my attention without even trying.

"Gravy, Hunt." I hear my name and feel a jab in my left arm as Ford asks for the gravy, apparently a second time.

"Sorry," I mumble, handing him the gravy boat and silently telling myself not to look straight ahead for the rest of this meal.

———

"Okay, but why didn't you just say *Titanic*? I would've gotten it then!" Mia protests, folding her arms over her chest.

"I said *The Wolf of Wall Street*. It's not my fault that your Leo knowledge only spans to who he dates and the *Titanic*," Liam jokes as he tosses the scrap of paper into the used pile.

Mia makes another grunting noise as she walks off into the kitchen to check on the dessert. I've been out of the game for the last couple rounds, and it looks like Ford and Abby are the winners. They're both suspiciously good at Celebrity Charades, it makes me wonder if they practice in their spare time or something. I personally prefer a good old fashioned board game. Give me *Sorry* or *Monopoly*, even a game of *Scrabble* is more fun to me than this one.

"Anyone need anything?" Summer asks the group, but I don't look up at her when I answer no. My plan for the foreseeable future—until whatever the hell this is goes away—is to speak to Summer as little as possible and only make eye contact when necessary.

But my plan is immediately shot to hell when she takes a seat beside me, knocking her knee into my leg.

"Are you all right there?" Her head tilts as she looks over at me. A piece of hair falling into her face that she quickly gathers, pulling all of her hair to her other shoulder, showing the silkiness of her skin, practically putting it on display for me.

I have *never* been so fucking affected by Summer Kincaid in my life.

Her and I have had plenty of conversations over the years, plenty of moments where our eyes have met or smiles matched, laughs collided and skin grazed. Yet sitting next to her on this couch has me absolutely fucking weak.

A grunt leaves my chest louder than intended.

"I'm good," I say, pounding my chest with a fist.

I risk a glance in her direction and am met with the smirk I've seen a hundred times before. The challenging one. The one that taunts me. The one that wants to push me. And test my willpower, my patience.

She lifts herself from the couch and makes her way into the kitchen, Abby on her heels. I've got half a mind to just gather CeCe's things and call it a night so I don't have to find myself distracted and longing for something I shouldn't be paying any attention to. But we haven't even had dessert yet and that's CeCe's favorite part.

"Chase, can you help with this?" I hear my sister call for me from the kitchen.

When I walk in, she's holding a jar of chocolate fudge and clearly struggling to get it open.

"Where's your husband? This is his job now," I quip, which earns me an exaggerated eye roll from Abby as she walks past me and out to the living room, calling Mia's name.

The jar opens in one twist and I place it on the counter, licking my finger where some of the fudge ended up.

"There's this one too, while you're at it." Summer casually slides the caramel jar across the counter as her eyes pivot to mine. Without breaking eye contact with her, my hand shoots to the right, gripping the jar in my hand. Summer's bottom lip is pulled in and I don't miss the way her teeth peek out behind her lip as she grins slowly.

"Nice reflexes."

"Nice dress."

I'm stunned by my quick witted response, but Summer's lips purse together and a proud smirk seems to overtake her face.

"Wow," I say, feeling like I just let all my fucking cards show. "Sorry, that slipped out."

"Don't apologize. It is a great dress," she says, offering a knowing smile as she pulls ice cream from the freezer.

She walks by me, flipping her hair over her shoulder as she does, leaving behind her coconut scent that has me downright feral at this point.

And I'm left standing in the kitchen like an absolute idiot.

———

"Are we about ready to go?" I throw the question over to CeCe once she finishes her ice cream, knowing she'll probably protest. She loves being around Nate and Mia's boys. She's pretty bossy with them, makes them sit for her "class", and gives them both chores to do. The boys take it willingly for now—I'm sure that'll change as they all get older.

"Where's your heart?" CeCe's eyes plead as she looks up at me.

"What?" I ask, confused.

CeCe waves a small pink foam heart in front of me.

"Oh, uh." I tap both hands on my pockets, knowing damn well it isn't in there.

"I found it!" I turn around to face Summer as she's holding a pink heart, the same as CeCe's and hands it to me.

"This is the one she gave me, so you better find yours. I accept iced lattes as thank you's," she whispers.

"Same colors mean best friends." CeCe smiles, holding her pink heart up to mine. Before she turns and walks away to grab her backpack full of things she brought over. It dawns on me that Summer and I are the only two CeCe gave pink hearts to.

"Thanks," I say to Summer, extending my hand to give it back to her. She reaches to grab it at the same time, causing our hands to collide and the heart to fall completely from my fingers. We both do nothing but watch it float to the floor, as if in slow motion, neither of us is too eager to bend down and get it.

I'm hanging on by a fucking thread and know I can't trust myself to be alone with her again.

CHAPTER TWENTY-ONE

SUMMER

The night of Friendsgiving felt like I was living in some dream world, where everything I did seemed to affect Chase in the same way that he's been affecting me for all these years. It felt good to see him squirm a little, to know—even if it was brief—that in some way he was tempted by me. But I'm still not convinced he'll ever go back on his "never kissing again" rule. It'll probably take a lot more than longing stares and hand brushes for him to cave.

I watched his body language that night, I studied how he moved around me, how he spoke and the way he tried to shield himself from ever looking my way. He seemed flustered when we made contact and downright mad at himself when he let his compliment about my dress slip.

I don't want to force anything with Chase, but I'm finding it so hard to understand the more I think about it. I wish I could read his mind, so I can see why he still wants this shield up with me. I've been doing everything I can to earn his trust when it comes to CeCe, and with that I've also been trying to help him realize he doesn't have to be so uptight all the time. He doesn't have to plan everything out to the tee. And he doesn't have to do everything alone. I know letting go of some control is hard for him, but I'm just hoping to help him realize that things can go a little off course sometimes and it will still be okay.

I admire Chase's dedication to the life he's built. The structure he's curated in their life and the safety and security he surrounds CeCe with. He's a better man than most, stepping up in the ways he has. But he has to let himself have some fun once in a while, he has to remember he's still important and appreciated for more than being a great football player and more than being a great parent, but just for being who he is as a man.

And maybe I'm the best person to help him see that.

––––––––

This morning, I found myself at the entrance of Chase's apartment building, even though I'm not needed for CeCe today. He offered me his second gym key card the other day and while I think he probably regretted it shortly after, he insisted I take it while mine is currently being renovated.

It's a hell of a lot bigger than mine—although, that shouldn't surprise me. His apartment building is much more upscale. The giant floor to ceiling windows are tinted so people outside can't just awkwardly stare in as I do squats or lunges and the walls are a softer grayish-white, making it feel a lot more serene in here than in mine where they're black and makes it feel like a dungeon.

As I'm walking around just to familiarize myself, every corner of this gym looks like it was so well thought out, down to the feminine products available to take in the women's bathroom.

I spend an hour rotating between some of the weights and cardio machines, taking my time as I have the entire place to myself.

The sauna is tempting as I walk by it on the way out. It's a small room behind a wooden door and I swear just standing outside of it you can feel how hot it is in there. When I open the door, the wave of heat hits me in the face and it takes me a second to adjust to how the air in here feels. There's a small bench that runs along the wall across from the door and then an even smaller one near the side, slightly hidden from the window in the door.

Taking a seat in the smaller area, I instantly feel the sweat start to double from what it was just from the workout. I can see the appeal though for these things. It's quiet here—calm and relaxing. The intensity of this heat feels great on my skin, too.

Leaning my head back against the wall, I let my eyes close and my body relax. I'm still not over the kiss with Chase and every time my mind settles, the memory of his lips on mine push through and invade my thoughts. It was perfect. *He* was perfect.

Sitting here alone, I let my thoughts get carried away. I let the memory of Chase's body against me work its way through my mind. I imagine how things might have progressed if we kept going. If his morals didn't pop out at the most inopportune time. I can feel the ache between my legs and I press my body down against the wooden bench as I arch myself forward.

There's a sound near the door causing my eyes to shoot open and I'm met with the man of the hour himself. Chase strides in quietly, adjusting the string on his shorts. I stare at his bare chest as he pulls his headphones from his ears.

"Oh, I can come back if you want some privacy." He returns the look, staring at my chest that's covered in sweat.

My eyes linger on his body for a moment before we meet each other at eye level and I smile as if I wasn't just picturing him on his knees for me. "You can stay."

He reaches for a knob on the wall, lowering the temperature before he takes a seat on the other side of the bench. I shouldn't be paying so much attention to every move he makes, but I've noticed it's not just me paying attention to him anymore. His eyes are on me just as much as mine are on him. A new development I'm beginning to love.

"Is Abby still with CeCe?" I ask.

He nods, running his hand over his shorts. "Yeah, she took her to the Rec Center for some arts and crafts event."

After this week, Chase's mom will be in town for a while and she'll be helping with CeCe a lot too.

"Oh, okay. This is my first time here, just so you know. It's not like I'm making it a habit coming to your apartment building all the time."

"I gave you the key card and expected you'd use it. No need to justify it."

I nod.

The way he looks right now is downright criminal. Beads of sweat are forming on every part of his body and I have this insatiable urge to just touch him.

"This thing is definitely not built for a crowd." I stretch my legs out in front of me, glancing around at the walls around us.

"No." His tongue coats his lips. "It isn't." His stomach flexes as he sits himself up more, pulling at the waistband of his shorts and all I want to do is run my tongue over his skin. His thigh tattoo peeks out—again only giving me a small glimpse of it as I stare at him. I can feel his eyes on me, too.

The warmth continues to build as we sit in silence for what feels like forever, but it's also a nice change of pace. Most of the time I feel like I need to fill silence with conversation, but right now sitting here and hearing each other simply breathe feels like enough as our eyes keep finding one another's from across the sauna.

The golden flecks in his eyes are consuming and my fingers long to skim against his chiseled jawline. "You're staring, Kincaid." The low rasp of his voice gets my heart pumping faster.

I can feel heat building in every crevice of my body as I

settle myself against the bench. "So are you." My words are a whisper.

Like a challenge neither of us want to back down from, we hold our eye contact until he slowly stands and walks closer to me. He's a tall man, thick and built, and as I'm seated here, he's towering over me, trapping me in his bubble and I never want to leave. His knee knocks into mine, spreading my legs apart as he gets close enough to touch and my skin wants to burst into flames.

"You have to stop," he warns, leaning down and tilting my chin up at him with his thumb and index finger.

"You first."

His hand releases my chin and he leans even closer, taking his palm and cupping the side of my neck into his grip. It feels possessive, yet I've never felt safer or more willing than I feel right now.

It's hard to think straight with his hands on me and even harder when I glance at his shorts and see that he's just as turned on as I am right now.

He slides his hand from my neck to my shoulder and skims my collarbone, lighting my body up with goosebumps as he does. I feel the pressure from his fingers as he rubs them over my skin and my chest pumps up and down as a whimper leaves my lips—begging him to keep his hands on me, to keep touching me. But he pulls away.

"You can keep touching me, Chase."

He takes a fallen piece of my hair from my face and tucks it behind my ear.

"No, I can't," he whispers. "If I keep touching you, I'll never be able to stop. I already can't fucking stop thinking about you."

His knee remains between my legs and I spread my knees further apart as I lean against the wooden bench. My head tilts back and my eyes want to close, but I keep them trained on him.

"What are you thinking about?" My fingers gently pull the drawstring on his shorts.

"Right now?" He skims his thumb over my bottom lip and then circles to the top.

Taking two fingers, he glides them down my chest. It's barely a graze as he feathers his way down to my stomach, stopping at the waistband of my leggings.

He smirks and leans his head back slightly before words roll off his tongue. "Peeling these flimsy leggings from your body. Spreading you out on this bench and tasting every inch of you while I watch those pouty lips of yours moan my name." His fingers slowly work their way back up in the same motion as before. "Feeling you coat my tongue and then burying my cock so far inside you that we both never recover." His hand stops just below my neck, and his fingers skim my collarbone as my breath stutters. "*That's* what I've been thinking about."

He stills in front of me, his gaze rotating from my eyes to my lips and my mouth goes completely dry. My hands shake and my clit *throbs* at his words.

To say I'm in shock wouldn't be enough. The man standing in front of me right now isn't the same one I've known all my life. He's not the same one I've known even the last few weeks. Because this Chase is *hungry*. He's tormented. He's downright distressed, caught between giving in to a want or trying to abide by what he thinks is right versus wrong.

He can see the surprise on my face when my bottom lip hangs slightly open. The faint sound of voices outside the sauna causes him to slowly back away and move toward the door.

"I've never seen you at a loss for words, Kincaid." The corner of his lip curves up into the sexiest smirk as he walks out, leaving me in a state of disbelief.

My mind whirls at the words he said to me. Chase said those words to *me*. I give myself a solid ten minutes to feel my legs again before I decide to get up and leave. I've never had a man's words alone be enough to render me completely still, speechless and quite frankly ready to explode.

Walking over to my car, I've never begged for a downpour more than I am right now. My body could use some cooling off and a bout of rain would do the trick.

Just as I get into my car, a text comes through in the group chat from Abby.

ABBY

While I'm waiting for CeCe to finish her painting, let me get your opinions! How does this dress look for the charity dinner?

A picture of Abby in a dark green dress pops up and I have to shift my focus from Chase's filthy mouth to the absolute smokeshow that is my best friend. I know she's still out with CeCe, so she must've taken this a different day. Because the background looks nothing like the Rec Center and every bit like her newly renovated, gigantic walk-in closet.

I'm sorry, I've passed away from how good you look in that dress

MIA

Ford will lose his mind

ABBY

Okay... so maybe it's too much for this event then? I don't want to be overdressed

You're the hostess, wear what you want. Plus, it's not possible to be overdressed! It looks so good on you, wear it and let your husband suffer all night

ABBY

LOL. You know I suffer seeing him in a suit too

Yeah, but not as much as this dress is going to
have him on his knees for you

MIA

It is a formal event, I don't think you'll be
overdressed. I still have no clue what I'm
wearing. Maybe something pink? My life is full
of the color blue and I'm about to add a third,
so wearing some pink for me sounds nice

I found this brown dress at the new little
boutique on Main months ago. Maybe I'll wear
that

It's been sitting in my closet since the day I bought it. On the rack I wasn't sure about the color, but when I tried it on—it took my own breath away. The slit goes up my thigh and it hangs off my shoulders so comfortably. I feel like it flatters me and my body in a way that makes me feel like I could walk a runway.

———

"You're late," Chase clips when he opens the door this morning. As if he wasn't just talking about fucking me into oblivion two days ago.

"Am I, though? What is time? Is it not just this illusion, a small reflection of change?" I joke while we both stand in the foyer.

His hair styled just right with a small piece curling toward the front. He swallows as we stand there looking at one another and I can feel the tension building by the second. I can feel the air thicken and the sounds from the living room drowning out. The walls feel like they could close in at any minute and just push us closer together.

Without another word, he reaches over my shoulder and closes the door. It quietly shuts behind me and he steps slowly to his left and out of my way, gesturing for me to walk in.

The television is on with one of CeCe's shows playing while she's completely enthralled by her coloring book in front of her. The dishwasher is going and I can hear a pot of coffee brewing as I walk further into the house. All of these sounds register, but I'm focused on the one causing the pounding in my ears and the throbbing in my chest.

"Be good today," Chase calls to CeCe from where he stands at the kitchen island, his fingers tapping away on his phone.

"Don't you want to wait for that?" I ask when I see Chase begin to walk toward the door with a coffee thermos in hand while the pot is still brewing.

His tongue runs between his lips, almost as if it were an attempt to delay his response.

"I, uh…" His throat clears and he slides his free hand in the pocket of his jeans. Black washed denim and a black t-shirt with boots has to be some kind of weakness for me because I'm melting in all the right places.

"That pot is for you. Thanks for your help," The words rush out, and I can't do anything but stare at him before he quickly turns and walks out the door.

The flip between naughty *Daddy* Chase and put together *Dad* Chase is something he has quickly mastered.

CHAPTER TWENTY-TWO

CHASE

It took every fiber in me not to push Summer against the wall in my foyer and kiss the attitude right out of her mouth this morning. If she's kissing me she can't make her smart ass remarks, right? God, what the hell is happening?

It was the same at Nate and Mia's the other night—an impossible urge to just devour her lips again. I was hoping time away from her and minimal conversation might alleviate some of this tension I'm feeling, but then I'm forced to be in close quarters with her again and the need becomes a hunger and the hunger becomes all consuming.

My phone vibrates in the pocket of my jeans just as I'm about to get changed for practice. My body feels absolutely wrecked from all of the extra recovery training I've been trying to get in. The sauna helped my knees, but did nothing to help my current Summer problem. The one where I can't fucking get her out of my mind and every thought I seem to have ends with us wrapped up in bed together.

SUMMER

Hey Daddy.

My skin instantly feels hot. Since when is she calling me *that*?

> You can't call me that, Kincaid.

SUMMER

> Guessing the picture of CeCe wearing a shirt that says "rad like dad" didn't come through?

I breathe a sigh of relief at the mishap.

> Oh, no. No picture came through.

SUMMER

> Figured. Let's circle back to the daddy thing though. Feels like a missed opportunity.

Fuck, I'll bite.

> How so?

SUMMER

> Well first of all, it's basically a term of endearment

> And second?

SUMMER

> Not sure if you can handle the second part, come to think of it. I wouldn't want to derail the rules you put into place

> Trying to break them?

SUMMER

> I might be.

That damn attitude.

I can't get swept up in the back and forth with Summer right now so I lock my phone and continue to change for practice. It boggles my mind, really. One minute I'm pissed off that she's clouding my thoughts and the next I'm wanting her to invade every piece of them. I can't fucking think straight when it comes to her lately.

"Hunt! We're going to mic you up for Sunday night's game!" Coach Aarons slaps my shoulder when I get back to the sidelines.

I hang my head, laughing at his statement and finally taking off my helmet.

"You don't want that, Coach."

"Ah, come on, old man. Let the people see how a team captain gets it done," another one of the defensive guys says to my left.

I don't take my role as a captain on the team lightly, I know it's something I've been chosen for by my peers, and that comes with responsibility and a level of respect. I've earned that over the last few years and being a play caller on the defense is something I take a lot of pride in.

It's surprisingly our only prime time game this season and with it being on a Sunday night, there's no way CeCe can attend with how late it'll end up running. I've already asked Summer if she can come stay with her and thankfully she'll be done working in time to help out. Although, another late night with Summer isn't exactly something I want to revisit, I'm once again out of options aside from her.

"Nothing exciting ever comes out of my mouth, so it'll be a snooze fest. Rethink this one, Coach."

His lips turn down and he shakes his head. "Nah, you're a captain. A play caller. You can do it."

Liam and Nate are both practically jumping up and down at the thought of me having to be mic'd up during a game. The last time this happened, I ended up slipping out that I was about to be a dad to the entire staff who was monitoring the microphone.

After practice, there are two more text messages from

Summer, one of them is a picture of my refrigerator and a paragraph about how it should be illegal to have things so organized in there. If I had to bet, hers is probably in shambles and would send me over the edge I'm sure. The second one was a little less judgy and a lot more… thoughtful.

SUMMER

I hope the picture actually comes through this time, because this moment was too sweet not to capture. She said one of her stuffed animals was in your bedroom, so she went to grab it. After like two minutes, I was concerned when she didn't come out right away and when I walked in, I saw this.

You should talk to her about him, Chase.

The picture is CeCe sitting in front of an old whiskey barrel in the corner of my room. The stuffed animal she was going to get was sitting on top of it and when she grabbed it, the frame must've come down with it.

I'd recognize the wooden frame she's holding anywhere. It's one of the few things I've kept that belonged to my dad. Quite a bit of his stuff was junk, if I'm being honest, and I know he would've thought so too. *"Get rid of that shit,"* he would've said.

Going through his life after he passed away was harder than attending his funeral, I think. That day was spent hearing stories from people who loved him, moments that made me laugh and cry and shake my head. But the stillness that followed—the silence and the sheer amount of time I had alone afterward was the hardest part.

I thought the day of his service would be the worst day of my life. Saying goodbye to the man who raised me, the man who never missed a game and always made the time. But it wasn't. There were people around constantly, making sure we had what we needed, almost afraid to leave me, my mom, and sister alone.

It was the days after, the weeks. When life for everyone else resumed as normal and all I had was the quiet around me and my own thoughts and memories circulating. The painful reminder that for everyone else who knew my dad—they were sad Jack Hunt had passed away, but they said their goodbyes and got to jump back into their everyday lives and routines. And while I tried to throw myself back into football and my way of life, it was just me desperately trying to avoid being alone and avoid having to talk about him because it hurt too fucking much.

CeCe's ponytail is falling out and the yellow princess dress is hanging off her shoulder. The stuffed animal is sitting next to her and the beginning of a smile coming together on her face as she stares down at the picture of me and my dad the night I got drafted. Cloudy eyes and proud smiles for both of us.

After taking a minute to let the photo sink in, I lock my phone and get changed. I don't talk about my dad much to CeCe—if ever, actually. I should, though. I know it. But it's so damn hard. The moment I think I can start sharing a memory or a piece of who he was I can feel the lump in my throat building and I just shut it down. She asked about him once earlier this year. My mom had just left from a weekend she was staying with us and CeCe questioned why I have a mommy and not a daddy. Kids are more intuitive and observant than we realize, that's for damn sure. I wasn't ready for the question and didn't know how to answer her without making myself miserable in the process—so I avoided it. I changed the subject after saying something about him no longer living here. It was selfish and wrong, but I just... I wasn't ready.

Summer knew my dad well. It was a trip seeing the two of them together. Come to think of it, they're actually pretty similar. My dad was just as sarcastic and witty as Summer. Calling things how he saw them and standing up for the little guy. She reminds me of him in that way, actually. Kind of reckless and impulsive, not always making the best choices, but always *trying* their best. The quick humor, and quite frankly, irreverence they both shared. Not taking life too seriously, I guess, is something they have in common.

He'd call her a spitfire and she'd joke that he was an old man when he'd make noises every time he got up from a chair. He'd always tell me to make sure I was looking out for her along with Abby.

———

When I walk into my apartment, I set my bag down near the laundry room and make my way toward the living room. I can hear faint sounds coming from the television. When I round the corner and glance into the living room, I see all of my dining room chairs lined up in a row. My barstools are on the other end and a fitted sheet is stretched across them, making a fort over the floor.

"CeCe," I whisper, but don't get a reply so I try to quietly move around the chairs and pillows set up in my living room.

When I poke my head around the side, I can see into a very cleverly crafted pillow fort. Couch cushions are lined up around the perimeter and pillows from CeCe's bed and her comforter are laid out with an extra comforter I had in the hall closet.

But the best part? CeCe curled up against Summer. Her teddy bear under one arm and the other resting right against Summer. Chocolate is rimmed around CeCe's lips and I find the evidence of Oreos and milk on the coffee table beside them. Summer's chest moves up and down as she lays there, eyelashes fanned over her cheekbones and I just watch both of them for a moment. Soaking in the sight of my daughter with a woman she loves. A woman who loves her just as much, if not more.

Deciding not to wake either one of them, I head to my bathroom and turn on the shower, letting the water warm up while I get undressed only to hear someone clear their throat just before I undo my belt.

"I'll clean it up, don't worry." Summer stands in my doorway, gesturing down the hall, no doubt referring to the fort. Her red shirt hangs off one shoulder, exposing the part of her neck just above her collarbone. Staring at Summer right now has my blood running to one place and as much as I want to keep forcing the thoughts away, I'm too fucking tired of fighting it at this moment.

"It's a nice fort," I say, smirking at her.

"We had fun making it. She asked if you could do it with us next time."

"Count me in." I pull the belt from the loops and toss it on the floor beside me. I catch Summer's eyes on my bare chest as she stands there.

"You mind?" I ask, cocking an eyebrow in her direction. It's definitely a bad idea to get undressed in front of her.

"No, not at all. Continue." She crosses her arms over her chest, getting comfortable as she leans against the frame.

"Kincaid." Her name rumbles in my chest.

"I'm joking. Relax. Have a good shower."

She leaves my room as swiftly as she entered, but my pulse is still pounding.

CHAPTER TWENTY-THREE

SUMMER

I thought he would've heard me tap on his bedroom door, but maybe the sound of the water in the shower drowned it out. It's a good thing I spoke before he unbuttoned those jeans, otherwise life as I know it probably would have ended seeing Chase in that state.

CeCe ate dinner and then wanted to build a fort and watch a movie—something I didn't hesitate to jump on. I remember making forts as a kid and thinking it was the coolest experience ever. She was so excited to start the movie, but I'm pretty sure we both fell asleep within the first ten minutes of it even starting. To be fair, we had a pretty busy day. Chase warned me that it would be a longer one since he was staying for some recovery training after practice, so I fully expected to be the one to get her dinner ready.

"She's having an early bedtime tonight, I take it," Chase says, noting the time and CeCe still sleeping in the fort.

"She ate dinner already and we brushed her teeth. She seemed really tired today, we were busy."

Chase kneels down in front of the opening in the fort and I hear his knees crack as they bend. He lowers himself even further to duck under the blanket and when he reemerges from the floor, he's already knocked over the two stools on the end and the fitted sheet is being stretched to its limit as he rises with CeCe in his arms.

Her sleepy eyes open and close slowly, and I whisper goodnight to her as Chase carries her down the hall and into her bedroom.

Taking the stools two at a time, I line them back up along the kitchen island and then go back one by one for the dining room chairs. There's zero percent chance I attempt to fold a fitted sheet so I toss it on the couch and fold up the comforter before grabbing both and putting them back in the closet.

"Thanks for today," Chase says when he walks out of her bedroom.

His eyes linger on mine for a moment, letting a deep sigh leave his chest. His hair is still damp from the shower and the pair of sweatpants he's wearing are making my imagination run amuck. The white t-shirt clings to his shoulders, letting every muscle be displayed. I've never looked at a man the way I look at Chase. And that sounds… awful to admit, considering I've been in relationships before and I've loved other men—at least I used the word, even though I don't think I truly meant it.

"You don't have to thank me every time I watch her, Chase. I like being with her and I'm happy to help you."

He nods and reaches into the cabinet above his refrigerator.

"Well then, thanks for the picture today. The one that actually came through."

I laugh, recalling the mishap from the first photo that apparently got lost in text message land somewhere.

"I saw something in your room, though, when I was in there. I wasn't snooping, I swear. But it caught my eye."

"Trust me, Kincaid, I've already assumed you've been snooping."

I gasp dramatically. "Rude."

We exchange smiles and he takes a seat at the island while I'm pulling my phone from the charger.

"You still have the guitar." I soften my features as he looks at me. I'm sure he didn't see that coming.

The sun's already setting and the golden hour is upon us as I can see pinks and oranges, causing the light in the sky to look softer and less harsh than it has all day.

The light drifts into his apartment and the rays bring out the golden flecks in his eyes. I wish I knew how to tell him how one look from him makes me feel. How the tenderness of his eyes make me feel at peace and comforted. How the stature of his body close to mine gives me so much safety and such a feeling of assurance.

He nods slowly. "I do."

A low roar of thunder stirs both of us to focus on the window, not seeing any dark clouds, but knowing it's probably coming.

"I loved hearing you play that guitar growing up. I remember you would just walk around the house strumming notes. I was in awe of you." A faint smile spreads across his lips. "Just another thing that had all the girls swooning, huh?" I joke.

I can tell he's reminiscing on those years too.

"Do you still play it?" My head tilts when I lean against the counter.

He exhales, his eyes closing briefly.

"I haven't in years. Used to… but now I just can't."

I nod slowly. "Can I show you something?" I ask, pulling myself up from the counter.

He nods and sits still like he's waiting for me to pull out my phone or something along those lines, but when I start to move down the hall he follows.

"CeCe did this. I thought it was sweet and wanted to show you."

The wooden frame that CeCe was holding earlier is back on the whiskey barrel in the corner of his bedroom, except this time there's a tiny pink foam heart sitting next to it. It's exactly like the ones that she handed out the other night around the dinner table.

"There was no prompting in this, by the way. She did it all on her own."

"The pink foam heart," he says softly, looking at the picture in the frame and letting himself smile for a change. "Did she ask about him?"

I shake my head no, seeing a sigh of relief leave his lips.

"It's okay to talk about him, Chase."

His hand pulls at the back of his neck and he sighs on a shaky breath.

"I know, it's just… Never mind."

My initial instinct is to comfort him. I can see the struggle in his features as he holds back. He's not a hugger, not someone who gets close to people–but I am. I touch my fingers to the inside of his forearm, feeling the strength that he physically exudes, but knowing that beneath the surface, he's soft and tender.

"Sometimes, it still feels like it happened yesterday and I guess that's why I just don't let myself think about it much or talk about him. It's fucking hard."

My chest constricts as I look at him. "I know. You were such a pillar of strength for your mom and Abby. Did you even let yourself grieve?"

He scoffs under his breath and it makes me feel like we shouldn't be diving into this. Like I'm forcing him into a conversation he isn't ready for, but when I open my mouth to apologize and change the subject, he cuts me off.

"I gave myself a day." His eyes find mine, a soft brown and slightly glossy. "I cried. I threw things. I cursed up to the sky and ultimately drank myself into an oblivion. And you know what it did?"

I shake my head, feeling a lump form in my throat.

"Nothing. It did *nothing*. He was still gone and I was still left with this pain." His throat clears and he pinches the bridge of his nose. "I gave myself that day. And now I handle my grief on my own terms. I process it how and when it feels right to me."

"Grief looks different for everyone. People handle it differently all over the world, but the bottom line is always the same. Knowing grief means we know love."

He presses his lips together before he looks back down to the guitar and inches closer to it, gripping the top of it lightly. He's looking at it as if he's wanted to touch it for years.

"He loved this damn thing. I only started playing it because he loved it so much. He took an interest in my football and I just wanted to take an interest in something he loved too, you know? I was never very good, but it was enough to impress girls in high school." His eyes shoot up to me and I roll mine. His minor skills definitely worked on me.

"I think I've only played once since he died. Every time I would go to pick it up, I'd hear him. I'd hear his two cents that I used to beg him to stop giving me, but now I'd do anything to have that back."

My eyes well up thinking of Jack. God, I loved him. He was a second father to me in every definition of the word. When he passed away I felt so much sadness for Abby and Chase, but a sadness for me too. My parents traveled so much for work, and Jack and Diane filled their shoes in so many ways when they were out of town. It doesn't compare to how Abby and Chase miss him, but he was such a riot. His kindness and sense of humor were things I always appreciated growing up.

"It makes you feel close to him, but that's hard too. I get it," I say. "But still, using the term 'used to' about something you loved so much is a pretty sad phrase in any language." My hand running through my hair, I risk getting a little closer to him. "Do you miss it?"

"Yes," he says without hesitation or second guessing. Like

he's been waiting for someone to ask him the question so he can admit it.

"You're right, it was one of the things that always made me feel connected to him, and I want to pick it up again. I want to be able to pass this down to CeCe, to give her a glimpse into something that he loved so much. I don't know, I fucking freeze up when I try," he professes, pulling it from the stand and taking a seat on his bed.

His curtains are open, letting the moonlight drift in and the sound of rain that's now drizzling is relaxing to say the least.

"You can play it for me, I won't tell a soul you serenaded me on this rainy night."

A small laugh escapes us both as I stare down at the strings, watching his fingers feather over them lightly.

"For all I know, I don't even remember how to play it." He chuckles, pulling it closer to him.

I'm not surprised Chase misses playing it. But I'm also not surprised he wants to avoid playing it either. Knowing him, he probably keeps it in this corner because it's not within direct eyesight when you're in the bedroom. It's almost hidden away, something to be kept a secret.

I take a seat next to him on the bed, feeling my pulse race as I get closer, but I can't help it. I know he set these rules into place, but I just… I want him to know that it's okay to let people in, to let people be close to you.

"Do you want to try?" I ask.

CHAPTER TWENTY-FOUR

CHASE

"Do you want to try?" she asks as she takes a seat next to me.

The very thought of playing this damn guitar right now feels impossible, but I also feel pulled to it.

I slowly nod my head, but my body stays frozen. I never thought that Summer Kincaid—my sister's best friend, my current babysitter, and the girl who used to drive me nuts for the better part of a decade—would be the one to have me considering picking this up again.

Summer scoots herself back further on my bed, settling against the headboard. Tanned legs extended, crossing one ankle over the other as she smiles at me.

I don't know how we got here. How we got from utter irritation to finding comfort in her.

I loosen my shoulders, nostalgia coursing its way through me. God, it's like muscle memory when I strum a few quick notes before stopping. Heat crawls up my spine and my neck begins to sweat before I feel a delicate touch on the back of my arm.

"Close your eyes and just play."

Her fingers pull away from my skin and I exhale, letting

myself find comfort in something that once brought me happiness.

"If this sucks, I don't want to hear it," I joke.

She releases a hearty laugh and repositions herself from where she previously was, moving closer to me, knees underneath her body as she sits by my side.

"No promises. Play me something and I'll try to guess what it is."

"You'll know this one." My voice hoarse as I glance up at Summer, already staring at me.

I'm not someone who gets nervous in front of a crowd—hell, I play football for millions of people every week—but something in this moment about Summer's eyes on me has my stomach flipping upside down.

It feels like riding a bike. The ease of jumping back into it and the calmness it brings me.

A, A, B minor, B minor.

I can feel Summer's eyes on me still. They've been burning into me since I got home this evening and in the last hour she's gotten more out of me than most people have in the last few years.

She smiles when our eyes meet and I know my willpower is about to be tested.

She looks breathtaking. She's a stunner in the daylight, but under the moonlight she's fucking magnificent. Her blue eyes sparkle like diamonds and her skin looks like porcelain—daring me to run my hands over it to feel its silkiness. Her head sways back and forth and her lips start mouthing the words once she recognizes the song.

"You're going to turn me into a puddle if you keep playing," she jokes. "Chris Stapleton is one of my favorites."

I bring the guitar down between my legs, resting it on the floor once I stop playing.

"'Tennessee Whiskey' is the first song I learned on guitar."

"Was it hard?"

"For me, learning anything on this thing was hard, but this particular song felt easier because I loved it so much I think." I laugh and stretch my back, turning my body to face hers.

"Can you teach me?"

My mouth opens to protest. To tell her I think we should call it a night before I let myself mess up again and fall into her lips. Fuck, I want to. But I was clear about where we stood and if I kiss her again, what the hell does that say?

"Not the whole song, just like, a little bit." She shrugs and sits up closer to me.

"Ah, I don't know, Kincaid. It's getting late and I…"

"Don't trust yourself?"

"Something like that," I confess.

"Trust me, then. Kissing you is the last thing on my mind. Bleh." She sticks her tongue out playfully. I know she's not telling the truth. I know I should still decline and not allow myself to be around her much longer. The temptation I've had over the last couple of weeks with her has been an actual nightmare in some cases. Jolting me out of sleep and withholding it all together.

But being around her is starting to feel like a *need*. Her presence has become a change in my life that I've been craving. I didn't realize how starved I was until I tasted her. And now, she's all I want.

"Just a few chords," I say, picking up the guitar.

Her smile widens and she pulls her hair back into a ponytail. I watch her tongue wet her full lips and I feel myself getting flustered already.

When she pulls her feet from under her and sits on the bed, I hand her the guitar, letting her get it in a comfortable position.

"Okay, I'm ready. Teach me how to be a rockstar," she jokes as I get up. "What are you doing?" she asks when I take a seat behind her.

"You wanted to learn. This is the best way."

I hear her swallow as I wrap my arms around her, holding her hands as they're delicately placed on the guitar strings.

"This is A," I whisper into her ear, guiding her fingers along the frets. "You'll do this one twice, count to six in between."

She strums once, and I silently count to six before taking her hand and repeating the same chord.

I'm making every effort not to breathe directly onto her skin, but with the close proximity it's hard to avoid. Every time I do, I watch her squirm a little. Her breathing picks up and she wiggles a little bit on the bed.

"Then B minor…" I begin to say, and she waits for my hand to reconnect with hers before she moves it again.

Her coconut scent is all I can focus on and it shows when I wait too long to tell her the next chord.

"What's next?" she whispers, but I don't answer.

She tilts her head up at me and I'm caught up in her stare entirely. Her lips part and I feel her warm breath on my cheek.

My heart is pounding, throbbing out of my chest and I can't fucking stand to sit here much longer with her like this.

Summer's eyes are pleading. I can hear her words even when nothing comes from her lips. She's telling me to fucking kiss her. To take her. To drop all the rules and boundaries I put up and just give in.

"I—um…" A hand runs down my face and I pull back slightly from her, creating some separation between our bodies. Touching her—in any way—seems to be a recipe for disaster.

Something is changing with me when it comes to Summer and I don't have any fucking clue how it happened or when or what the fuck to do with it. I know she's waiting for me to act on it. She's waiting on me to say something, to do something, but my body stills and I can't articulate a sentence. There's this foreign feeling stirring inside of me.

I'm suddenly *nervous* around her.

"Sorry," I say with a shake of my head. "It's another B minor."

Her features soften, and she looks at her fingers on the guitar before pausing. Against my better judgment, I lean forward, trying not to have my chest flush against her back as I reach my hand over hers.

"Like this," I say quietly, and she nods, letting my hand guide hers.

"Relax your hand a little bit, Kincaid." I can feel her body tense up the further along we get.

She peers up at me through dark lashes, two bright blue pools staring back at me as her fingers rest on the strings under my hand.

"Better?" she whispers, sending a shiver up and down my spine.

"Perfect." I manage to get out on a shaky breath.

She smiles and then removes her hand from the strings, taking the guitar and placing it carefully on the bed beside us.

I've got about 3 percent of my willpower left as she stares and turns to face me. Her chest is rising and falling almost in rhythm with mine.

You can't fucking kiss her again.

The words ring in my ears and I'm hanging by a thread to stay focused on them. I should be getting up and ushering us out of my bedroom and getting her on her way. But if I stand up right now, the fact that I'm so fucking turned on will be too obvious.

She stands from the bed and turns, stopping when she's just in front of my legs. Her eyes roam from my thighs and up my chest until she finally meets my gaze again and I see it written all over her face. If I kiss her, she'll welcome it.

Instead of waiting for me to do anything, she comes closer, letting her leg hit the bed, causing me to lean back slightly. She bends to bring us face to face and rests her hand on the side of my cheek as she leans forward. My heart feels like it fucking stops the second she breathes on my neck.

"Thank you for the lesson," she whispers. Her thumb lightly feathers my jaw as she pulls away and leaves my bedroom.

And I'm left just trying to wrap my head around how the woman who has done nothing but rile me up as long as I've known her, is now the same one to make me completely weak for her.

CHAPTER TWENTY-FIVE

SUMMER

The Knights have the eight o'clock game this evening, and while I wish I could be there in person, I've got the next best thing. CeCe snuggled under my arm, popcorn to my left on the end table and the sounds of Sunday night football coming from the television.

After she got changed into her pajamas, she suggested we both have matching braids before bed and I couldn't say no to that. And while I'm not the best at braiding my own hair, hers looks photo worthy.

"Look at those shoes," I say, giggling with CeCe.

One of the players is shown on the screen with a pair of bright orange cleats. I know there are many reasons why the players will sometimes wear special cleats, and the ones this guy has on are definitely eye-catching. Bright orange with white stripes, similar to a tiger and bright yellow splatters of color all over them.

"I like them," CeCe declares, taking a sip from her juice.

"Me too." My words are jumbled through my mouthful of popcorn.

The kickoff begins and in typical fashion, they do close ups of a lot of the players. We see Liam right away on the sidelines as the other team won the coin toss so our defense is on the field first. Liam's chiseled jawline stands out and his stoic game face is such a difference from his off the field persona. He's the definition of being on stage and doing his job for sixty minutes every week.

Along the bottom of the screen we see the player introductions coming up. CeCe shouts when Chase shows up, declaring the college he went to while his picture sits in the bottom right corner.

"Go, Daddy!" I yell, mimicking her excitement.

If only she knew that my excitement wasn't solely for her benefit because I do actually love watching Chase play. I have ever since high school. He was good back then, better in college, but he's downright unstoppable in the NFL.

"Why isn't he smiling?" CeCe asks when she notices his blank expression.

"All the good smiles are for you," I say, squeezing her a little tighter.

She giggles at the contact and we continue to watch the first quarter of the game before I glance down and see her eyelids closed, still holding an empty juice box in her hand and head leaning heavily against my shoulder.

"Come on," I whisper, pulling her up into my arms the best I can.

Chase makes this look so effortless when he picks her up and carries her into her bed, and I'm over here trying to maneuver it without tripping over my own feet.

When I get her into her bed, she's awake, but sleepy. I'm certain the moment I leave her room she'll be passed out again.

"Good night, my girl." I run my hand over her back and she makes a small sound before drifting off again.

As the game progresses, I decide to clean up a little bit so there's less for Chase to do tomorrow. There are some dishes in the dishwasher that I unload, and while I'm at it, I take the broom out and clean up some of the crumbs I noticed on the floor in the dining room.

While I'm cleaning up I can still hear the game in the background. Ford just scored a touchdown and the current picture is his obnoxious new end zone dance he's come up with. I'm convinced these are things he and Abby must rehearse at home. He looks like he's attempting some kind of moonwalk, but then he skips and he flexes his arms in front of the camera. Since when is he so showy? I laugh to myself.

That's your husband.

I text Abby with the dancing man emoji.

ABBY

Isn't he a dreamboat?

MIA

He's something.

I laugh out loud at the text exchange. I know we're all watching it from our respective couches—or in my case, while holding a broom in Chase's apartment.

I've officially created my own little cozy space for the remainder of the evening. Complete with a lit candle, the fireplace on, and a glass of lemonade while I get comfortable on the couch to watch the final quarter.

The camera pans to Chase and I see him on the sidelines laughing with another one of the defensive players. His hand runs through his sweaty hair and I want so badly to run my own fingers through it. I wanted to kiss him the other night—even though I know it's against his "rules."

"Well, at least the Knights are looking like themselves tonight. I know they didn't anticipate being this low in the stand-

ings this late in the season, but let's face it, when you've got Liam Evans as your quarterback and Chase Hunt on the other side of the ball, you're never actually out of it."

I smile to myself at the commentator's mention of Chase as if I have any claim to him, but even still it makes me blush. There's something so attractive about seeing a man excel at what he does, but even more than that—it's exciting. Chase isn't just good at his job, he's exceptional at it. He's an All Pro, he's a Super Bowl Champion, he holds records for the Knights that I doubt will be touched for years to come. And while all of that is admirable, the best thing about him is still his heart. Even if he guards it from most people.

The game comes to an end, leaving the score at an embarrassing fifty-two to fourteen and I know that means the guys will be in a good mood.

My phone dings with a text message nearly an hour after the game has ended, jolting me out of a small cat nap I was apparently taking on his couch.

CHASE

Not so bad, Kincaid.

I bite my cheek at his response to the picture I sent him of CeCe's braid and then another one comes through.

CHASE

I hope you're up. I'm on my way home.

He hopes I'm up? Why? Thoughts swirl in my mind, but it's probably to make sure I can leave.

I quickly gather up the blankets, organizing them on the couch the same way he keeps them. The coasters are all back in their normal spots and I've wiped up any of the condensation that may have landed on the table. I feel wide awake after that small nap I took and even more so after getting the text from him. Lately, there have been moments, albeit small ones, but times where he's just playful enough to make me think he enjoys being around me.

The front door opens as I'm sitting on the couch scrolling my phone and I hear a grunt as I stand up and walk toward the kitchen. Chase is standing at the island, his bag near his feet and his eyes dark, like the deepest part of the ocean.

"Hi," I quietly say, offering a quick smile.

"Hi." He exhales the word and places his hand on the counter.

My eyes shoot to where it lands and then back up to him. He doesn't say anything more, but he's staring at me so intently, as if he's studying every move I make.

"So, um, CeCe was great. She fell asleep in the first quarter… and I brought her to bed. Boy, you make that look easy."

Still nothing. No words, just him staring at me and his head tilts every so often as I move my hands while I talk. I'd think it to be creepy if I wasn't so insane already and find everything Chase does attractive anyway.

"I know you don't love it when I clean, but I just picked a few things up."

This time his tongue slowly glides between his lips as he watches me and I feel a wave of heat rush through me.

"Great game, by the way. Funny how Jefferson couldn't make a tackle last week, but then tonight he doesn't allow anyone to get past him," I say, trying to get something out of him, but still… crickets. "Tough crowd," I finally blurt out with a shake of my head, reaching for my purse that sits on the stool.

Chase's hand still sits firmly on the counter, but his breathing has increased slightly since I started talking. I'd have to assume my incessant rambling is just raising his blood pressure, though.

"You're probably exhausted, so I'm going to get going. But I'll see you during the week. Have a good night, Chase." I slide the strap of my purse onto my shoulder, inhaling and giving him one more quick smile before I walk by him and toward the door, but finally he speaks.

"Stay."

I jerk my head up to get a better look at him and I see his eyes narrow slightly as he stares down at me.

"Stay? Stay where?" I ask. He's been ignoring everything I've said for the last five minutes and now he asks me to stay?

"Here."

"I'm going to need more than one word answers."

A whiff of his scent makes its way into my nose and I feel myself becoming entranced by him.

His body shifts, turning to face me completely and he takes my purse off of my shoulder and places it on the kitchen island.

"I had fun tonight on the football field for the first time in a long time. Real, true fun."

"Well, that's good," I manage to say.

"I didn't go out there with a running list of things in my head that needed to get done after the game. Or a checklist in my mind of things to accomplish during the game. My mind was clear and I felt… I felt carefree. For the first time in a long fucking time, I focused on more than just the next thing I had to do. I felt present."

"Living in the moment sometimes isn't so bad after all, huh?"

He smiles and the most gorgeous brown eyes shine as he looks at me.

"I thought about you when I walked into the hallway after I left, and again when I got in my truck. A third time when I pulled into the stadium for the game tonight and many, many more moments between kickoff and right now."

My mouth goes dry at his confession and I feel my pulse race as he inches closer, placing a warm palm on my cheek and I instantly sink into his embrace.

"Tell me to stop," he whispers against my skin, but I won't. I don't want him to.

"No," I answer softly.

The most handsome, devilish grin comes out to play on Chase's face and I feel like somehow I've awoken a beast and I'm so eager to meet this side of him.

"I've been trying… So. Fucking. Hard. To get you out of my head, Kincaid. You don't belong there, it's not right to want you the way that I do." His thumb feathers over my lips, and I close my eyes momentarily as the ache between my thighs grows stronger.

"It's okay to give in to what you want," I say in a shaky breath and look up at him.

"I haven't been so good at giving in lately, but…" Chase's hand lands on my hip and I almost crumble at the contact. He gently guides me back until I hit the wall and he presses his body against mine. I can feel his cock against my stomach and I take a deep, stuttered breath as he pushes himself against me.

Feeling Chase's body like this against mine is overwhelming in the best way possible and seeing his eyes darken with desire as he stares down at me makes me ache. For years, I've longed to be the one he looks at this way. And I tremble under his touch when his fingers dip into the waistband of my leggings.

"Fuck, you're beautiful." He gently tugs on the braid in my hair and I whimper, which only causes a sly grin to form on his face before he yanks it a second time and all bets are off. My head falls back at the same time his mouth engulfs mine and we immediately pick up where we left off weeks ago.

My hands pull his hair, grasping at whatever I can to somehow get even closer to him. Both of his hands reach for the back of my thighs and as if I'm weightless, he picks me up and my legs wrap around his waist. He moans into my mouth when I pull his body closer to mine and then walks us to his bedroom, not allowing our lips to part.

Chase quietly closes his bedroom door behind us and I hear him flick the lock before he lays me on my back in his bed. He towers over me, breaking our contact only for the smallest moment before I'm pulling him back to me. His scent instantly covers my body as I'm writhing underneath him, wanting this to go further.

I feel Chase's thigh between my legs and he rocks against me, bringing me an unexpected feeling of so much pleasure and there's still layers between us.

"Fuck," he breathes, lips still just hovering above mine. "I want to touch you."

"I want you to touch me, Chase. I *need* you to fucking touch me."

His chest rumbles as he takes his fingers and lightly runs them over my collarbone. He's such a damn tease I can't stand it.

"Chase, I've been a patient girl, but…" I begin, bucking my hips at him and feeling his thigh again push into my center.

He sits back on his heels, looking handsome as ever as he pulls his shirt from his body and then brings both hands to my hips as he slides my leggings off, but leaves my underwear in place.

"Patient girls get rewarded."

CHAPTER TWENTY-SIX

CHASE

Summer spreads her legs further apart as she lies back on my bed. A pair of white lace underwear are all that separate me from seeing the most intimate part of her. Ever since I kissed her, I've been dying to see other parts of her, *taste* other parts. Something sparked after we kissed. And something within me came alive that I didn't think would find its way to the surface again. At least, not for a while and especially not with Summer. She's been a welcome addition into my routine, fun even. I know for certain that CeCe has loved having her around.

I run my hands up her legs, savoring everything I'm seeing tonight as I watch her try and press her thighs together to stop the ache. When I reach her center, my thumb grazes over her underwear and she sucks in a breath at the touch.

"Sensitive?" I grin at how quickly her body jerked in response.

"Mm-hmm," she moans.

Summer reaches down toward me and pulls my face against hers, clashing our mouths together as she rocks underneath me. She's wet, I can feel it. And fuck, I love it. She's not afraid to take what she wants and she's vocal about what she needs. It's the sexiest thing and makes me want her even more, knowing she's dying for my touch.

"*Please*," she begs against my lips, and I pull one of her legs up further, moving her underwear to the side and opening her up for me.

Slowly, I slide two fingers through her pussy. A deep moan leaves her chest as she presses her head back against my bed, nearly arching her whole body.

"God, you're so fucking wet, Kincaid. It's so hot."

My thumb finds her swollen clit and I circle it slowly. Her body rocks against me and she whimpers every time I flick her clit with my finger.

"Is this what you've wanted from me for all of these years?" My lips press against her ear while my fingers push inside of her.

"Yes." Her voice is becoming rough and desperate.

I pull my fingers from her briefly to get a taste as her head tilts back.

"Keep your eyes on me. You should see how much I fucking love this." Licking my fingers clean, I smile down at her as she stares. Her blue eyes watching my tongue pick up every last drop.

Her body shudders under me still, and I waste no time finding her clit again—causing her sounds to get louder, only fueling me further.

I circle her clit over and over, feeling how messy things are getting, knowing it's making me hard as a fucking rock right now.

"Chase, oh God," Summer pants as she bucks against my hand and I rub my palm against her clit as my fingers curl inside of her.

"Come on, Kincaid," I taunt against her ear. "Let me see you come undone."

I slow my movements slightly before picking up the pace again and I watch her body fall into rhythm with my fingers as she swivels her hips.

One of her hands slips under her shirt and cups her breast as she quickly pulls the straps from her bra down.

"Let me," I say, moving her hand out of the way and taking her entire breast into my palm, feeling how warm and full it is.

The way her body feels is driving me absolutely wild. I squeeze her nipple and run my thumb over it, both movements eliciting a moan from her. Her hand grips my hair and she pulls aggressively as she cries out.

"It's so good. Fuck, Chase, I'm—" Summer's body shakes and she completely falls apart beneath me, coating my hand in everything she has to offer as moans echo around the bedroom.

Without hesitation, I find her mouth and take her bottom lip between my teeth, sucking while she digs her fingernails into my back. I rock my body against hers, letting her come down from her high while still wanting to feel her all over me. She's made a goddamn mess and I love every part of it.

Summer's breathing evens out and she wipes the back of her hand over her forehead. "I could do that again." She chuckles.

"Me too," I admit, pulling myself from the bed to grab her a towel.

"I don't think I've ever been so, um… messy." She leans up on her elbows as I run the towel over her thighs so she's more comfortable.

"I like your mess." My hand runs over her lower stomach as I lie back down, trailing toward her back and I feel her body recoil slightly. "Are you okay?"

"I'm very okay." She laughs. "You're just touching my back fat." She laughs again and brings the pillow to her side.

"Your what?"

Her eyes roll playfully and she turns on her side to face me.

"Just this." She squeezes near her hip. I have no fucking idea what makes her think there is anything to criticize.

"What the fuck? Who said that?" I demand.

"No one had to tell me. I can see it." She shrugs, seeming unbothered, to be honest; but if it doesn't bother her then why the hell even make the comment?

"This," I say, running my thumb over her skin, "is perfect. Healthy. Desirable."

"Okay, well then, it's just something I'd like to tone up and I guess I feel weird about you seeing my body like this. I don't know."

"Do you not realize how beautiful your body is?"

Rather than hit me with a sarcastic remark or joke, she stills. Her tongue wets her lips as she stares at me.

"I'm not saying there aren't things to love. I do love my body. But you know, we get older and things get *bigger.*" She emphasizes the last word. "I'm not a tiny woman, Chase."

"And thank fuck for that." My hand grips her chin, pulling her face toward mine.

"Tonight was the first time I saw your body in an intimate way, touched you intimately… and you know what I was thinking the entire time?"

She shakes her head as I'm still holding her chin gently.

"All I was thinking about was why I didn't do this sooner. Why didn't I see this sooner? Why didn't I see how fucking incredible you are? Feel how fucking perfect you are." I grab her hand, skimming it over her warm skin. "Your thighs? I want to touch them all the damn time. Hips? The perfect curve that drives me fucking wild. Your lips? Eyes? Arms? Fucking toes… What else do you want me to talk about, Kincaid? I've noticed it all lately and there isn't a damn thing about you that needs criticizing. I want to lick every damn inch of you."

Her eyebrows crease when she looks at me, releasing a slow,

steady breath as she pulls me closer, planting a soft kiss against my lips.

"Are you a feet guy? Because, I'm so sorry, Chase… but I just can't get on board with that." She laughs, pulling a similar sound from me before she shakes her head. "Tomorrow, don't try to hit me with anymore 'no kissing' rules, okay?" She says.

I grab her thigh, pulling it over my leg as we lie face to face.

"I'm serious, Kincaid."

I used to think she was the most confident woman I know, but I'm seeing now we all have our insecurities. I'll repeat my words everyday if she needs to hear them.

She nods her head at me, taking her fingers and gently running them through my hair while my hand roams her thigh.

"I can't seem to follow my own rules anyway," I choke out, getting caught up in the way she feels. The smoothness of her skin and the warmth that radiates.

"What are rules if there's no one around to break them?" she jokes and wiggles her body even closer to mine.

"You're reckless," I say, my fingers feathering her neck.

"Well, one of us should be."

Summer smiles innocently, and I grab her body, hoisting her on top of me as I turn on my back, forcing a gasp from her mouth as she feels my cock between her legs.

"Fuck," she moans as her hand reaches between her legs and she feels the bulge against her pussy.

"I just needed to feel you again for a minute," I say.

Summer begins to circle her hips on top of me.

"Fuck, you can't move like that," I groan, balling my hand into a fist.

"Why?" She seductively tilts her head and moves her body back and forth.

"Kincaid," I growl, pressing my head back into the bed. "You know that only turns me on more."

Her tongue wets her lips and before I know it she's rocking

against me harder. "You're hard as stone, Chase. I need another." Summer takes her hand and moves her underwear to the side completely, letting her clit rest right against the ridge of my dick through my shorts.

Right now, I'd let her have endless orgasms to make up for all the time I was such a fucking idiot.

"Use me, then. Ride my dick. I want to watch you get off again."

"And you?" she asks, rocking her body against mine.

"When you go, I'll go. Believe me, I'm hanging by a fucking thread."

I lean myself back against the headboard, keeping her body lined up against mine, but this time I remove her shirt completely. I want to see her perfect breasts and feel them against my tongue. Summer breathes in sharply when I sit up.

"Oh, even better." She moans at the slight change in position.

Summer's hands pull at my neck as she rocks herself back and forth and I bring my mouth around her pebbled nipple, sucking as she moves faster against my dick. It feels so fucking good like this, I know the real thing would absolutely wreck me.

I have a feeling Summer is close when she starts gasping for breath every few seconds and her body moves fiercely against me as I suck on the swell of her breast.

"Yes," she cries out.

My lips move from her breast to her neck and I drag my tongue across her skin.

"Again," she begs. "More."

We both moan at the same time and I feel my legs nearly go numb as she screams my name louder than ever before.

"Oh fuck, Chase!" she calls out before I cover her mouth with my own, colliding our lips into an explosion of fireworks as her orgasm pierces through her. I feel her body jerk against me in quick movements and then they slow down. My own orgasm instantly rips through me the second I see she's satisfied. My head falling to her shoulder and a loud groan leaving my chest as I ball up the comforter beside me.

"God dammit," I whisper and lift my head to face her.

A hand goes up to cover Summer's mouth and the most schoolgirl giggle leaves her lips.

"Did we just... *dry hump*?"

I hang my head back against the headboard, letting out a chuckle as well.

"Fuck yeah, we did."

I stare at her intently, before pulling her toward me for another kiss. This one is slow and mindful, allowing us to savor the feeling.

Being with Summer intimately is the last thing I ever expected, but now that we've dipped our toes in, I want all of it.

"I meant what I said." The back of my hand strokes her cheek before she slides off of me, grabbing her shirt from the bed.

"Which part?" She cocks an eyebrow playfully, and I stand from the bed.

"All of it. No more rules. I can't... I can't seem to stay away from you and I'm starting to think it's just because I don't want to."

I hand her a towel as I grab one from the bathroom while she sits on the edge of my bed in her shirt and underwear. Tanned legs outstretched in front of her and lips pouty and red from all of our contact.

She shakes her head back and forth slowly with a chuckle.

"What?" I ask.

"It's just... I've always wondered what it would be like to have your attention."

My feet shuffle me even closer to her, taking her hand in mine to pull her from the bed as she shimmies back into her leggings.

Our fingers interlock as she stands in front of me and all I can think about is how I missed it. How'd I miss Summer going from this annoying kid with a crush, to this absolutely beautiful woman standing in front of me? How was I so blind?

"Yeah?" I say, tucking a piece of stray hair from her braid behind her ear. "What are you going to do now that you have it?"

CHAPTER TWENTY-SEVEN

SUMMER

I pull myself onto my tiptoes and kiss him. Soft and lingering for a moment before pulling away.

"I'm going to savor it." My hand presses into his chest, feeling the coarse hair under my fingers, knowing tonight is something out of my wildest dreams. "I'm also going to even the score some time soon. You've made me come twice now, I have some catching up to do." I smirk, running my hand down his chest to the band of his shorts and he hisses as he breathes in.

"Good night, Chase." I pull away and leave, knowing that this time if he tries to put up another wall, it might actually break me.

———

Waking up this morning after the events of last night has me feeling like I'm floating on a cloud. There's a fluttery feeling churning in my stomach and I keep smiling to myself as I'm getting ready for work.

The Rec Center charity dinner is Friday and the plan has always been that Chase's mom Diane would be in town this weekend to help with CeCe while he attends the dinner. It did cross my mind that maybe he'd just ask me instead now that I've been helping out, but he said she's still making the trip here. I've been excited about the charity dinner since Abby mentioned it months ago, but now nerves have crept their way in. It baffles me, as someone who feels confident in the majority of situations, how Chase is still able to make my knees wobble sometimes.

I keep replaying the moments of last night as I'm driving to work and can't stop myself from feeling hot and bothered all over again any time I think about how his hands felt on my skin. Or how he sent me well over the edge not just once, but twice… and there easily could have been a third.

Chase admitting how he was feeling yesterday came as a shock, to say the least. I could tell he'd been resisting an urge of some kind, but I never expected him to say so much. To share just how much of *me* he was thinking about. It was easy to get caught up in the physical parts of what was happening. Hell, I've been dreaming of experiencing Chase in that way for years, but the emotional moments we shared? The vulnerable pieces where I made a comment about my body and he so quickly tried to rewire my thinking. I can't remember a time I've ever said that out loud to anyone else. But I think part of me was worried Chase was thinking it. Like he skimmed my side and I needed to call out my own flaw before he could?

"Morning!" I hear as I'm stepping out of my car.

Damien quickly takes my attention from last night to the present as he walks up to me with a smile on his face.

"Hi!" My greeting is more enthusiastic than normal, granting me a suspicious eyebrow raise from him as we walk toward the building.

"Did you have a good weekend?" he asks.

I swipe my badge at the doors as we enter, "It was great, how was yours?"

"We went to that new farmers' market that just opened, it was amazing. Someone was selling freshly squeezed orange juice and I bought much more than I need for someone who doesn't really even drink the stuff."

"Oh, sounds fun," I say as I place my purse down.

The ER is already buzzing. A lobby full of people and most rooms already occupied.

Thankfully, the morning flies by with the amount of patients I've seen and the afternoon follows a similar suit as I stay busy and on my feet. I had enough time to inhale a protein bar, a stick of string cheese and a bag of chips before it was time to get back on the floor for the second half of my shift.

"What room is the cardio consult?"

My head turns quickly at the sound of Drew's voice coming down the hall.

"In seven," Damien answers him, stepping between the two of us.

"Oh, okay. I thought Summer had this patient?" Drew looks at me impatiently, waiting for me to answer but again Damien speaks up.

"No, I have this one, Dr. McCall." Damien leads Drew into the room, and while I have no problem working alongside Drew when necessary, I'm thankful for friends like Damien who will step in sometimes.

"What was that?" I ask when Damien comes back to the nurses' station just before our shift ends.

"You're in a good mood today. *Extra* good," he emphasizes with a raise of an eyebrow. "I didn't want him ruining it." Damien shrugs, and I bite my cheek to hide the smile that's daring to break loose.

"Thanks," I say, nudging his shoulder.

———

MIA

Which one looks better?

Mia sends two pictures in the group chat, both of her in floor length dresses with similar necklines. Except one is a light purple and the other one is navy blue and seriously stunning on her.

ABBY

What's Nate wearing?

MIA

Whatever I tell him to once I pick my dress

They both look so good, but I vote for navy!

ABBY

I like them both!

MIA

I'm kind of leaning toward navy too, but I
wanted to wear something lighter so I'm stuck!
I'm going for... which dress is going to make
me look hotter so my baby daddy will want to
get it on when we get home. You know?

You could wear hot garbage and he'd be
crawling to you.

ABBY

That's true.

MIA

Okay, navy it is.

My hair is doing the thing where it doesn't actually want to cooperate with my vision for the night so I'm about to toss my entire idea and just leave it down like I normally do. Every time I try to pin the pieces up in the back, I can feel them falling and they don't feel as secure as they should be.

Dammit. I mutter to myself with a bobby pin between my teeth. My arms officially give out after another try and I revert back to my tried and true. Leaving my hair down in loose curls and then pinning one side back completely.

Grabbing the dress from my closet, I step into it carefully. The fabric shimmies over my hips and up my torso as I pull the straps up and let them hang from my shoulders. I didn't get a chance to put any self-tanner on this week, so the slit that goes up to my thigh definitely exposes my paler skin, but at least I shaved, right?

Giving my hair one final fluff, I grab my clutch off the bed and apply a tiny amount of lip gloss before taking one more look in the mirror and heading out the door. I've only talked to Chase once since we took things further last weekend, but I've had a hell of a week at the hospital and if I wasn't working, I've been sleeping.

———

Liam places both hands on my hips as he comes up behind me, spinning me around to face him.

"Careful, Evans. Almost gave me whiplash," I say, pressing a finger against his chest as he hugs me.

To his left is a wall of a man with long, thick legs and strong shoulders. A pair of honey brown eyes with flecks of gold and the most perfect scent I could get drunk off of. Chase stands tall and confident, dressed in a perfectly tailored pair of khaki pants and jacket, a white button down underneath with a tie and a dark brown watch on his wrist, pulling the whole look together.

Liam releases me and I look over at Chase as he takes a step toward me.

"Hi," he whispers in my ear when he pulls me in for a hug and my insides feel warm and tingly.

My arms wrap around his neck as he pulls my waist closer to him.

"Hi." I blush, feeling like a little girl in his arms.

"I'll tell you something, these dinners get more and more extravagant every year. Why isn't your sister a party planner?" Mia walks up beside us just as Chase lets my waist go, but his hand dangles dangerously close to mine at my side. Brushing our pinkies together every time he moves.

"This is her party planning," I say, waving my hand around the room decorated like a celebrity wedding reception.

Champagne colored lights cover the room, giving it a warm and glowing feeling. While the tables are perfectly placed throughout the room with just enough space to comfortably walk through and mingle. The centerpieces are stunning—truly something out of a fairytale with white flowers cascading down and tea candles on every table.

"It's amazing," Mia says.

"What's amazing?" The hostess herself walks up, wearing the same green dress she showed Mia and I the other day in our text thread.

"You are, little sis." Chase locks his arm over her shoulder and pulls her closer. "You outdid yourself this year. The place looks great."

"Oh, thanks. Having some extra time since Summer has been helping you has actually been helpful for me."

Chase nods, kissing her cheek before letting her go and I link my arm into Abby's.

"Can I borrow you for a minute?" I ask Abby and then glance at Mia. "Both of you?"

I can feel Chase's eyes on me, but I'm bursting at the seams to tell the girls what happened between us.

The three of us walk toward the bar and down a quiet hallway outside the doors and into an art room.

"What's going on? You look incredible, by the way. This color is gorgeous on you," Abby says.

"Thanks!"

Tossing my hair over my shoulder, I lower my voice slightly and look at Abby first.

"Is it weird if I share something that happened with Chase?"

Her eyes widen and lips pursed together as she smiles. "In moments like this I just pretend he isn't my brother because you're my best friend and I want to know."

"I knew something would happen," Mia says, adjusting the strap on her dress.

"I hoped something would, but I wasn't sure… except last weekend, when he came home from the game, something *definitely* happened."

"Did you sleep together?" Mia's voice gets louder.

"No, but we fooled around and… I may or may not have—but definitely did—experienced two of the best orgasms of my life." I bite my lip remembering that night, feeling turned on all over again.

"Two?" Abby gapes at me.

I nod my head up and down, heat spreading across my cheeks and my chest. I can feel my body ramping up for a repeat. Seeing Chase tonight just revved my engine even more than normal.

"Hot." Mia smacks her lips together and then runs a hand over her baby bump. "I'm reminding myself that three is enough," she blurts out in a laugh.

"Honestly, I just liked being close to him. Like skin on skin kind of close. We've hugged before and you know, high fived, been in close proximity, but like *that?* I was actually burning. My skin just went up in flames immediately, I don't know how else to describe it. Everything felt… perfect. He said he'd been thinking about me. How he wanted me. It was unexpected, but in the best way."

"I'm really glad he finally got his head out of his ass."

Abby reaches to hug me and Mia joins in, creating the perfect mega hug between my best girls.

"I know." I nod my head against her shoulder.

"It's so typical of him to think he could resist you, though. You're good with CeCe, you're smart, fun, and you're kind. Plus, you know… you're insanely hot."

A loud, unexpected laugh leaves my chest as I pull away from the girls. I don't need the ego boost, but I'll always gladly take one.

Being with Chase last weekend only made a few things clearer for me. One being my feelings for him aren't going anywhere any time soon, or ever probably. And two, how badly I want *more* of him.

CHAPTER TWENTY-EIGHT

CHASE

"Where have you been?" Liam asks when Summer takes a seat next to him at the table.

"Girl things." She pats his shoulder casually and scoots herself in, pulling her hair behind her ear.

She's a damn goddess in that dress.

The way it hangs from her shoulders, exposing the part of her neck I fucking love. There's a slit in her dress, a *high* slit, that has my memory of her thighs playing games with me. Those thighs of hers had me in a goddamn trance and the way her leg peeks out with the slit has me feeling like a hungry, rabid animal. Her gold rings shine every time she talks and moves her hands around in an animated way. And I can't even look at her lips without wanting to kiss them.

"Chase?" Abby says my name loudly. "Hello? Do you want something to drink? The waiter is asking."

"Shit, sorry, yes. Uh, glass of whiskey. Neat." I shake my head and run my sweaty hands over my thighs before risking a glance across the table at Summer.

The corner of her mouth is pulled up into a smirk and her chest is rising and falling with deep breaths as she looks at me.

"Careful," Nate says, leaning into my ear.

I pull back, looking at him, confused.

"Did you mean to be so obvious?" he asks with a smirk before taking a swig of his beer.

"Oh, fuck off."

Nate barks out a laugh causing the rest of the table to look our way.

"Summer, you look good." He diverts attention back to her, and I watch as her eyes roll and she laughs.

"I know." She shrugs. "Thanks, Camp." Her words are directed at Nate, but she's staring at me. In nearly the same eye fucking way I've been staring at her all evening.

It does amaze me how publicly Summer comes off as incredibly confident, almost arrogant in some ways, but behind closed doors she very easily expressed her insecurities. I know we all have them. Little things about ourselves we don't particularly love or would like to change, I guess I just never expected Summer to be so open about hers. She's physically stunning, yes, but she's beautiful beyond that. I've never met someone with as much life and joy as she emulates.

I feel my phone buzz in my pocket and pull it out discreetly to take a look while people around me are still mingling.

SUMMER

Here. So you don't have to stare all night.

Fuuuuuck.

Summer's text comes through with a picture of her in the dress standing in front of her mirror at her apartment. She must've taken this just before coming here tonight. My mouth waters at the way she's posing, letting the slit in her dress do its job and giving my dick a reason to start aching.

It's a nice dress. I like it.

SUMMER

I like your suit.

Her reply to me comes almost immediately, but when I glance up she isn't across from me any longer. I swivel around in my chair trying to find her when suddenly my eyes land on her figure near the bar. She's leaning against it, hair brushed completely to one side with her eyes sparkling from all the way over there. That dress really outlines the curve of her hips and the shape of her body. Something I've barely noticed until recently, and now it's all I can fucking see.

My phone buzzes another time and I see her set hers down on the bar.

SUMMER

And I like your face.

I like your face.

SUMMER

Your hands.

Your thighs.

I pull at the collar of my shirt, loosening it as much as I can without looking sloppy for this damn dinner that I suddenly have the urge to leave. And take Summer with me.

Summer comes back to the table along with Liam, Nate, and Mia. All taking their seats as we wait for Abby and Ford to make a quick speech before dinner is served and the rest of the night continues.

She peeks at her phone, but Mia grabs her attention and I watch as they talk for the next couple of minutes. One of the assistant coaches takes a seat at our table next to me, striking up small talk just as some of the lights come on a bit brighter.

"Your sister knows what she's doing with these dinners," he says.

"Yeah, she does."

As Ford begins talking, we all move our attention to the stage. He's practiced the speech with me and the guys a couple of times to make sure it sounded okay and not "dull"—as he put it. Although, with the charm that follows Ford Anderson everywhere, I'm not sure anyone would ever use that word to describe anything he does.

I quickly throw my hand over my phone as it buzzes, creating more noise than before with how quiet the room now is. I feel eyes on me, but see Summer's name pop up and know I can't resist the urge to check the message.

SUMMER

These thighs?

Another picture. In real time.

I'm a strong man. But this woman is making me so damn weak. Her hand sits gently on her upper thigh as her fingers pull the slit open just a little bit more in the picture. The silkiness of her skin has my mouth hanging open and my blood pumping.

Kincaid... you're killing me.

SUMMER

I can just tell you where I want my thighs, if that's better?

Don't fucking tempt me to bring you into one of these rooms.

SUMMER

Promises, promises.

Ford and Abby finish their speeches and the dinner plates are served, but my appetite is now for something a little more blonde.

Get up, Kincaid.

I send Summer the text message and rise from my seat, quickly making my way toward the doors that head to the main lobby. With everyone else focused on eating and schmoozing, I can't imagine I'll be missed.

My strides are quick as I head down the hall and I hear heels clicking behind me, but she never says a word. She just follows my lead.

Once I enter the last room down the hall, I let the door close behind me and wait in the dark. The only light from a lamp post outside shines dimly through the window and there's a soft light that comes in when Summer opens the door.

Before she's even fully in the room and the door has a chance to close, my body finds hers and presses her against the wall. Summer gasps as my hand lands gently on her chest, inches away from her neck.

"Mmm," she moans, and I lean into her further, putting one of my knees between her legs.

My hand slowly creeps up, gripping the base of her throat softly and I can feel her pulse racing. Her blue eyes sparkle against the darkness and she bites her bottom lip with a smirk.

"Look at you, being risky… spontaneous, even," she taunts.

"You…" I breathe against her cheek. "You're making me reckless."

My free hand finds the slit in her dress and I cup the back of her thigh, pulling her leg up and around my body.

Summer grinds herself against my thigh between her legs and I let my hand roam her smooth skin, never wanting to let it go.

"Fuck, Chase." She pulls my tie and I slam my body into hers one more time, pressing against her as I bring my lips down to her.

She's all tequila and lime as I savor the taste. Her hands go into my jacket as she pulls at my shirt, untucking it. The sounds that Summer makes are enough to drive me wild, add how she feels, how she tastes, it's all too fucking much.

My fingers feather her inner thighs and I feel her body twitch when I run my thumb down the middle of her underwear before peeling the material to the side and sliding my finger down her center slowly. Summer moans against my lips and becomes more fervent in our kiss. Her nails scrape the back of my neck as she tries to pull us closer to one another.

"Fuck," I say when we briefly break apart. Placing my fingers in my mouth, I suck her arousal, savoring the way she tastes against my tongue.

She inhales a breath before she reaches for the belt on my pants.

"My turn for a taste." She fixes her dress but then sinks to her knees right in front of me.

Her fingers pull the belt from the loops and she takes it off completely, letting it fall to the ground beside us making a thump noise just before she slowly tugs at the zipper. My hand reaches down, cupping her cheek and pulling her to look up at me before she does anything further.

"I don't want you doing anything just because you feel like you owe me. You don't owe me *anything*."

"I know," she says with a smile and pulls my pants to my thighs, leaving my boxers in place.

Summer rubs my cock from outside of my boxers, slowly with a firm hand. Like she's feeling every outline, every vein, and ridge. Each touch makes me feel harder than I was the moment before.

There should be alarms ringing in my head. Something telling me to stop this. To grow up and not have a girl on her knees for me at a formal event. Something reminding me that this is my sister's best friend. But nothing comes through. There's nothing in this moment that makes me want to stop. It's the opposite, in fact. It's a voice asking me what the hell I've been doing all these years? Why have I never noticed this woman? Why it took one lonely night of weakness and good conversation to force me into kissing her—only to realize that I should have been doing it this entire time.

"God, you're a tease," I finally spit out.

"I waited *years* for you to touch me. Sixty seconds is noth-ing." She smirks, gathering her hair and tossing it behind her before she pulls my boxers down just enough to free my cock.

I watch as a devilish grin spreads across her face. My head falls back and I hiss in pleasure the moment I feel her tongue touch the tip. She pulses against it briefly before she slides her tongue from the tip up to the base and back down. A drop of pre-cum almost falls, but Summer's quick and her tongue swirls to get it.

When I notice a piece of her hair falling into her face again, I reach my hand down and grab hold of it, yanking it slightly and exposing her throat as she gazes up at me.

"Show me you can take it," I challenge her, and as expected, Summer doesn't back down.

She wraps her hand around the base and squeezes gently as she pulls my cock into her mouth and sucks, then licks just along the rim.

"Fuck!" I yell out, balling my hand into a fist at my side. God, she feels good. I knew she would.

Summer swirls her tongue around a few times before releas-ing, and I'm trying to keep it together but know that she's too damn good at this for me to hold out much longer.

Then, Summer does something I'm not expecting. Something I fucking *love.* She drags her tongue to the base and back up, putting just the tip in her mouth and sucking before her tongue pulses right at the tip over and over. Her fingers run up and down the underside. It's like she has a fucking tell all handbook on the things that drive me wild.

"Fuck, Summer," I moan.

I can feel her teeth as they skim up and down and I bring my hand into her hair. "You're so perfect. Your mouth is fucking perfect."

She takes me even further down her throat and sucks even harder than before as my legs start to buckle underneath me. Summer moans below me, and I feel everything begin to pulse.

"You gonna swallow, Summer? You want me down your throat?"

She moans again, nodding with my cock in her mouth as my orgasm rips through me.

She takes every drop. Every last fucking drop. She even goes back for seconds when she isn't sure she got it all, sucking one more time before I shiver at the touch of her.

I watch as she slowly begins to rise and I'm pulling my pants back up, noticing the puffiness of her lips. The fullness is what I can't get enough of. Everything about Summer gives me this feeling of always wanting more. I take my thumb and skim it over her bottom lip, feeling the warmth beneath my finger.

"This mouth."

She takes my hand into hers, interlocking our fingers between us. "What about it?"

Her glossy eyes are piercing into me. "Add it to the list of things I like."

CHAPTER TWENTY-NINE

SUMMER

My skin is on fire as we walk side by side down the hall and back to the ballroom where all of our friends have probably noticed our absence by now. I feel Chase's eyes on me every now and then, but I keep my focus forward, fixing my dress as I continue to the doors.

The taste of him still lingers on my tongue and I'm relishing in the state of control I just had over him. Over the man I've been hopelessly in love with for as long as I can remember. He was just at my mercy. All of these physical encounters lately only have me fiending for more. For all of it, all of him.

Chase opens the door and holds his hand out for me to go in first. The room has cleared out a bit, but still plenty of people are around as I walk back to our table.

"Nice of you to rejoin the party." Mia smirks at me as she butters a piece of bread in front of her. She's the only one sitting at the table when I take a seat.

"Well, I couldn't just leave. I have to thank the host and hostess for inviting me to such a thrilling event." Refilling my water glass from the pitcher, I take a sip, leaning back in my chair. I can see Chase standing at the bar talking to Liam and Nate.

"Oh, I'm sure you've had quite the thrill tonight," Mia says, smiling at me with a small shake of her head.

Chase glances over to me from the bar and winks as he brings a glass of whiskey to his lips.

If we're trying to hide anything, we're already doing a shit job of it.

———

My time with CeCe lately has been scarce due to Diane being in town, but Chase still mentioned needing my help this morning.

He's been going on and on about his knees bothering him quite a bit lately, so I guess this morning he's hoping to get some additional therapy done on them. We haven't seen each other since the charity dinner on Friday and I was tempted to offer my services, a massage for his knees that might lead to more, but figured that innuendos at eight in the morning might not be his cup of tea.

"So, who made the pancakes?" I ask CeCe while she dips her fingers through the syrup on her plate.

"Daddy." She beams up at me, chocolate smeared all over her lips as she licks them.

"Really?" I'm surprised that Chase had time to cook before he left this morning.

"He was up really early."

Hmm. Maybe his knees were bothering him and he couldn't sleep? I'm sure I'm thinking way too much into this, but CeCe seemingly answers my question when she continues talking.

"He wasn't tired anymore. When I'm not tired anymore I get up too."

"Well, that makes sense." I swipe a damp paper towel over her lips.

"Daddy isn't tired anymore." She smiles as I pull the paper towel away and for some reason her statement makes my eyes all of a sudden feel heavy, and a small lump forms in my throat. "We played a puppet show last night!" she exclaims, hopping down from the stool and racing to her bedroom.

Chase has been tired for the last three years. Even with Abby helping him, he still forced a lot of the load on himself. It doesn't take any kind of specialist to look at Chase and say he's overwhelmed, but he'd never admit it out loud. He'd never flat out say, "I need help."

In the last month, I've watched him shed a small layer of that. He's still overprotective and has his routines, but he seems to be enjoying himself a little more and accepting the fact that my purpose right now is to help him. I noticed it the day he asked me to come over at the last minute. Chase and last minute are two things that rarely go hand in hand. He's a planner and an organizer, he doesn't just "forget" something—but that day I think he understood he was juggling more on his own than he needed to.

CeCe comes back into the kitchen as I'm loading the breakfast dishes into the dishwasher and shows me the dolls that they were playing with last night. One of them has long black hair, but it's pulled back in kind of a wonky looking braid and then there's another doll with blonde—almost yellow looking hair—with a braid as well. Except that braid actually looks pretty well put together.

"We did braids," she says, taking her fingers and smoothing out the small pieces on the side of the one with black hair. "Here."

She places the blonde haired doll on the counter next to the sink.

"Wow, she's so beautiful." I smile as I press start on the dishwasher and wipe my hands on the towel.

"Summer," CeCe says, looking up at me as I pick up the doll. She's wearing a purple dress with one shoe missing.

"Yeah?"

"She's Summer too."

"Oh yeah, she does have the same color hair as me." I smile and walk toward the living room with her.

"That one is Daddy's favorite."

My brows crease slightly as I take a seat against the couch on the floor with her.

"Oh?"

She nods and puts both dolls next to each other on the floor before she starts making multiple trips back and forth, bringing out a bunch of stuffed animals for us to play with.

I giggle to myself at the thought of Chase putting on a puppet show with his daughter, using a doll named Summer.

When Chase walks in the door later, I hear him place multiple bags on the floor as he shuffles around in the foyer. CeCe wastes no time running toward him where they meet in the kitchen and I can hear a different energy in his voice.

Usually, when Chase gets home from practice or a meeting, he sounds exhausted. But today, there's a pep in his voice and his step when he walks toward me as I'm putting the pillows back on the couch.

"Do you have any plans for the rest of the day?"

I eye him cautiously, "No…"

"Okay, good." He turns around quickly, leaving me confused at his question.

As I enter the kitchen, I see CeCe sitting on a barstool, rummaging through one of the bags he brought in and pulling out all sorts of Christmas decorations. Garland, lights and ornaments begin to pile up in front of her and I tilt my head, again in confusion at what he's doing.

"CeCe, careful not to break any of those ornaments, put them on the counter gently." He hauls another bag from the floor onto the counter, and I just stare. Not knowing what to do or what to say.

Chase isn't an overly festive person. Between him and his sister, Abby got the holiday gene. Last year, I remember he had a small fake tree in the corner by the fireplace, and I'm positive he only had it for the sake of CeCe.

"What's uh… what's going on here, Buddy the elf?"

"Great movie." He points at me and hands me the last plastic bag from the floor. "No idea what's in here, can you take a look?"

"Sure…" The word drags out slowly as I study him.

The blue t-shirt he's wearing is covered in glitter all down one side. "Where'd you get all of this?"

"Mia." He shrugs as if it's the most natural answer in the world and I'm some kind of idiot for even asking.

"You got Christmas decorations from Mia?"

"I bought some, but the stores didn't have a lot. Abby is busy so I knew I couldn't ask her right now, so the next option was Mia. She said these were extras she didn't have space for."

Decorating for Christmas is one of my favorite things to do. I don't do much in my apartment because it's just me and I'm not there often, but a tree and lights are always a must. Anything to make it feel more like the Christmas season in Florida when the weather still feels warm.

"Oh," I say, smiling.

CeCe takes a bunch of the garland into her bedroom and Chase lets her have free range on decorating her room however she wants to. It's pure chaos when I walk in, but she loves it.

"What prompted you to want to decorate all of a sudden?" I

ask when it's just the two of us while CeCe finishes her bedroom.

He stills briefly, holding a string of lights in his hands that he just tested to make sure they all work and looks over at me.

"I've felt… I don't know… compelled lately to make things more fun for CeCe. I saw all the Christmas decorations at the facility today and I heard Nate talking about driving the boys around to look at lights this weekend and I just thought I needed to start making more memories like that with her. Bedtimes can be pushed back and candy canes can classify as dinner every now and then, right?"

My smile widens as I walk closer to him. "Right."

The back of Chase's hand skims the side of my bike shorts as I stand in front of him. Creating instant goosebumps down my legs.

"Since you aren't busy the rest of the day…" His other hand discreetly feathering the small of my back under my sweater. "I was hoping maybe you'd want to come pick out a tree with us."

CHAPTER THIRTY

CHASE

Two weeks left until Christmas sure hasn't left me with the best options for a damn tree. It's almost like part of me forgot the holiday was approaching, even though I'm reminded of it every time I step outside of my apartment.

I don't hate holidays, I just don't get overly into them like a lot of people do. I've never had more than a small tree in my place aside from when my sister lived with me and did the decorating. But how fair has that been to CeCe? Sometimes, I think I forget she's still a kid and needs that magic and wonder.

"This one is a little sad looking," Summer says, tugging at the branches.

We've been to three tree farms and haven't found one that CeCe is jumping up and down for yet. I have half a mind to go to the local store and pick up a fake one, but CeCe was so excited when I mentioned getting a real one, I can't go back on that now.

"This one!" CeCe shouts behind me.

The tree is lopsided and barely as tall as me. The branches are still a lush dark green, though, and as I stare at it, looking at Cece and then back to the tree, I feel like I could work with this.

"I knew you'd find the best one they had." Summer places a

hand on CeCe's head as I leave them standing near the tree and head to the guy at the front to pay.

Hauling it upstairs shouldn't be this difficult, but branches are scratching my face and the tree stump is wet and dewy from sitting in water. Summer snorts as she tries to help and we both end up pulling the tree in opposite directions, but I'm stronger than her and end up pulling her body down nearly on top of the tree itself as we walk it down the final stretch in the hallway.

"Looks like you've got it," she breathes out, laughing.

Summer could have gone home hours ago. She could have said no when I asked her to stay and decorate or go shopping for a tree. She didn't have to make CeCe hot chocolate and help hang a Christmas banner in her bedroom. She wanted to. She wants to be around CeCe just as much as I do and it pulls at something in my chest.

When it comes to dating women, I'm a package deal with CeCe. I've never introduced anyone to CeCe, primarily because I haven't actually dated anyone in years. But the thought of ever bringing a woman around her made me feel so fucking uneasy. Summer and I aren't dating, in fact, we're not doing much of anything aside from fulfilling a physical need we both seem to have. Except, something in me wants there to be more. Summer's always been around, but she fell into our lives last month in a more consistent way and now I don't know how the hell we're supposed to just stop seeing her when the season is over and I don't need the help.

We've spent the afternoon getting the tree set up and decorated. Summer said she didn't want to take away the father and daughter experience from CeCe, so she mostly sat back and told us where ornaments were needed as CeCe and I decorated the tree. A lot of them are clumped together at the bottom, nothing really matches and she basically just threw the tinsel on the tree in one spot on the side. But it's perfect.

"Here," Summer says, handing me a small star to place on the top.

"Come here." Scooping CeCe in my arms, I lift her toward the tree. "It's not done yet. You need to place the star on the top."

She stretches her arm, reaching for the top and I hoist her up a little bit further, guiding her hand to place it where it needs to go.

"Perfect." Summer stands near the side of the couch, holding a cup of hot chocolate in one hand and a bowl of her overly buttered popcorn in the other. And when I look at her in this moment, I see something I couldn't have predicted, something I never expected I'd want with Summer.

I want more.

More of this. More of her. More of her with my daughter. More late nights and early mornings. More smart ass remarks and flirtatious comments. More text messages, the dirty and the sweet. More walking into my home after a long day and seeing *her*.

"Thanks for your help," I say to Summer as the day winds down.

She rolls up the sleeves of her blue sweater, cuffing them just below her elbows. There's a peacefulness about this evening. CeCe is laying on the couch watching a show before bed and Summer and I just finished going over the next two weeks when I'll need her help. With my mom still being in town, Summer won't be around too often to watch CeCe, but that doesn't mean I don't want to see her.

"You should hang some Christmas lights outside," she says, staring through the sliding glass door.

When I don't answer I hear her mumble under her breath, and I just shake my head knowing Summer can't stand a silent moment.

"Or, you know what? They have twinkling lights you can hang that I bet CeCe would love."

She presses her hands together gently. A little tick I've noticed she has sometimes.

"Are you all talked out for the day?"

A low chuckle leaves my chest as I lean one hand on the counter and position my body toward hers. She inhales and her eyelashes flutter my way.

"Go on a date with me."

She pulls her head back. "What?"

"I want to take you on a date. Will you go on a date with me?"

"Just the two of us?"

"Well, that's generally what a date is, isn't it? It's been a while since I've been on one, but I don't think the premise has changed."

Her cheeks turn red as she looks at me blankly. I imagine the same thoughts are running through her head that ran through mine earlier when I had this idea. We've never intentionally hung out just the two of us, there's always been a reason, an event, an outing, a storm—putting us in the same place at the same time.

"Okay…" she says slowly.

"I'll make arrangements with my mom for CeCe," I assure her.

"Okay," she says with more enthusiasm this time, pulling at the hem of her sweater.

"Eight o'clock tomorrow night, I'll pick you up."

"Oh." Her eyes widen in front of me. "Like a real date *date?*

"Well, yeah. What'd you think I meant?"

"I just… I think I'm in shock. Chase Hunt just asked me out on a date… I have to get home and add this to my diary."

She brushes her hand against my abdomen and even the slightest touch sends all the blood in my body rushing south. A smug smile spreads over Summer's face and she backs away only leaving me wanting more as she says goodbye to CeCe, and waves to me from the door.

"Tomorrow." She points at me with a smile, and I nod.

———

We only have a couple more games left in the regular season and therefore practices have felt a lot more intense than usual. We're in a position to be in the playoffs, but we won't get that first round bye week that we've become so used to having. Wildcard weekend is where we'll begin and hopefully continue our playoff run.

"What are you staring at?" I ask Liam as I approach him on the sidelines. His focus is on the group of reporters in a circle on the opposite side of the field.

"What do you think that's about?" he asks me, gesturing to all of them talking.

"Player interviews, probably."

"Nah," Liam says, shaking his head. "Look. Just watch her."

When he says *her*, I look more closely, seeing the woman he's talking about is Demi Sanchez. She's a sports reporter who has handled a lot of our team interviews and game day reports for years. She's also very active in Nate's foundation. She hosts a podcast and did a live show at one of his events last year, sharing her own experience with mental health and she had a handful of athletes on the panel to talk about their struggles too.

Demi wipes her cheek as two other women stand around her, one clutching Demi's arm in what looks like it's meant to be a comforting manner. I've only ever seen Demi be as professional as they come. So, I'm surprised when it looks like she's having a personal moment out on the field.

"I knew something was wrong," Liam yanks his helmet from his head. "I'll fucking kill him."

"Whoa, whoa, whoa. Who are you talking about? Kill who?" I ask.

Nate walks up to us with a bottle of water in his hand, squirting it at Liam like a child.

"Cool off, man."

"Did I miss something?" I ask again.

"Mia told me about an article she saw last night about Demi and Brandon." Nate shakes his head, and we all watch as Demi regains her composure and walks back into the building, out of sight.

"Yeah, we've all met him. Nice guy." I say.

Liam scoffs and spits on the field. "Piece of shit guy."

"The article said that Brandon had an affair and left her weeks ago. I don't know how much of it is true, but you know… leave it to Mia, she'll find out what happened."

My jaw drops. "No fucking way."

"Please, let me run into that motherfucker at an event or better yet on the street without press so I can level his ass," Liam mumbles as he walks by us and to the locker room.

Nate and I exchange looks and Ford jogs up beside us as we begin to make our way in as well.

"Well, well, well…" Ford says immediately. "I hear someone's got a date."

Nate's head spins toward me and I don't bother trying to hide it or downplay anything.

"Yeah. I'm taking Summer out tonight."

"My guy," Nate says, slapping my shoulder. "I take it your *no kissing again* rule flew out the fucking window."

"Yeah, about immediately after I made it, to be honest."

Both of them laugh and shake their heads as we enter the building.

CHAPTER THIRTY-ONE

SUMMER

If sixteen-year-old Summer could see me now… standing in my closet picking out an outfit to go out on a date with Chase Hunt, she'd never believe that after all this time the pining paid off. I can't help but feel giddy about tonight. I know I'm outside Chase's comfort zone when it comes to his type. I'm still very aware that, at the end of the day, I'm a person who challenges him, forces him to see and react to things differently. I'm not always certain that's something he likes, but he did ask me out tonight, so I have to assume he doesn't completely hate those things about me.

After landing on my outfit for the night and putting the finishing touches on my curls, I give myself the tiniest of all pep talks. I always say the nervous feeling and the excited feeling are really just the same. They go hand in hand and while I'm excited and ready, I'm also very aware that this is something high school me would have lost her damn mind over.

The knock at my door surprises me, even though I was fully expecting it. He's right on time. Exactly on time. Like my phone *just* changed to eight o'clock.

I quickly slip my feet into my heels and give myself one final glance in the mirror by the door. I went with a light pink dress that falls to just below my knees with a small slit up the side. When I open the door, Chase is wearing a navy blue suit with a white shirt underneath. The top few buttons are undone, letting his chest breathe a little and I feel like I could crumble at his feet.

Chase in a football uniform is *hot*.

Chase in a suit is downright *captivating*.

"Damn," he says as I open the door.

"Right back at you."

He blushes as we both stand at the door on either side of the threshold, taking in the sight of each other.

His hand extends to mine, pulling it to his lips and he plants a soft kiss on my knuckles, before intertwining our fingers together.

"Ready to go?"

I can only nod at his question, allowing him to completely take the lead for the night.

The restaurant is fancy when we walk in. I've never been to this area of town, but it feels like it's built for country club members and very, very wealthy people. The waiter places a bottle of champagne on the table just as we take our seats and I look around feeling as if I don't belong in a place this nice.

"So, uh, how was your day?" he asks and it instantly feels… weird.

"It was good. How was yours?"

"It was good."

We both nod and reach for our glasses at the same time. I watch as Chase almost spits out the champagne he just took a sip of, but he holds himself together.

"You can order a whiskey," I let him know.

"Yeah, I might. I just thought champagne would be nice."

"It is," I say, tipping my glass in his direction.

Date Chase is nervous and hesitant. He looks so out of his

element and I can't figure out if it's me, if it's him, the place, or a combination of all three.

When the waiter comes back over, he goes over the specials and places a basket of bread down in front of us. Like starved animals, both of us reach for the bread, practically tuning out everything fancy the waiter says.

"Do you think I can get chicken tenders and fries here?"

Chase chuckles, pressing his lips together and he glances around the room. The chandeliers sparkle and there is classical Christmas music playing from the speakers. A giant tree in the back that you can see from every angle of the room and the water glistens out back.

"I'll get you chicken tenders and fries, come on." A grin makes its way across his face. He leaves a hundred-dollar bill on the table and grabs my hand as we briskly walk out of the restaurant.

There's a small chill in the air as we walk hand in hand down the block toward the parking garage where his truck is. Without a word, Chase's blue jacket covers my bare shoulders and he nods at me before he takes my hand in his again, squeezing it tight.

"That place was fancy," he says the moment we get into his truck.

"A little too champagne for our beer taste," I joke. "But the place was beautiful."

"I have an idea… if you can just go with it," he offers, and I nod with excitement. The night hasn't started exactly as I had always pictured, but that feels on brand for Chase and I in a way.

He pulls into Louie's parking lot before turning to face me. "I'll be right back," he says.

My fingers fidget in my lap as I sit in his truck waiting for him to return. I hear a song I love playing from the radio so I reach for the dial to turn it up and notice it's coming from his Bluetooth. I wouldn't have expected him to just leave his phone unattended, but it's sitting completely unlocked in the center console and when I glance at the playlist, it says *Summer's Cleaning Jams.*

He added my playlist to his phone?

Maybe it automatically syncs with his Alexa device?

A moment later he emerges from the building, carrying a large to-go bag. He's rolled up the sleeves on his white button up and my desire to straddle him in the driver's seat of his truck just rose tenfold.

"Tenders, wings, fries, mozzarella sticks, and pretzels."

He places the bag on the floor in the backseat and the truck smells just like Louie's, minus the beer, and I can't wait to dive in.

"You're listening to my playlist," I say as he puts the truck in reverse and his hand spreads open on the steering wheel, doing that hot spinny thing that guys do when they drive.

"CeCe asked for it a couple weeks ago when we were at home. A lot of the songs grew on me. Guess you've got good taste, Kincaid." He smiles with a shrug like it's nothing, but it doesn't feel like nothing to me.

Since Diane is at his house watching CeCe, we take the food to my apartment. Chase takes it upon himself, setting everything up and we both get comfortable on the couch with plates full of everything we love.

"Sorry about that restaurant," he says, wiping his mouth with a napkin.

I wave my hand in the air at him, "Are you kidding? The place was gorgeous. But you know, I just… I don't need fancy. This is perfect. It was a sweet thought, though, and now it's just a funny thing to look back on."

"There's one more thing I wanted to do tonight. I have to go get it from my truck, though. I'll be right back."

My eyes narrow, suspiciously, but also with excitement.

"Okay…"

He kisses the side of my head, right next to my temple before he heads out the door. It's quick and soft, like a routine, a common thing he does all the time and it fills my stomach with butterflies.

The door swings open and shut as I'm cleaning off the table and boxing up the rest of the food we didn't get to eat before placing it in the fridge. When he rounds the corner into the kitchen, he places a stack of board games on the counter with a prideful smile.

"Are you sure you want to do this?" I ask, playfully. "I don't lose at board games."

"You're all talk, Kincaid." His index finger wags in front of me, and I drag my eyes from his hands up his arm to the jawline that's sharp enough to cut glass.

He takes the pile of boxes into my living room, placing one in particular on the coffee table and the rest he moves to the corner.

"Scrabble it is," I say confidently, tossing my hair to the side and taking a seat opposite him on the couch.

After some time, the board in front of us is filled with short words, basic words, some naughty words and the name Don. I thought about challenging him about using a name, but technically, it's a word so I let it slide.

Although, the moment he tries to play "qe" as a word, I draw the line.

"It's not my fault you're out of letters." My voice raises and I start laughing while he pulls the letters off the board.

"You got away with using the word mote, what the hell is a mote?" He stands, placing both hands on his hips. His competitive edge doesn't just end at football, he's the worst at losing games. I love it.

"Mote," I say after pulling up the Scrabble dictionary. "a tiny piece of substance." I rise from the couch, getting into his personal space to gloat for a moment.

"You know I don't like to lose, Kincaid." He pulls me by my hip closer to him.

"I know. You're *such* a sore loser."

His fingers pulse against the fabric of my dress before he holds them steady in place, bringing his lips dangerously close to my ear.

"I fucking love this dress," he whispers against my skin. "Now, take it off."

"You lost, I should be the one giving the demands." My fingers begin to run down his chest, but he's quick and spins me around in one swift movement, pulling my back flush against his chest.

"Feel that?" he asks, his cock pulsing against my back.

I nod as I lean back, feeling how hard he is.

"Take off your dress." His voice is nearly a demand.

His hands run down my body, pulling me closer to him with every touch. My clit throbs at the attention he's giving me. I can feel the zipper slowly sliding down the back of the dress as he brushes my hair to the side, his fingers grip onto my arms and I shimmy out of the dress, pulling it down with my fingers when it reaches my hips.

"You have got to be fucking kidding me," he says, turning me around to face him as I stand there in a matching black lace bra and underwear set. He stares and then looks away briefly, only to bring his eyes back, but this time they're burning with so much desire, so much hunger. He moves even closer, backing me up into a wall and my chest pounds with anticipation.

"Do you like it?" I ask, slowly circling the fabric around my nipple with my fingers.

My other hand hovers over my stomach, just below my belly button but he pulls it away and drops to his knees in front of me, kissing my lower tummy.

He doesn't answer my question with words. He pulls one leg

over his shoulder and tugs my underwear to the side. Spreading me open with two fingers just before his mouth devours me. The contact is sudden, but so welcome. I feel his tongue against my clit immediately and he circles over and over. I pull him closer to me, pressing his face against my center. His mouth around my clit is unbelievable.

"Oh, God. Chase," I pant as he sucks. I feel his fingers slide into me while his tongue continues to swirl over me. "Yes," I hiss as my head falls back against the wall in a slam.

He reaches his other hand up, cupping my breast and I place my hand over his, holding it in place.

Chase's tongue takes me to places I've never been and the way his fingers curl inside me has my orgasm building to new levels.

"More," I call out, and Chase looks up at me. I can see myself coated on his face as he briefly pulls away, but keeps his fingers thrusting in and out as he licks his lips.

"You going to come for me? Let it out. Let me see you get messy again." He smirks, bringing his face back between my legs and I press him closer to me again, needing to feel the friction against my clit as his fingers drive in and out.

Goosebumps line my skin as I feel my orgasm building and building with each dirty thought of Chase. His mouth on me is unlike anything I've ever felt before. I moan out his name again as my body begins to convulse, jerking back and forth against him while he squeezes my nipple.

Waves rip through my entire body as my orgasm sweeps me away and my back arches from the wall. Chase holds me in place and keeps his tongue against my clit as everything I have to offer coats his face.

"Oh, God." I shudder, finally coming down from the high.

"I could get used to seeing you like this," Chase says as he rises to his feet. He presses his body against mine, his hands finding their way into my hair as he brings his lips down to mine.

My hand reaches between us to unfasten his belt and he lets

me pull it from the loops before his hands reach for the back of my thighs, picking me up and carrying me into my bedroom. When my back hits the mattress, I sit up slowly and reach my hands behind me to unclip my bra. I let it pop open and fall into my lap as Chase watches intently.

A low rumble sounds in his chest while he blinks his eyes slowly with a soft smirk before he pulls his shirt from his chest and lowers himself on the bed as I lie back. His mouth finds my nipple and he takes it between his teeth, gently pulling as a whimper falls from my lips.

His eyes scan my body. They linger between my legs as I spread them open for him, still in nothing but the underwear from earlier.

"You looking like this should be a goddamn sin." His voice husky and low.

From his back pocket, he pulls his wallet out and grabs a condom, placing it on the nightstand before turning his attention back to me.

"For weeks, I've wanted to know what it felt like to be inside of you." He leans forward, taking my underwear from both sides of my hips and gently sliding them off.

"God, Chase," I say, throwing my back against the pillow. "Please."

It feels like some cruel and unusual form of torture to be played with like this. Chase tosses my underwear to the floor and my legs instinctually open wider. My clit is already throbbing again for his touch.

My skin tingles as he skims his fingers over my inner thighs. There's no rush in his movements, even though everything inside of me wants to tell him to please, *please* fuck me.

He's as tempting as they come, hovering over me with his unruly hair dangling above my face, his wilderness scent drawing me in and his hands teasing me with every single touch.

"I need you," I whisper against his lips, pulling my face up to meet his.

"Here?" I whimper at the feel of his thumb as it glides slowly against my pussy.

"Yes."

The mere touch of Chase's hand sends shivers flowing through my body as he breathes against my neck.

He begins to remove the blue suit pants from his body as he pulls himself up onto his heels. His boxers slowly follow and my breath stutters, as if it's the first time I'm seeing him like this. At the charity dinner, the room we snuck into was dark, I went mostly by feel that night, which didn't disappoint. But seeing Chase like this makes me tremble. After he slides the condom on, he slowly brings himself back down toward me, letting his lips feather mine ever so slightly and I instantly feel my body weaken under him.

"You drive me fucking wild." He sucks on the divot of my neck briefly. "In all the worst ways," he whispers as he moves lower and kisses my collarbone. "And the best." He plants his lips on the swell of my breast and my back arches as he moves further down, swirling his tongue over my nipple.

His body rocks against me, but he doesn't push inside me. I'm spread so damn wide, my clit is screaming for something more. As if he can read my mind, he slides his hand between my legs and pinches my clit and I wouldn't be surprised if someone on the other side of this wall heard my scream. He groans at my outburst and slides his fingers down my center.

"Don't tease me, Chase. Be a good boy and fuck me."

His chuckle vibrates above me and he grins like I've just given him a green light to commit a crime.

Chase lines his cock up against me and I lift my hips as he slides himself in.

"Oh, fuck!" I cry out, my words are mumbled by my erratic breathing.

I can feel him moving slowly as he eases into me. He shudders above me with every movement, filling me so completely.

"God, Summer. Fuck." Chase brings his forehead down to mine and my hands lock behind his neck as his body shivers above me. "You feel so good."

He pulls out slowly and then thrusts back in, giving me an unimaginable sense of pleasure.

"Oh my god," I gasp. He pulls out again and then back in.

"I know," he whispers. "I know. But you don't have it all yet."

My breathing becomes a heavy pant as I process his words. Chase begins to move quicker, each thrust starting out with the smallest speck of pain that turns into the greatest pleasure.

"More." My hands roam his back, pulling him closer to me as he shoves his cock inside me again and again.

Feeling our bodies collide this way is pure euphoria. There's a piece of my soul that feels like he takes every single time his body slams into me. He's commanding and possessive, but still gentle and tender.

As mindful as he's being, I know he wants to unleash more. I want him to give me more.

"Fuck me harder, Chase."

He grunts and instantly our movements become erratic, near animalistic and he brings his thumb to my clit at the same time he pushes inside me.

His movements continue at a steady pace until he pulls out completely for a moment, wiping the back of his hand over his forehead.

"All fours," he demands.

He pulls me by the hips, flipping me onto my stomach and I arch myself for him, placing my face on the pillow.

I glance back at him through the hair falling in my face. "No pressure, but this is usually my favorite position."

"I think seeing you in any position is my favorite."

Both of his hands grab a hold of my hips just before the pressure of him pushing into me takes my breath away.

"Might need that pillow to drown out your screams." Chase shoves in again and I feel my entire body nearly fold at the pressure of him inside of me.

My whimpers are muffled by the pillow. His hand wraps around my hip, finding my clit once again as if he has the perfect map to my body. His fingers move in circles and my body stiffens as he moves faster against me.

"Chase," I call out, unsure if he's even able to hear me. My orgasm builds up as he continues to thrust in and out in rhythm with his fingers circling my clit.

"That's it. Come on my cock." His words a near growl before his head falls against my shoulder and I feel his body shudder.

"It's so much, too much, I—" My words are cut off by the way my release tears through me. There's little I can do to slow my body down as my hips keep moving, letting my orgasm completely consume me.

I can feel Chase's movements slow and become steady, his thrusts intentional as he holds my hips and I can feel his build up.

"Oh, fuck, fuck, fuck." His words are quick and low when he moves, until finally he stills behind me, and my body falls into the mattress.

CHAPTER THIRTY-TWO

CHASE

My hands just want to keep touching her. I can't help but feel territorial over this woman lately, even more now that we've experienced each other this way. If any part of me thought sleeping with Summer would be awkward, I couldn't have been more wrong. Being with someone has never felt so goddamn right.

I glance at her from the corner of my eye, her bare chest rising and falling with deep breaths. She runs her fingers over my thigh and I let out a sigh at the touch.

"I've always wondered what this whole thing looked like," she says as she turns on her side to face me. Her breasts fall in front of her and it takes extreme self-control to not put my lips on one.

"I want to add to it." I touch the ink on my skin as she traces the lines.

"What do you want to add?"

"I want to add an anchor near the compass. And the coordinates need a touch up too."

She nods at me, but her eyes still remain glued to my leg.

"I've only ever been able to see to the bottom of the

compass." She laughs to herself, skimming her fingers up my thigh toward the ship I have tattooed. "The ship and the coordinates are new to me."

There's a pink tint to her cheeks when she finally glances up to me. I run my hand down her body, pulling her thigh over my leg, feeling the warmth between her legs on my skin.

Summer pulls the blanket up over both of us, snuggling herself closer to me as she does. She smells like coconuts on the beach as she nestles further into my body and my arms wrap around her.

"These are all for your dad, right?" she asks, her head resting on my chest as the fan spins above us.

"Yeah."

"But you have them in a place that almost no one will ever see?" she questions.

"I guess they're for me. My way of… grieving."

I feel her nod against my chest.

"I can understand that. He warned me about you, you know?" She chuckles, and I pull my head back a little.

"What? When? And why?"

She laughs again as she trails her fingers over my chest. "At the party you had before you went to college. I was only fifteen, I think. But everyone knew I had a major crush on you. I never tried to hide it, though. So I guess that part is on me."

I try to think back to that summer before I left for college, but truthfully it's in bits and pieces.

"Your dad came up to me while I was sitting on the porch watching all of you guys play football in the backyard. He handed me a bottle of water and sat down right next to me. He was making jokes as you guys all ran around, telling me who he thought out of your friends might get drafted."

"Who'd he say?" I ask, curiosity needing to know where he was wrong since I'm the only one of my friends who actually did.

"None of them," she whispers. "And he didn't say it in a rude way. More just like a scout, observing, you know? He said Randall was good, but had no discipline. Vick was smart, had potential, but probably wouldn't stick with it long enough to make a real go at it…"

"What about me?"

"He said you'd be a first round draft pick."

A labored chuckle leaves my chest as a small lump forms in my throat before I force it down.

"I challenged him, of course. Said he was just saying that because you were his son, but he threw it right back to me. He said you had a lot to learn, a lot of growing up to do, he had a whole list of things you needed to do before you'd be ready. But he was sure you'd do them all."

I pull Summer closer to my chest as we lie in bed and my memory races through my time in college in a flash. Every workout, every meal plan, every practice and game. All the nights I said no to parties, to dates. The weekends I would come home for a quick visit and my dad wouldn't mention a thing about football, he'd let me be home, he'd let me rest and recharge. He always told me that my home should be my safe space. The place I would refocus my mind and recharge my body. I still try to abide by that even today.

"Jack," I whisper, shaking my head, and Summer laughs.

"That day he also told me that boys are stupid." She taps my chest and I feel her breath against me as she giggles. *"He's not ready for you yet, Summer Rose."* She whispers the words.

"He said that?"

Her head nods up and down against my chest. "I remember it like it was yesterday."

"I'm sorry," I say, pressing my lips to the top of her head.

"Why?"

"Because I was stupid." The words are slow to fall from my lips while I hold her.

"Yeah. But that's okay."

Since I've known Summer, I've never given her much of a second thought. Her crush was always just that to me. A simple crush, by a silly little kid who probably didn't even know what she was feeling. But I was wrong. God, was I so fucking wrong.

I pull her leg closer to me, pulling her on top of me as we lie here talking about the past. About moments where I should have noticed her. Her body stretches out and she lays on top of me. It doesn't feel sexual, even though neither of us are even dressed, it just feels intimate. Close. I tuck a piece of hair behind her ear as she rests her head on my chest on top of me. I can feel every curve of her body on my skin and the way she fits so perfectly.

"You are your name, that's for sure."

She laughs and I can feel the rumble in her chest against my abdomen.

"Hot and unpredictable? Yes, I know."

"Yeah, that… and…" Laughing to myself, I keep my hands roaming her back. "I don't know, I just want to make my time with you last. Lately, every day feels like the best day and it just reminds me of when you're a kid and it's summertime. You just always want it to last. The days are long and full of fun. It's the thing we all always look forward to."

"I think that might be the sweetest thing anyone has ever said to me." She giggles, resulting in a smile as she pushes her face toward mine and kisses my lips softly. "I know you can't stay overnight, but five more minutes of naked cuddling?"

I grin at her, reaching down and pulling her up closer to me. "Six," I whisper against her earlobe.

Alexa pops up with a reminder this morning for the captains' meeting I have with the coach in an hour. In other words, though, it's basically me and three of my closest friends in a room together talking about the rest of the season and then the play-offs. Something we would be doing either way.

My mom is here for one more week and then she'll be back home. It's always nice having her around and I know CeCe loves it, but she did ask the other morning if Summer would be coming over to play. I had to laugh at the way she worded it. But I also appreciate it. With Summer, CeCe never feels like she's being babysat, she looks at it as someone who just comes over to hang out with her and I fucking love that Summer has made her feel that way.

I've been talking to Summer every single day since our date. Whether it's been quick texts in the morning and at night or full blown conversations throughout the day, I've loved it either way. A new feeling of hopefulness fills my chest as each day passes. Officially making her mine is something that has consumed my mind for a while now and my mood feels like it's shifted drastically even in just a few weeks. I don't feel as burnt out and having someone around to talk to at the end of the day has felt good. But before I make anything official with Summer, the first girl I want to talk to is CeCe.

"Morning, Peanut." I slide a paper plate with a muffin on it in CeCe's direction. She's been sleeping in my bed with me while my mom's staying in her room. It's been hard to get a good night of sleep with a three-year-old tossing and turning every hour, but I've managed.

"Morning," she mumbles through a yawn and pulls herself on to the stool.

"I have a question for you," I say, leaning my elbows on the counter across from her.

I watch as she pulls the muffin apart, starting with the top pieces first.

"Would it be okay if I spent more time with Summer? I know she's your friend."

Her face perks up and her eyes widen as she licks the chocolate from her fingers.

"That's okay." She nods. "You can be her friend too."

"Yeah?" CeCe's fingers push her hair from her face, coating the strands in chocolate as she does. "What if she was my girlfriend? Would that bother you or would that be okay?"

Part of me feels ridiculous asking my child permission to date someone, but I know it's the right thing to do. My decisions aren't just mine anymore. Everything I choose in this life affects CeCe, and having her input on this is important to me. I know Summer would think so too.

CeCe sits there for a moment, chewing her muffin as I stand here waiting for her to answer.

"What's that?" Her head tilts as she chews.

I guess I should have anticipated her not exactly understanding the concept of what a girlfriend is.

"Well, I'd take her on dates. She'd probably spend more time with us."

Before I can think of other ways to describe it, she starts to nod her head up and down and then puts another giant piece of a muffin in her mouth.

"I think it's okay." Her words are muffled by the food, but I'm able to make out what she's saying and it sends a sigh of relief through my body.

My mom walks inside from the balcony just as I'm about to kiss CeCe goodbye and she offers me a small nod with a smile before I leave.

———

"How was the date?" Nate's the first one to enter the conference room after me and doesn't waste any time trying to get the gossip.

"You mean your wife didn't tell you?" I joke.

"She did. I just want to hear it from you." He chuckles, tossing his notebook on the round table between us.

"It was fun."

"Where'd you take her?"

"I tried Antonio's… but it just wasn't us. Ended up getting Louie's and going back to her place."

Liam and Ford walk in the room in the middle of their own conversation before taking a seat as well.

"And?" Nate urges.

"What are we, fifteen?" My brow raises in his direction.

"I think we all just want to make sure you… you know, it's been a while for you, big daddy." Liam's head jerks back and forth as his eyebrows wiggle, assuming our conversation.

"Yeah, I'm going to have to draw the line there, man. Some things you just don't get to know." I shrug, taking a sip from the coffee cup as we wait for Coach Aarons to join us.

"Means they did." I hear Liam whisper to Ford next to him, and all I can do is roll my eyes.

The moment Coach Aarons enters the room, it's all business and Liam's game face is perfectly plastered on his face as we discuss the rest of the season.

The air is finally cool and crisp when I leave the facility. Christmas is fast approaching and I've spent every free moment on my phone or computer ordering all the gifts CeCe has been casually mentioning she wants. The other day it was a unicorn puzzle, then she wanted this new doll she saw on a commercial. Last week, one of the other girls in her gymnastics class was wearing a leotard that had a bunch of princesses on it, so, of course, she wants that too.

"Anyone here?" I call out when I step inside my apartment and don't hear a sound. I wouldn't be completely shocked if my mom had decided to take her for a walk downtown.

She's been saying for years that I should move somewhere that CeCe has more space to be outside. And while I don't disagree with her, the housing market is fucking insane right now and the thought of moving and uprooting the life we have here feels exhausting and intimidating. I'd also have so much to consider too, I can't just decide to up and move.

"We're in here," my mom calls out, and I head to CeCe's bedroom.

When I walk in, CeCe is sitting on the side of her bed wearing one cowboy boot, one sandal, a princess tiara, and some kind of feather scarf draped around her shoulders.

"What's going on here?" I ask as I take in the sight of complete chaos.

"Cleaning!" CeCe shouts as she waves a wand around in front of her.

My mom just looks up at me from her spot on the floor with an overwhelmed expression on her face. "I seem to have started a project that is taking longer than I thought it would." She laughs but then shrugs her shoulders.

"Mom, you don't have to do this. You shouldn't be sitting on the floor sorting through her clothes."

"Am I too old to be sitting on the floor?" She eyes me.

"That's not what I meant," I say with a sigh.

"I'm fine, really. We've been having fun. If you have anything more you need to do today or anyone you want to see, take advantage of me being here and do that. I'm going to take her to Abby's in a bit, so we won't be in here much longer." She smiles at me in a way that only a mother can when they know what you've been up to.

I didn't have to tell her that I was taking Summer out the other night. She's known that Summer has been helping with CeCe lately and when I told her I was going to dinner, she simply smiled, patted my shoulder, and told me to take care of Summer.

"Maybe I'll just get in a quick workout downstairs," I offer as I stand in the doorway. CeCe's completely consumed by all the clothes around her, trying everything on at once—she barely notices I'm here.

"That sounds like a good idea."

When I walk out of CeCe's room, I pull my phone from my pocket. Learning Summer's routine has been tricky, considering she doesn't exactly have one. She isn't like me in the sense that her days are relatively similar each day and her plans are written down anywhere. She flies by the seat of her pants in a lot of cases. But one thing she did let slip is that she enjoys working out in the afternoons instead of the morning.

Hi

SUMMER

Did you implant a GPS tracker on me? I just walked into your building.

I'll never tell.

SUMMER

Can't say I'd be that mad if you did.

Heading to the gym?

SUMMER

Walking in now.

Good, I'll come meet you.

SUMMER

Didn't you workout already? You don't need to pull a double.

If you're going to workout, I want to workout with you.

SUMMER

Come find me then.

CHAPTER THIRTY-THREE

CHASE

I quickly change and head downstairs to the gym. The door swings open and music is playing from the speakers as I make my way around the corner to the open weight room. I don't see anyone, but I hear weights clinking together and I keep walking to follow the sound.

Summer's easy to spot with her dark red leggings and a white tank top against all the black equipment in this room. She's lying back on the bench press, headphones in her ears while I watch her lift the bar over her head. Her whole body works to push the barbell up. Her legs twitch and her chest puffs out. She blows a breath out as she goes for another rep.

I lean over above her, placing my hands under the bar for support, but still letting her do the work.

Her eyes sparkle as she smiles at me and I help her place the bar back on the rack before she sits herself up and pulls her headphones out.

"Shouldn't do that without a spot," I say, brushing the hair from her forehead.

"I knew you were coming. You'd rescue me if I needed it."

"What if I changed my mind? Decided not to show up?"

Summer stands from the bench, but keeps one knee on the padding as she leans closer to me, her hand lightly skimming my thigh.

"You're a gentleman. A gentleman wouldn't stand a girl up." Her words are whispered against my lips and just when I think she's about to kiss me, she licks her bottom lip, letting me feel a small amount of warmth from her breath before she pulls away.

"You're right, I'd never stand you up," I say, grabbing her wrist and pulling her back toward me.

"But there are plenty of other things I'm thinking of risking my gentleman's card for." My hand cups her ass as I pull her closer to me, eliciting a gasp from her lips before I cover her mouth with my own.

When I pull away her body sinks down slightly, her fingers holding my arm for balance as she blinks her eyes quickly.

I smirk to myself seeing her regain her composure.

"Are you okay there?" I tease.

Her eyes dart up to me like daggers and she shakes her head as she pulls away.

"Not cool." She laughs, fanning herself. "Stop trying to get me all hot and bothered while I'm trying to workout."

"Just making sure everyone in here knows you're spoken for."

Summer places her hand on her hip, narrowing her eyes at me in a stare.

"There's no one else in here."

"No?" I glance around the empty room, seeing the TV's play to a bunch of empty machines.

"But you knew that." She tugs at my t-shirt as she walks by me, leaving a devilish smirk behind.

Summer sets her water down next to the free weights and picks up the set of dumbbells as I watch from where I'm standing.

"Come on." She gestures her head toward me. "Don't make me workout alone."

I really should take it easy, I already know my joints need some rest before the game on Sunday. The team trainer took a look at me the other morning and made me lie on the table for almost an hour while she tried a few different things to relieve some of the pressure my legs have been feeling.

Sweat trickles down Summer's chest as I stand in front of her. I did the bare minimum today—mainly spent my time staring at Summer, realizing how strong and resilient she is. Fuck, watching her is motivating as hell.

"My legs are dead," she says, leaning herself against the wall.

Her blue eyes gaze up at me as I inch closer to her and she lets my hands cup the back of her thighs. On a whim, I lift her up, pressing her against the wall and her legs instinctively straddle around my waist.

I can feel my cock throb at the feel of her body against mine. She feels like fucking heaven in my arms. Like the other night in her bed, I just didn't want to let her go.

"Did you walk here or drive?" I ask.

Her fingers feather against the nape of my neck, a touch I've grown to fucking love.

"I walked. It was my cardio."

"Want me to drive you home?"

"Where's CeCe?" She asks.

"Her and my mom took on the project of cleaning out her closet." I laugh. "But then they were going to see Abby."

"Mmm." Summer leans against me and then pulls herself up closer to me.

"Sure, you can take me home."

"I need to grab the keys to my truck first, hold on tight."

With her body still latched onto mine, I take us upstairs to my apartment where my keys are sitting in the bowl near the door. Summer shimmies down from me quickly.

"Bathroom," she says, pulling her hair from her scrunchie and walking down the hall. I watch in confusion as she passes the bathroom in the hallway and walks toward my bedroom. My door closes behind her and I give her a minute, waiting for her to come back out, but that doesn't happen. Instead, I hear my shower turn on.

I waste no time walking down the hall into my bedroom, quickly glancing in CeCe's room and seeing it's empty. It's a disaster, but an empty disaster. As I walk in my room, I'm met with pieces of discarded clothing. Socks, a tank top, a pair of leggings all leaving a trail to the bathroom door that's closed. The dim light is on when I slowly push the door open. Steam from the shower hits me immediately and my feet land on a sports bra on the tile followed by a pair of underwear. When I glance to the right, I can see Summer's outline in the mirror as she stands on the other side of the glass shower.

My head swivels to the fogged glass and I can make out the shape of Summer's figure. The curves of her hips and the swell of her breasts. I'm staring. Caught completely in a trance. How the fuck could I not? She's a damn vision clothed, but undressed? She's incredible.

Without a word, she slides open the door and points the shower head to the side so water doesn't spray out. She steps aside, standing there showing every piece of her to me. My eyes work their way over her skin. Her taut nipples, the redness of her shoulders where the warm water is hitting.

"Oh, come on." I gawk at the perfection standing before me.

"Don't make me wait much longer," she taunts.

I'm quick to pull my clothes off as she stands there. The water hits my skin as I enter the shower, feeling a sting when she moves the shower head back to its normal position.

"Trying to burn me, Kincaid?"

"Burning you is the last thing I want to do right now." Summer's hand runs down my chest, slowly approaching my throbbing cock. I can feel the blood pulsing through me as it rushes to where her hand is dangerously close.

She sinks slowly to her knees and her tongue traces the water droplets that fall on my abdomen.

I can't believe I get to have Summer like this. Can't fucking believe she's on her knees in my shower for me or that I've been on my knees for her, been inside her, felt her walls pulse around me as we both lit up into an explosion the other night.

She kisses my thighs as water runs down her back, her tongue slides against my stomach.

"Want to keep playing games or are you going to let me fuck your face?"

One of her hands slips between her legs briefly, getting a moan out of her before I reach my hand behind her neck, gripping her head to look up at me.

The hint of a smirk lines her lips. She slowly slides her tongue between her teeth and I gently release my grip the second her tongue swirls around the tip of my cock. I suck in a breath at the feeling. She slides her tongue up and down, slowly, like she's savoring the taste. She kisses the underside and I jerk back at how that feels. Every time she touches me, it makes me harder than I was even a second before.

I don't have the patience for the teasing anymore. I'm not strong around her like I once was. She makes me crumble like a house of cards every fucking time.

"Take it, Summer. Fucking take what you want. My cock belongs to you." Her hand squeezes me at the same time her mouth wraps around the head and she sucks like it's a goddamn lollipop.

My hand slams the wall of the shower as I steady my breath, grabbing her hair in my free hand wrapping my hand around it. The feeling is sensational. With every pull, I can feel myself getting closer and closer to spilling down her throat. She licks up and down and lets me hit the back of her throat. When she glances up, her eyes look watery, but she shows her teeth in a smile, skimming them all the way down. Goosebumps erupt all over my skin as she takes me deep again.

"Fuck, fuck, fuck!" I groan. "That's it. You're such a good girl taking all of me like this." My encouragement seems to only fuel her. Her hands grip my thighs as her tongue swirls over me again and I can feel my body begin to jerk faster at the strokes of her tongue.

"Up here." It comes out commanding, but she licks her lips as she stands. "Do you trust me?" I ask, staring into her blue eyes.

She nods, but I need the words. I need to hear her say it.

"Use your words. Say it."

"I trust you," she says confidently, pulling her hair out of her face.

"I'm tested before every season. Everything's negative."

"I'm on birth control," she says quickly. "Let me feel you."

The warm water splashes against my back as I lift her up, pressing her body against the wall and lining my cock up with her.

Summer's pussy felt so fucking good the first time, I can only imagine how it'll feel with no barrier between us.

Slowly, I slide my cock in, letting her get used to the feeling for a moment before I move any faster. She moans as I move deeper and I feel her body stiffen slightly.

"Almost." I push in further and then out, creating a rhythm that she quickly falls into.

"God, yes." She digs her nails into my shoulders as she pulls me closer to her. "You need to push harder."

I've never been with a woman who told me what she wanted. Not in the way Summer does. She knows what she likes and what she needs and she isn't afraid to say it.

"Fuck." My hands grip her thighs, holding us in place as she cries out and I thrust harder, trying to keep us steady.

She brings her hands into my hair, pulling at the wet strands and my mouth closes around her nipple. My tongue swirls while she pants against me. Her head hangs between us as she watches me suck her nipple.

"Just like that," she whispers, slowing her own movements against me. "Fuck, Chase."

My cock slides in and out of her pussy with ease. A motion we're both so content in. With a slower movement, I can readjust my footing, keeping her pinned against the glass wall as I push in and out. My hand reaches between her legs and I run my thumb over her clit. She's so swollen, so ready to combust, I can feel it the second I pinch with my fingers.

"Come for me," I whisper against her cheek as my fingers play with her pussy.

She doesn't answer me with words, but her sounds say enough. I flick her clit with my fingers, fast, and then slow. Building her up and then letting her breathe for a moment before I pick up the pace again. I can feel her pussy beginning to clench around me as her orgasm builds.

"I'm so close."

"Me too," I moan as we hold nothing back, fucking in my shower like there isn't a perfectly good bed less than ten feet away.

"Chase, oh my—" I cover her words with my lips as she shudders. Her body moves back and forth and I move both of my hands to grip her thighs, but her scream breaks our kiss and she gasps for air as she closes her eyes in pleasure.

My own orgasm is mounting with every pulse of hers. I can feel my walls crumbling as she continues to bounce in front of me. Perfect, full breasts sitting nearly eye level with me.

"Fill me up, Chase." She takes my face in her hands and runs her tongue over my bottom lip.

I thrust one more time before my body vibrates, letting the best goddamn orgasm rip through me.

She slides her body down mine, resting her head against my chest as we both recede from the orgasms that left us breathless.

"Hey." I run my hands over her face. "I said something earlier in the gym that you didn't question me on."

"What's that?" Her arms wrap around my waist as we stand together, letting the water continue to fall around us.

"I said you were spoken for, even though we haven't actually talked about it. But it's something I've thought a lot about."

"You have?" Her voice carries a shock.

"Yeah… I—I want to see where this could go. If we can date, be a… a couple." My words feel like they're rushing out. I haven't asked someone to be my girlfriend since I was a kid. I barely know if I'm even doing it right.

"You asking me to be your girlfriend?" She swipes her thumb over my jaw as she stares up at me.

"Yes." I sigh. "I want you to be my girlfriend."

Her face softens. The blue of her eyes deepen and she brings both hands up around my neck.

"Chase, I've always been yours."

CHAPTER THIRTY-FOUR

SUMMER

Every inch of my skin has been on fire for the last twelve hours. When Chase dropped me off last night, I felt like I was leaving my heart in his passenger's seat and I've never felt more okay with that than I do now. I've been with other men before, Chase knows that, but telling him I've always belonged to him wasn't a lie. And I don't think he thought it was either.

I remember agreeing to date the quarterback in high school because he was so adamant about bringing me as his date to prom. I agreed to it out of boredom, in a way. The guy I wanted wasn't giving me anything and here was this perfectly nice guy practically falling at my feet, so I said yes to a date that resulted in my first serious relationship where he ultimately cheated on me. I feel like, in one way or another, I've been wronged by every guy I've let close to me. Any man who has ever whispered sweet nothings into my ear about how amazing I was or how much they loved me, never thought twice about hurting me or letting me down.

I settled, more often than I care to admit, with men who didn't mean much to me when I look back now. My heart has always been with Chase.

When I lived in Miami, I went on a handful of dates with this guy who was a regular at the bar I worked at. He sweet talked his way into me giving him my phone number and I eventually let him take me to dinner a few times. The more time we spent together, the more he seemed to actually pull away. I noticed it quickly—not that he attempted to hide it too well, though. When all was said and done, he told me that dating me just felt like "a lot", whatever that meant to him at the time. I didn't ask for clarification or challenge him, I let his excuse be his out without any kind of question. Thinking back on it now, I wish I would've asked what the hell he meant by it. Drew often made me feel like I was too much too. He'd tell me to settle down at the bar all the time. One night he apologized on my behalf to his friends because I was yelling at the television while we were watching the Knights play an away game. He looked embarrassed the entire time. That should've been my sign.

As someone who considers herself overall pretty confident and of the opinion to take no shit—I sure as hell have taken quite a bit of shit from weak ass men. And that stops now. No more small men. No more men who want to stare at my chest one minute and then tell me to calm down the next.

Abby's face lights up my phone screen as I'm lying in bed, still reeling over last night and the memory of Chase's hands all over me. I texted her when I got home last night and told her to call me when she woke up. Telling her my teenage dreams came true last night is first on my list this morning.

"Morning, Sunshine." I smile into the phone when her face comes into view.

"Hi," she croaks out before she coughs all over the screen. She moves the phone away from her face and I see Ford laying next to her. I'm certain he's naked. Either that or he just wears his shorts real, *real* low.

"Cover up, Anderson," I call into the phone as he takes it from Abby's hands. "Is she okay?"

"She's got a little bug I think, but she'll be okay."

I nod at him while he looks off the screen and watch his eyes as he looks at her. Ford stares at Abby like she's the single greatest thing he's ever seen. It makes me wonder if from the outside anyone would say that about Chase when he looks at me.

"What'd you want me to call you about?" Abby asks when she comes back to the screen. She takes the phone from Ford as she sits up in her bed against the headboard. His head falls into her lap and her attention is on me, but I see her fingers running through his hair at the bottom of the screen.

"You guys are making me want to have sex at eight in the morning. Stop fondling each other, I can't handle the tension."

Ford's laugh carries through the screen and he pulls the phone back down to him. "I'd love to have sex right now, but I can't until I get a test done in a couple days—doctor's orders."

"He's going to be unbearable for that time, I hope you know that," I say to Abby. "But I have to tell you about last night. If sixteen-year-old Summer could see me now…"

Abby chuckles, and I take a sip of my coffee before continuing.

"Chase and I are actually going to try and date, I guess. He very sweetly—and shyly, I might add—asked me to be his girlfriend."

"What?" Abby leans forward, nearly choking on her own saliva as Ford sits up abruptly too. She puts both of them in focus on the screen and my cheeks feel warm as I place a palm over them. "I'm so happy. I'm kind of shocked, but also not that shocked. You've been spending more time together, I figured he was bound to realize how perfect you are."

"My guy." Ford beams on the other end of the screen and I see him pull out his phone, which I can only assume he's reaching out to Chase right now, too.

"It caught me by surprise. I mean, he's definitely let his guard down a lot more in recent weeks when it comes to himself personally. But his home life, football, his dad life, when it comes to CeCe—all of that has still been pretty much the same. Very on routine with everything there. Almost like he's finally just making time for himself, you know?"

"Mm-hmm, yep. That's what he needs, though. Everything in his life has been pretty lined up and well-practiced for a while. But he completely forgot how to be just Chase. Of course, only you could bring him back." Abby laughs as she pulls her legs up to her chest.

"So how are you feeling? Aside from the coughing." She's been pretty private about all of her fertility stuff, but she fills me in when she feels up to it.

I've taken the approach of sending her texts every now and then letting her know I'm thinking of her and whenever she wants to fill me in or catch up, my door is always open. It feels like she appreciates that route so she can share things on her terms and when she's ready, versus someone needing an update every step of the way.

"I feel okay. I'm exhausted. But I've got a good little caretaker here." She rubs Ford's bicep and he kisses her forehead.

"Good. You still have my apartment key, right? Just in case you need to check your blood pressure or need an extra heating pad, you know, anything, right?"

"I have it if I need any of that stuff, thank you."

"Okay, good." I nod my head.

"By the way, will you be here for Christmas?" she asks.

I sigh, thinking about the holiday. I'm looking forward to it, but my parents asked me to come home for it for the first time in years. They're usually out of town, but this year they've decided to come back to Florida.

"No, actually. Can you believe my parents will be home this year? So they're having a bunch of family over."

"Oh my gosh, well, that's exciting, though. It's been almost a year since you've seen them in person, right?"

I pause, thinking back for a moment and counting months in my head. "Yeah I guess so. My mom emails me all the time, though, so I'm not completely out of touch with them."

I keep seeing Abby swat Ford's hand away from her as she talks and it makes me feel like I'm invading their time together. "I can let you go, I just wanted to let you know that dreams do come true."

Abby belts out a laugh and so does Ford. "I'm going to text him and tell him not to fuck it up and to treat you like a fucking queen," Ford says, pulling the camera closer to his face.

"That's not necessary," I say, shaking my head.

"Give me the phone." I hear Ford say to Abby and she clicks her tongue before handing it over to him. "Love you!" she calls out as the scenery begins to change.

"Where are you taking me? Have you put clothes on yet? I swear to God, Anderson, if you're talking to me naked, I'll kill you."

"Relax," he says, flashing the camera at his waist to show a pair of shorts. "Listen, you're like a sister to me, Summer. Chase may be my teammate and my brother-in-law, but I'll still sucker punch him if he hurts you."

Ford's overprotective, big brother thing he's been doing with me lately is actually pretty sweet. It's hard to get annoyed with him when he's just looking out for me, even though I want to tell him to chill out, back off and stop being so macho. It's kind of nice having him in my corner.

"Thanks," I say, smiling at him.

"Look at my palm tree," he says, quickly changing the subject and facing the phone out toward his backyard. I can hear Abby in the background telling him to stop talking about the palm tree.

"Uh, looks great."

"Yeah, I just had it planted." His voice is full of pride before Abby's voice gets closer.

"We're going to let you go," she says, stepping in front of him.

"Love you," I call out just before we disconnect the call.

There's an obvious pep in my step as I'm getting myself ready for work today. Curling my hair feels fun and not tedious, pulling my scrubs up over my hips doesn't make me groan at the couple of jumps I do to get them in place. I feel happier than I have in a while.

Before I walk out the door, my phone dings with a text message from Chase.

CHASE

This will be waiting in the family suite for you Sunday. Wear it.

A picture of one of his jerseys pops up on the screen. It's a special edition throwback jersey with his name and number on the back. It's one of the only jerseys of his I don't have, until now.

That sounds a little bossy.

CHASE

Good.

CHAPTER THIRTY-FIVE

CHASE

FORD

Roundhouse kick right to the face if this goes
south

> Why would you assume it's going to go south?
> And why would it be my fault?

NATE

Because Summer would never fuck things up
with you.

LIAM

Roundhouse kick to the face and then a good old
fashioned WWE smackdown diving knee drop.

> What the hell is that?

LIAM

I'll attack you when you're least expecting it
and take you to the ground.

NATE

All of this during the off season of course.

> Okay, enough.

I grab my charger from the nightstand to plug my phone in and end this conversation. Summer told Ford and Abby about our relationship status and since then I've received an influx of messages from not just the guys, but the girls as well. All warning me not to screw anything up.

Last night, Summer stopped over briefly to drop off some things for CeCe. My mom insisted she stay for dinner since she conveniently made so much food. It's been nice having my mom around lately, but I know she's also itching to get back to her retired life of travel and relaxation in a couple days. She leaves the day after Christmas and I know CeCe will be sad to see her leave, but she'll be excited to have more time with Summer again.

When she asked if she could stop by to drop off something she bought for CeCe, I assumed it would be a coloring book or a new set of crayons, something simple that they always use together, but I couldn't have been more wrong.

Summer rolled an entire cart of goodies in behind her. Some coloring books and crayons, sure. But there were new stuffed animals, a few books for her, craft supplies for painting and drawing, and then a bracelet making kit. The look on my face when she stepped through the doors probably alluded to my absolute shock, but Summer carried on like it was nothing.

"Can you believe Santa dropped all of this off at my house early?" she said to CeCe as she kept pulling things out of the cart.

I know she'll be with her parents for Christmas this year. I also know she feels indifferent about that. Her parents have always been very nice and generous people the handful of times I've actually met them. They were honestly really fucking absent most of Summer's life, even though Summer seems to have actually preferred it that way. I don't think there's any bad blood between them, but she made it sound like a chore to be going home for the holiday instead of staying around town like she has in recent years.

With our game today, I feel like I definitely should have done more rehab on my knees than I have all week, but I've been busier than ever as of late. I haven't had much of a personal life in years, resulting in early bedtimes, little plans aside from dad life or football, and certainly no company. I've enjoyed the last few weeks more than I think I even want to admit. Summer still even gives me a hard time about my calendar that dings with meetings and appointments.

The sky's the brightest shade of blue when I step out of my truck and begin walking into the stadium today. It reminds me of the color of Summer's eyes and picturing her eyes makes me picture her face, and then her body and her on her knees for me… all thoughts that shouldn't be in my mind as I'm about to prepare for a football game.

"He's here!" I hear as I'm walking into the locker room.

Nate smiles as I approach him and I notice the new hair right away.

"Got tired of having to shampoo and condition the hair?"

"Luke grabbed a chunk of it after he got ahold of the peanut butter jar. Needless to say, I couldn't stand the smell so I'm back to short hair."

Laughing, I pull my boots from my feet and take a seat on the chair in front of my locker just as Liam comes up beside me.

"There you are, we thought maybe all of our threats had you scared." He smirks.

"Your empty threats," I correct.

"Fuck if they are. I will physically hurt you." Ford comes up to us, holding a cup of coffee.

I give him two thumbs up just as Coach Aarons walks into the locker room, bringing everyone's attention to him.

"Morning, gentlemen," he begins. "Big day. Let's focus on this game, stay tough and ready. Depending on how things are shaping up around the league and within our own game, we'll see if we keep starters in or rotate you guys out. I don't want any fucking around today; no one slacks off. Just because we're in the playoffs already doesn't mean we hold back. No stupid fucking injuries. Keep the penalties to a minimum. This is a team of champions—you need to play like it. Go do your job."

"Who shit in his cheerios this morning?" Liam mumbles when Coach Aarons walks out. "All the f-bombs. The black windbreaker instead of red. Who's that man and where is our even-tempered guy?"

"That guy abandoned ship when we decided to lose fucking four games in a row earlier in the season," Nate scoffs, bringing his shirt off over his head to get ready.

Liam isn't wrong, though. Coach has become a lot tougher recently and takes most of his hardest shots at Liam and the offense, in particular.

I direct my attention back to my locker, pull out my uniform and suit up for today's game.

"It's a hot one today," one of the assistant coaches' remarks as we stand on the sidelines. The first quarter is almost over and the score is sitting with a sad goose egg on either side.

"Hear you got a girlfriend." One of my teammates standing beside me nudges my shoulder.

"Yeah? Where'd you hear that?"

I watch as the center snaps the ball to Liam and he gets it out of his hands within a second, sending the ball soaring down the field where one of our wide receivers is sprinting for his life, fighting off a cornerback trying to make the catch. He misses the ball, but a yellow penalty flag is on the field and I see Liam clapping as he stares up at the jumbotron.

"MVP." He nods out to Liam and all I can do is shake my head. Liam's a gossiper if I've ever fucking met one.

"Holding, defense number thirty-six. Automatic first down."

Our sideline claps at the referee's call, which brings our offense down the field significantly.

"If he didn't hold him, he would've caught it. Probably saved a touchdown there," my teammate comments, and I nod. He's probably right. Our wide receivers are fast and tall, not usual for them to miss a catch unless someone interferes.

After the penalty and a couple more downs, Liam is able to run it in himself for a touchdown. The crowd erupts, sending chills up my spine and I look up into the second level suites, knowing my daughter and Summer are somewhere up there looking on.

Halftime goes by quickly—as it usually does. A quick breather, bathroom break, drink of water and a few words from the coach and we're back on the field. The sun is sweltering as the day is progressing. I'd still choose an outdoor field to indoor, but fuck, we are getting our asses handed to us in this heat. Even in December, it's still a fucking nightmare.

Coach Aarons has kept the starters in so far. We've been hoping to bump our playoff seed number up with a win today and a couple of losses by other teams. The teams we've needed to lose, have done it. So, the fate of where we stand now in the playoff picture is left completely in our hands. Where it should be. Our games and our standings should always come down to us. Right now, we're hanging on, but field goals aren't going to cut it the rest of the game when Tennessee is only ten points behind us and has a solid running game.

The fourth quarter begins and it's evident that everyone on the field, on both sides, is gassed. Aside from the heat, it's been a physical game. We're in the playoffs no matter if we win or lose, it just affects where we sit. But Tennessee has to win to even make the playoffs in their conference. If they lose, they're done. And knowing what it feels like to be in that position, they aren't going down without a balls-to-the-wall fight.

As the defensive play caller, I pay attention to how the

offense is lining up. I watch as their tight end sits back toward the quarterback. It looks like he's going to be a blocker for someone else to carry the ball, but instincts tell me it's a fake and he'll run up the middle unblocked to wait for the ball to be thrown his way. We've got a four man rush up front, which should cover their linemen, but leaves that tight end to break loose if that's their play.

My eyes scan the quarterback as he sets up under the center. He pauses before quickly dropping back into a shotgun formation and the center lunges the ball back to him once he calls the play into motion.

Three receivers fan out wide, but our corner and safeties are all over them. Their quarterback does some fancy footwork, darting to his left further away from me. I hold off for a few seconds, anticipating he's going to throw the ball immediately, but since he doesn't my next step is to sack him. At first, it feels like a pointless feat. He's quicker than me, but I just need to get close. I'm bigger than him, and I can take him down if I can just get closer.

The moment I'm within arm's reach, he fires the ball from his hands and I swerve from tackling him to avoid a costly team penalty, but it doesn't take me completely out of harm's way. One of their linemen breaks free and in an attempt to block me from hitting his quarterback, he takes me to the ground. His hit felt legal. On the jumbotron watching it back, it looked legal. But the way my knee bent, it felt like every piece of ligament in my leg was tearing at the same time.

"Fuck!" I yell out from the field as the medical staff come to my aid. I try to stand up and walk it off, but they tell me to stay seated for the moment while they do a quick assessment.

"Do we need a cart?" one of the staff asks and before anyone can answer, I interrupt.

"No. I can walk off. Let me up," I say, shrugging one of the staff members off me.

They help me to my feet and I'm able to limp off with some assistance. Coach Aarons makes eye contact with me when I get to the sidelines, but doesn't say anything. He doesn't have to.

"We'll need x-rays, come on." The team doctor throws my arm around his shoulder as he helps me off the sidelines and into the locker room.

A million things run through my mind. I'm praying CeCe was asleep or occupied or something during that play. She's never seen me get hurt and I'm not sure how she'd react. Playoffs start soon and having to sit out would be such a blow to our team and to my whole fucking mood.

I can hear the doctor and some of the medical staff talking as they do the x-ray. I've known most of these people long enough to pick up on when things don't look so hot.

"Just tell me," I grunt out, pulling my gloves off my hands.

"It's a sprain, Chase. I'm sorry."

My fist slams the table I'm lying on. Knee injuries can be hard to come back from and all that's running through my mind is that I'm not ready to be done with football. I'm not ready to go out like this.

"We'll ice it now. You'll need to take it easy, rest. You're in good shape, Chase. I don't see this being anything detrimental, just rehab it the right way. We'll make sure you get in with the physical therapist, do some recovery movement on it soon."

"Playoffs are out of the question, though." It's not me asking them, it's my need to say it out loud. To tell myself that my season right now has come to an end.

"Playoffs are out of the question," the doctor confirms.

CHAPTER THIRTY-SIX

SUMMER

White knuckled, I clutch my purse as I head downstairs. The hit he took didn't look pretty on the screen and once they took him back into the locker room, he never came back out. Muffled conversations are happening all around me as my head swirls with different scenarios. I hear fans saying things like "he's done" or "there goes our playoff run" and my heart rate picks up thinking about those things being true.

When I get down to the players exit, I find myself waiting an awfully long time before *anyone* even walks out. It's like the entire team has stayed back or something. Slowly, team members begin to filter out of the double doors. My phone dings with a text from Mia, letting me know that Diane is taking CeCe home.

God, CeCe. She watches every second of the games she can. When the other team tackled Chase, she didn't flinch at first. She's seen tackles happen often, but it wasn't until the rest of us gasped in the suite as we saw the replay on the screen that she looked back and forth between me and Diane. Looking for one of us to give her more insight into what just happened. When Diane told her that he was just going to get checked out in the locker room, she seemed to take that well. I don't think she understood what it could potentially be yet.

I know Chase has been dealing with knee pain all season. To my knowledge, he hasn't had any injury to them in the past, but you'd have to assume after a lifetime of playing a contact sport like football, your joints would eventually start to feel some aftereffects.

"He'll be a bit, Summer." Nate extends his arms to hug me as he walks out.

"Is he okay, though? What did they say after the game?"

Nate looks me in the eye and shakes his head. Shrugging his shoulder, he says, "You know him. Anything other than telling him he's fine isn't going to sit well with him."

My shoulders drop and I nod at Nate as he turns to walk away.

Almost thirty minutes later, I see Chase hobble out of the doors with a pair of crutches assisting him. He's working hard to keep himself steady and I can tell he's pissed off. Telling him it'll be okay is a waste of breath, even though it's the first thing I want to blurt out. I know one of his first thoughts had to be CeCe, though.

"Your mom took CeCe home. She saw the play, but I don't think understood what actually happened. I'm not sure if your mom will explain it to her or wait for you."

He nods, placing a hand on my shoulder. Whether it's for balance or out of a need to touch me, I'll take either right now.

I've seen Chase look frustrated. I've seen him sad and angry, but he looks hopeless right now. He doesn't even comment on the jersey he brought for me that I'm wearing. In fact, he doesn't say much of anything, but I tell myself not to take it personally.

"I don't really know what to say right now," I admit as he stands in front of me. His head hangs and I tilt mine underneath his, looking up at him. "Can I ask what the doctor said?"

I'd have to assume the crutches aren't a sign of good news, though.

"It's sprained, just need to keep weight off of it for a few days," he mumbles.

He says nothing more as he starts slowly making his way to his truck. His expression doesn't change as we walk and I slow my pace so he doesn't feel like he needs to rush. I can tell that alone is driving him crazy. A few fans are hanging around and calling out his name. He raises his hand to give them a curt wave, but nothing else.

"Well, can I do anything for you? Um, drive you home? Cook something? Do you want any ice packs or anything? I have a bunch of stuff at my place."

"No," he says quietly, still making his way to the truck.

"Okay…" I sigh.

"Where did you park?" he asks bluntly.

"Oh, not important. I just wanted to make sure you're okay."

"Get in and tell me where you parked so I can drive you to your car." He tosses his bag in the backseat of his truck before pulling the passenger side door open.

Everything in me wants to argue and tell him to not worry about me at a moment like this. But debating him will only annoy him. And I can already tell he's hanging by a thread before losing his cool. He's pissed off. He's upset. He feels like he let the team down. I know him so damn well… I can see those thoughts weaving their way through his mind.

He closes the door behind me and makes his way over to his side of the truck before pulling himself in.

"A sprain shouldn't mean any surgery, so that's good at least," I whisper as he takes the final turn to the lot I'm parked in.

His shoulders rise and fall in a quick shrug and I can tell he doesn't want to even talk about it right now. When he pulls up to my car, his hand reaches for mine, giving it a quick squeeze as he offers the smallest hint of a smile and then turns to face forward again.

I sigh, realizing he probably just needs some time to process all of this.

"I'm sorry about your knee, Chase." I pull the lever on the door and let myself out.

———

I decided not to text Chase after I got home from the game the other day, but I had to check in yesterday. I sent him a text message about a new documentary I thought he might like. He responded, telling me he'd check it out. He also included a smiley face emoji, so I took that as a win. When I asked if he needed anything he responded with a simple no. I guess I shouldn't have expected much else, but jumping into action is quite literally what I've been trained to do when someone gets hurt, and it doesn't sit well with me that I'm not doing that for him.

I'm trying to find the balance in wanting to help and be there, but also not overstepping. It's the last thing I want to do right now, but this morning the urge to see him in person is too strong to ignore. Simply a sign of life is really all that I'm looking for.

> I leave tomorrow to spend the holiday with my parents. Any chance you're taking visitors today?

My text sits on delivered for the duration of my shower, the entire time it takes me to get ready and then even while I start packing a small bag for my quick trip home. Once I finally sit down to eat something, my phone dings and I can't get to the message fast enough.

CHASE

Sure.

A sigh of relief leaves my chest. Chase and I haven't been officially dating long, and yet it feels like I've lived a thousand lives with him already.

Before I get to his apartment, I stop at the store to grab a few snacks for him and CeCe and a couple things for Diane to do with CeCe to help keep her occupied. Abby said she's been bringing her over to their house the last couple of days just to give Chase some peace and quiet.

I tap lightly on the door and hear shuffling on the other side. Shit. I should have asked Abby for a key or something so I'm not making him walk to the door. Off to a great start, Summer.

"Hey." My voice is soft as he pulls the door open.

"Hi." His face is lined with scruff and his eyes resemble that of a sad puppy. He swipes a piece of hair from his face and I glance down at his knee. Now in a brace since the swelling must've gone down.

"I feel obligated to ask even though I'm sure it's not great, but how's the, uh…" I gesture down to his knee and that earns me a chuckle as he closes the door behind me.

"It's been better." He grabs a water bottle from the counter and takes a seat on the couch.

"Did they say how long your recovery will be?"

"Could be up to six weeks."

"Okay, *up to* six weeks, so it could be less then?" I ask with a hint of enthusiasm in my voice.

A sarcastic laugh jumps from his chest, and I immediately know I said something that's annoyed him.

"Sure. It could be less. Either way, I'm missing the playoffs."

I stay silent after his response, feeling my ears starting to ring and cheeks begin to feel flushed.

The nurse in me immediately grabs another pillow to prop up

under his leg and he doesn't protest as I push the pillow underneath him and then grab another one and prop it up behind his head.

"Thanks," he breathes out in a deep sigh. "You're not at work, though, you can relax."

"Habits." I shrug, taking a seat on the loveseat opposite him.

"I brought some snacks, a few activities for CeCe. They're in that bag," I say, pointing to the plastic bag hanging by the chair. "Do you want me to cook dinner for you tonight?" I offer.

"No, that isn't necessary."

I nod at his answer. Trying to talk to him right now feels like pulling teeth and I don't know if I should keep trying, if we should just sit in silence, or if I should just leave.

"Should we watch something? I'm sure we can find a documentary that neither of us have seen. I tend to steer clear of any that are about reptiles, because gross. But I'll build up the courage for you if you want."

A noise leaves his chest that sounds like it could be a laugh, but also a grunt at the same time. He shakes his head back and forth, pulling both hands over his head in a stretch.

His arms flex under the t-shirt he's wearing and I can see a bruise under his arm, assuming another reminder of the hit.

"You don't have to sit here with me, Kincaid. I'm on pretty limited activity. There's nothing for you to do here."

"I wasn't expecting a lot of activity," I say, standing from the couch and walking toward him. I take a seat next to him on the couch and run my hand over his cheek before placing it on top of his hand resting on his thigh. "I was just hoping to see you. Maybe help with a few things that you might need help with. I can also just be quiet, moral support too, if that's what you're looking for."

"You? Quiet?" He chuckles to himself, and even though it's a slight insult, I'll take it because it's more than he's been giving.

"I mean… I'll try my best." I shrug, and he pulls his hand out from under mine.

"I'll be fine, Kincaid. I don't need a babysitter."

I scrunch my face together in confusion. It's like one minute he seems accepting of me being here and the next he's bothered by it. It's very pre-kiss Chase.

"I—I know that. I'm just here to offer help or at the very least check in. That's what friends do, that's what people in relationships do."

His lip twitches. "Right." He sighs and attempts to pull himself up from the couch. He gets to his feet and steadies himself before he moves. He barely bends his left knee as he makes his way to the kitchen island.

"Is there something I can get for you?" I don't understand why he's being this stubborn. A little stubbornness wouldn't shock me, it's Chase. But refusing my help completely is just… stupid.

"I've got it," he says, reaching for the laptop on the counter and tucking it under his arm as he walks himself back to the couch.

"I'm going to say this as a nurse, not as your friend or girlfriend. But you need to keep your weight off of it and keep it elevated. Tell me everything you need by your side and I'll bring it to you so you can stop getting up so much."

"I've got it," he says again with force.

I watch his footing stutter as he stops just steps away from the couch. His face turns away from me, but I can still see the wince. His eyes squeeze together and his breath snags.

I walk over to his side and take him by the elbow to help him back down. His body feels rigid and resistant, but he keeps his mouth shut.

"Sit down, I'm going to get some ice for you. We'll do fifteen minutes on and off." I get the pillow back under his leg, lifting his thigh gently.

The ice machine makes an unnecessary amount of noise as I fill a Ziploc bag and I'm kicking myself for not just bringing over one of my many ice packs I have.

"Thanks," he mumbles. "But I—I think you should go, Summer. I'm still just battling with myself over this and you don't deserve the crossfire of my piss poor attitude."

Well, that's honest. I take a step back, hands on my hips as he rests his head back on the couch.

"Chase—"

"Summer, please." His words are a plea. One I can't ignore. I don't want to overstep, but my God, I can't understand why, after all this time, he can't just let me in and let me stay there.

"I'll leave," I whisper. "But Chase," I say, relaxing my body, "When you're friends with someone… When you're in a *relationship* with them, helping them and supporting them is what you do. When something happens outside of these four walls, you have to know that there is someone within them who will be there for you. I want to respect what you're asking and I want to give you your space, but I'm not going to stop checking on you." I wave my phone in front of me. "Keep it charged."

I lean down, gently brushing my lips against his cheek before walking away and out the door.

———

"That's bullshit and you know it." Mia pushes the cabinet closed after she grabs cups for the boys' water. "Do you know what I would do if Nate ever tried to shut me out and stop me from helping him?"

"You wouldn't let him."

"No. I wouldn't. It's different when you're friends before you become more. You know them on a deeper level. There's more to the story than just meeting and falling in love—there's history and there's familiarity. You can call his bluff. He can call yours.

You know ticks and grievances. But you also know when they need your love the most." Mia's feisty when she's pregnant and it's a side of her I've grown to love. Soft and sweet little Mia gets put away for nine months when she's carrying a baby.

I chuckle as I'm helping her put dishes away. "Can I be honest with you about something?"

"When are you not?" She smiles my way.

"I've never cared about a relationship before. I know that sounds terrible. But I've never cared about the long haul or the big picture. So, being impulsive all the time, doing what I wanted, regardless of what might've been 'right' in the moment, never *truly* mattered to me. I've always kind of been fine with the whole 'whatever happens, happens' mantra. I didn't care if things I said or did bothered any other guy because I was being myself. But with Chase… It's not that I want to change anything about how I handle myself, but I just *want* to care with him. I'm not even sure I'm making any damn sense right now." I sigh, getting frustrated with the words I can't seem to put together. "I want to be the best version of myself. I see—"

"You see the bigger picture; you want the long haul. I get it, it makes sense," she says, dropping a towel onto the counter.

I slowly nod. "I still gave him a piece of my mind, though. He needed it. But I just… I don't want to fuck it up."

"Believe me, any fucking up would not come from you."

CHAPTER THIRTY-SEVEN

CHASE

The second Summer leaves, I'm kicking myself for the way I acted. It isn't her fault that I'm sitting here in a knee brace, but I can't shake the thought that this is why I don't get close to people anymore, this is why people are kept at arm's length. When you let people in, you open yourself up to getting hurt— physically, mentally, emotionally. And my brain won't allow me to let go of the fact that instead of doing extra rehab, or maybe preparing my body better, I was spending time with her. All of that was my decision, I could have easily opted to spend my time elsewhere, and she would've understood without question, but I didn't. I let Kristen's old words linger in the back of my mind from the night she left. Telling me that I wasn't giving her enough, doing enough, before she ultimately told me she wasn't interested in anything I was trying to offer.

THREE YEARS AGO

"What the fuck, Chase? I asked you over and over what time you'd be back and you never responded to me."

"I was at practice, Kris. I didn't have my phone on me. I'm sorry. I texted you as soon as I got back to the locker room."

She whips a bag out from underneath the bed and grabs a handful of clothes from the floor. Whether they're clean or dirty I couldn't tell you. Our life has been in complete chaos since we brought CeCe home, but it's also been some of the best days of my life. The other day, she napped on my chest and held my finger the entire time. It was the sweetest fucking thing and I couldn't resist sending a picture to the guys.

"I can't do this myself. I don't want to do it by myself."

"You aren't by yourself. I was at practice. It's my job, Kris. I said I'm sorry that I didn't get back to you. You're acting like I was out at a goddamn bar or something and just ignoring you. That's not me and you know it."

I glance into the bassinet where CeCe is still fast asleep, thankfully. Two months old or twenty years old, I won't argue with her mother in front of her.

For the life of me, I can't piece together why something like this is all of a sudden making her so upset. She stopped working before CeCe was born and moved in here because I told her I would take care of both of them. I didn't want her to feel any more overwhelmed than I could already tell she was. I had thought maybe taking some pressures off of her with work would be helpful and she agreed at the time.

"I don't know how to do this," she whispers, and my heart aches for her. "I don't know if I even want to and it makes me feel terrible. But it's the truth."

"Hey, listen." I cup her face before pulling her close to my chest in a hug. She's frail and her skin feels ice cold. It's easy to see she's struggling now that I'm staring at her like this. Is this my fault? Should I have taken more time away from the team once CeCe was born?

"You're figuring it out. We both are. You're doing a great

job, Kris, and I'm so sorry that this is hard. But you can do this. I'm here to help you."

She pulls away from me briefly before she glances at the clothes spilling from the bag she half packed.

"But I don't know if I want to. I'm only twenty-three, Chase. Being a parent wasn't exactly on my list of things I wanted to do before thirty."

Panic starts to flood my thoughts and my body tenses. She never told me she didn't want this.

She begins emptying the dresser where her things are, placing them into the bag and all I can do is stare at her. What in the hell is going on right now?

"What are you doing?" I finally ask after she zips the bag.

"You've made me feel like I have to do this myself. Whether or not that was your intention, I'm still here day in and day out doing this. And I don't even want to be. I'm not ready for this and I'm forcing myself to be. But I'm tired of it."

"How... how have I made you feel that way? Please. Explain it to me. Because if I'm not at practice, or playing a game, doing my job, I'm here."

"This," she shouts. "This is your job." As she points to the bassinet.

I don't know what I'm missing, but there's something she isn't saying. There has to be. Everything we're doing right now is exactly as we discussed before CeCe was even born.

"She never sleeps." Kristen laughs, but it's filled with sarcasm. "Until, of course, right at this moment when I'm trying to make a point."

"It's never been my intention to make you feel like you were in this alone. If anything I've said or done has made it seem that way, then fuck, I'm so sorry, Kris. Because this"—I wave my hand around the room and then take her fingers in mine—"you, CeCe, this imperfect little life we have here is what I want. It's my priority and the most important thing to me."

"That's the difference between us, though, Chase." She pulls her hand from mine and takes a step back. Her hair falling over her shoulders. "I don't want it."

"What do you mean? Where are you going?" I trail after her as she walks around the room like I'm a lost fucking dog waiting for her to throw me a bone.

"I'm going to stay with a friend for a while to give myself time to sort this out."

"What friend?"

"Don't try to make me think you're jealous. I've known since the beginning we were just fuck buddies who happened to get pregnant and you wanted to be the good guy and stick it out."

"Would you rather I have been a deadbeat and just fucking left you? I've wanted to be a dad my entire life. Yeah, the circumstances are different than I thought they would be, but who the hell cares?"

She lets out an exasperated sigh. "I'm leaving, Chase."

The finality of her words cut threw me like a knife. Kristen and I are two people who aren't in love and I know that. I've tried like hell to make her life as good as it could be ever since we found out she was pregnant. I was shocked when I found out, so much so that I all but accused her of sleeping around by asking if she was sure it was mine. But I never thought about leaving her to do it alone. I never thought about anything other than doing the best I could do raising a baby I wasn't expecting, but wanted with my whole heart.

"If you need some space for the night, then fine. I won't try to stop you."

"This isn't just for the night. I need my life back. You can think I'm selfish and a horrible person, God knows that's what your sister and her friends will think the moment you tell them. But I'm playing a part here that I don't want to play."

"Kris, if you don't want to be with me then I can accept that. We can work this parenting thing out and just be friends. But

don't leave her. She needs a mother. If you're upset with me, take it out on me. Scream at me, key my truck, hit me for all I care. But don't take it out on her. Please, don't do that to her. Don't leave her."

"You know why you'll be better at this then I will ever be?" She comes closer to me, dropping her bag at her feet without even glancing back to CeCe.

My eyes are burning and my brain is short circuiting trying to process what's going on.

"You're selfless. You'll put her first because you want to. I thought I could force it, but I can't keep playing house when I'm not ready for it."

PRESENT

The door swings open and CeCe comes barreling into the living room, but stops when she reaches the couch, careful not to even touch me. She's carrying a bunch of papers she must've colored while she was with my sister. I swear, at the rate she colors, draws, and paints, I'm going to have an art gallery in my apartment soon.

"How are you doing?" my mom asks when she walks in behind her.

"Fine." I pull CeCe onto the couch next to me, giving her a kiss on the cheek before she wiggles away and heads down the hall to her bedroom.

"I see Summer stopped by," she says, gesturing to the bag she left.

"She did… for a bit."

"Oh, Chase… don't do that. Not with Summer," she says with a shake of her head.

"Do what?"

"Push her away when she's trying to help you. I know you." Her eyes narrow at me suspiciously.

"I wasn't trying to push her away. She's just a lot sometimes, Ma, and I'm still not in the mood to deal with people. It doesn't feel fair to have her here and take my frustration out on her."

"She is a lot." She nods in agreement, but it's one of those sentences where you know there's more coming. "She's full of a lot of life. A lot of heart. A lot of love. She's always been that way, honey. Don't expect Summer to change that about herself, even for you."

I let her words sit with me. Let them simmer on the surface before they really sink in. She doesn't say anything else before she begins to help CeCe put some toys away and get a few things ready for Christmas Eve dinner tomorrow night.

Summer *is* a lot.

But a realization begins to settle in as I replay my time with her recently. She's a hell of a lot to handle and for the longest time I looked at that as being a burden, a challenge I didn't want to take on. I called her "trouble" a lot when she was a kid. Hell, up until a year or so ago, I think I even still threw that out every now and then.

I used to think of Summer and associate words like immature, irrational, downright annoying sometimes. But after spending so much time with her as an adult, especially lately in such close quarters, I can think of about a million different adjectives to describe Summer that are so much better than those. It makes me feel like a real asshole for having that opinion of her when I didn't even know her. Not really at least.

She's selfless. Honest. Full of life. Joyful. Free spirited and open minded. And God, she's sexy, even when she doesn't feel like she is. She has her insecurities, and even those I find irresistible as all get out.

She didn't deserve my shit mood today. And I shouldn't have been so fucking short with her since my injury. Letting Summer into my life has only made it better and I've got to get my fucking head out of my ass if I plan on keeping her in it. I know my window to do something about it is closing quickly. If there's anything I know for sure about Summer, it's how much pride she takes in being able to stand up for herself. Which is exactly what she did today. She's strong, resilient, and compassionate. She's exactly the kind of woman I'd want around for my daughter to look up to. She *is* the woman.

"You're on my shit list." Ford points his finger at me when he walks in.

I've barely left my couch in days, and I'm starting to think there will forever be an imprint of my ass on the cushion now.

"Don't have to tell me. I know."

Abby joins me on the couch, decked out in head to toe Christmas colors and leans her head on my shoulder.

"You hit her with a little mood swing, didn't you?" she says quietly as she sits next to me.

"I feel bad about it. You don't have to rub it in."

I feel Abby's head move against my shoulder. "I know you do. And I don't mean to. She said she was just going to give you some space. But it didn't sound like she was mad or anything."

"She left this morning, right?"

Abby nods, and Ford walks over with a plate of food and stands in front of me, looking at my knee.

"Not to sound like a dick, but it's a grade one sprain buddy. Rehab it properly and you'll bounce back fine."

"I plan on it."

Christmas Eve dinner goes by quickly and CeCe makes out like a bandit from my mom and her aunt and uncle. Holiday food always hits the spot and I never eat dessert like I do on Christmas. The cookies my mom makes were always my favorite growing up, that part hasn't changed in thirty-two years.

"Hey, Ab," I call out to my sister as she's packing up leftover snickerdoodle cookies for Ford. "Do you happen to have a key to Summer's apartment?"

My sister smiles at me from the kitchen as CeCe lays under my arm, watching *Frosty the Snowman*.

"Yeah, I'll leave it for you."

CHAPTER THIRTY-EIGHT

SUMMER

"In your last email you said you were helping Chase with his daughter quite a bit, how is that going?" my mom asks as we sit around the fireplace, drinking our coffee this morning.

"It's great, she's the best kid. I love being around her."

Yesterday, Abby sent me a picture of her and CeCe while they were at Chase's for dinner. I checked in with him earlier, but it was a brief conversation on my end. I'm trying to give him the space he wants and since I'm two hours away that does make it easier at the moment to not just show up at his house.

He sent me more than just one word answers which was nice and unexpected. Knowing Abby, and with Ford's recent interest in my wellbeing, I'm sure they both told him to stop being so stubborn yesterday. In all honesty, though, Chase has every right to process what he's feeling how he sees fit. It's never someone else's job to tell another person how to handle their stress or emotions. What works for me, may not work for Chase. I get that.

I push too hard sometimes, I know that. It's like I know that eventually he's going to get to a mindset where he's hopeful again and just wants to focus on recovery and I just want to get him there quicker. Skip all the wallowing parts and just jump to the part where he feels better. But that's not realistic.

"She's adorable," my mom comments. "She looks exactly like him. What's the deal with her mother? Is she just not in the picture at all?"

I never know how much Chase wants people to know about Kristen. I don't even know the specifics of the night she left, but I know it left him with a lot of trust issues. In a lot of roundabout ways, he's basically said that he couldn't convince her to stay. That their downfall was his fault. Something I wouldn't believe for a second.

"Not right now."

"And now, you're dating?"

I nod at the way my mom says it. I think for most of my life she's been worried I'd just lust after Chase forever and never give anyone else the time of day. She's half right. My feelings for Chase never wavered.

My childhood home isn't one that you'd really desire to go back and visit. I don't have any bad memories here—I rarely have any at all to be honest. My bedroom was turned into a study after I left for college and the room across the hall that used to be just a free for all where any random things would end up, is now a spare bedroom. So even when I come to visit, it's not like I'm staying in a room I grew up in. Despite the lack of nostalgia I feel being back here, it is always nice to have some time with my parents. My dad's never one for much of a conversation unless he's asking me about work, but my mom always makes an effort to keep up with my work life and personal life.

The Christmas tree glimmers with white lights and perfectly placed ornaments all organized in the most ideal way. It's nothing like the state of the tree CeCe decorated. She threw anything and everything on the tree and Chase just smiled and called it perfect. It was perfect. The day he asked me to shop for a Christmas tree with them was the first day I felt like I belonged next to him. I didn't feel nervous at the thought of someone like Chase wanting me.

I tell myself I'm confident and I'm strong because I believe I am those things. But I'm also just a girl who has been head over heels for the boy down the block all my life, who desperately wanted him to notice her. And now that he has, I'm afraid to lose it.

After my mom and I finish our very brief catch up, I take a seat outside on the porch. The cooler air makes it easier to sit outside while my parents and grandparents are inside the house. A moment of stillness and silence is actually appealing. I don't often get moments like this living downtown in the city.

"Summer, honey, your phone is ringing."

"Thanks," I say as my mom hands me the phone.

Chase's name is flashing on my screen for a FaceTime call. It takes me by surprise at the same time it makes my stomach flutter.

"A FaceTime call, how'd I get so lucky?"

"Summer!" CeCe shouts into the screen as her face comes into view.

She has on the cutest pair of reindeer ears and a sparkly green shirt as she sits on the couch. I can see Chase's shoulder next to her. He tries to get his face in the picture, but CeCe is the one holding the phone, which means I'm probably going to get motion sickness from all the moving she's doing with it.

"Hey, my girl! Merry Christmas!"

"Look!" She shoves the camera screen in front of a giant unicorn stuffed animal and starts telling me all about it. She named it Corn for unicorn, and honestly, it's fitting.

After more back and forth with CeCe, she abandons the phone on the couch and I'm left with a picture of a ceiling fan spinning before I hear Chase's voice and his face comes into view.

His soft brown eyes and five o'clock shadow. The jaw made of steel and a small piece of his hair curling just near his forehead. He looks well rested. More alert. He's the picture of perfection as I stare at him.

"Hey, Kincaid." His voice is low, almost a growl, but it makes me smile.

"Hey."

"Merry Christmas," he says, pulling the collar of his t-shirt.

"Back at ya. How are you feeling?"

"Like I owe you an apology."

My lips press together as I glide back and forth on this rocking chair.

"I'm not mad at you, Chase."

"Doesn't matter. I was a dick." He whispers the word dick as close to the phone speaker as possible, pulling a laugh from both of us. "When are you coming back?"

"I actually work tomorrow, so I might drive home tonight because I forgot to pack scrubs. Two days here with my parents has been just lovely." We both laugh again. "But there's no reason I can't come home later tonight."

"When you get back can we talk?"

My head nods up and down, giving him a smile before I hear CeCe in the background and know that our conversation is coming to an end. He smiles before he disconnects the call and I place my phone in my lap as I continue to rock back and forth.

Chase—as stubborn as he may be—is always someone who will apologize. I'd say it's a testament to his parents, raising him to be emotionally mature enough to recognize when he feels like he's hurt someone's feelings, but I feel like it goes even deeper than that. Being on the receiving end of so much pain for so long, I think it actually hurts him to think he's hurt someone else. He knows what that other side is like a little too well, and as tough as he may be he doesn't shy away from communicating. He's as honorable and thoughtful as they come.

Swaying back and forth in this chair, I'm fully convinced if I let myself sit here much longer I could easily fall asleep. So forcing myself to get up is a must.

But I just need two more minutes.

I can't believe I forgot to pack freaking scrubs.

CHAPTER THIRTY-NINE

CHASE

The afternoon drifts into evening as I sit outside on the balcony. CeCe is inside with my mom, cleaning up and making a new mess at the same time. There are a million things I want to say to Summer. So many words that barely feel adequate enough.

"Come on, Pops. Help me out, here," I whisper into the sunset and close my eyes.

I wait for something to happen. A breeze. A bird. A butterfly. Anything I can chalk up to feeling his presence and feeling his guidance. I wait another moment before I hear the sliding glass door open behind me and CeCe quietly makes her way outside. Her fingers gently touch my forearm and I scoop her up into my lap.

"Why are you sad?" She points to my face, looking at me with a set of eyes that match mine.

That match his.

"I'm not sad." I kiss her forehead as she leans against my chest. "I have you."

She smiles up at me as an idea pops in my head. I knew I wanted to do something for Summer, but the picture wasn't clear until now.

"Hey, do you think you can help me with something for Summer?"

CeCe nods her head with enthusiasm.

———

"Come on, Peanut." I grab CeCe's hand as she steps out of my truck and we take it slow as we walk through the parking garage. Walking on my knee still aches like a bitch, but the swelling has gone down quite a bit in the last few days. With every slow step I take, it's a reminder of how badly I want to take back the way I spoke to Summer the other day. I'm not that guy. I'm not someone who dismisses people I care about, and I let my frustration with myself bleed out into my interaction with her. She didn't deserve it, and even though she said she wasn't upset by it —it doesn't mean I feel good about my actions.

We walk into the lobby and I let CeCe press the elevator button so we can head up to Summer's apartment. CeCe is carrying the new purse she got for Christmas with who knows what inside, but it's filled to the brim. She needed help closing it and when I asked her to take some things out she said she needed it all.

Toddlers.

Knowing Summer is planning to come home tonight will hopefully give me an opportunity to see her before she goes into work tomorrow morning. I'm thankful my mom will be in town one more night so I can slip out this evening, no matter what time Summer gets back. Hell, I'd wait outside her apartment door if I could.

When I twist the key that Abby left me into the lock and turn the knob, CeCe bolts in ahead of me carrying her purse and one of the lighter grocery bags I brought. I know Summer doesn't keep much food stocked in her apartment since she said she isn't here for many meals, but I made sure to stop at the store on the way over and grab a few snacks I know she likes to have on hand.

Her apartment smells like coconuts when I walk in and set things down on the kitchen counter. There's a small picture in the corner with a photo of her, Abby, and Mia from the night we won the Super Bowl a few years ago. It's fucking wild to me now, looking at a picture of Summer and seeing the woman I want to be with versus just looking at it and seeing my sister's best friend. It's amazing what can change in a matter of days, moments.

"Can you put the peanut butter in the pantry?" I ask, pointing to the door to my right.

CeCe nods her head and grabs the peanut butter along with a box of Summer's favorite Oreo flavored protein bars and puts both of them in the pantry.

"Can I have cake?" CeCe questions when she pulls the single slice of red velvet cake from the bag.

"No, that's for Summer."

The fact that red velvet was the only cake flavor left was something that couldn't have happened by coincidence. It was purely something that was just meant to be. I've learned a lot of small, random things about Summer recently. Most things I was surprised I didn't know, considering I've known her all of her life. But red velvet cake is her favorite, her least favorite is carrot cake.

There are a few things I already knew though, which I think surprised her. I know she can't sleep with her hair up. It has to be down. And she can't take a test with her hair down, it has to be up. She likes peanut butter and honey on her waffles and pays for the extra storage on her cell phone even though she has no idea what the cloud is. I know she once broke her arm jumping into a canal from an old bridge in our hometown. She played on the powder puff football team for homecoming week her senior year. I remember because she very annoyingly at the time would text me while I was at college about different plays she wanted to run, asking for my opinion, even when the game didn't mean anything.

I didn't see her then. She didn't register to me as anyone other than a girl who was not shy at all about her crush on her best friend's older brother.

Carefully, I place the egg container on the bottom shelf and close the refrigerator door, taking a look around to see if there's anything on the counter that I missed. CeCe has taken a seat on the couch while I wipe down the counter after some water spilled from the vase with the flowers and I grab a small piece of paper from her drawer along with a pen to jot down a quick note.

I'm glad I checked with my sister before coming over here. I wouldn't want to invade Summer's privacy, but Abby assured me that whatever I had planned to surprise Summer with was worth it. I sure hope she's right.

Summer's dresser is jam packed with clothing when I open the bottom drawer that Abby told me I'd find her scrubs in. This woman has more clothes than anyone I think I've ever met.

I pull out a pair of the navy blue scrubs and fold them up nicely, placing them on her nightstand with a protein bar, bottle of water and two ready-to-pop bags of popcorn with extra butter before closing her bedroom door behind me after I walk out.

"Okay, I think we're ready," I mention to CeCe.

She starts pulling things from her purse and laying them on the floor.

"Wait," she squeals.

I watch as CeCe places pictures she's colored all around Summer's apartment. Many of these I haven't even seen before. She puts one on her coffee table, another on the TV stand and then I watch her place another one basically just in the middle of the floor. The last thing she pulls out of her purse is a string of beads and she reaches up, placing it next to the flowers.

"Okay." She smiles, zipping her purse and walking toward me.

I take CeCe's hand as we step out into the hallway, closing the door and locking it behind me.

Opening my eyes to everything wonderful that Summer is was a long time coming. I'm sure to everyone around me it was so fucking obvious. I just didn't see it. I didn't give her the chance. I missed it. People search their whole life looking for something I found two miles from where I grew up. Summer's always been there. And I missed it once. I'm not missing it again.

Summer's like that one random wildflower that starts to bloom surrounded by all the concrete on a sidewalk. She pops up, giving beauty and character among something that most people might deem ordinary. She took the shell of a man I was becoming and put some color back into my face. She brought joy into CeCe's life.

She's anything but ordinary.

CHAPTER FORTY

SUMMER

"This is why I don't listen to the radio," I mumble to myself as I'm pulling into my parking spot after hearing the same ten songs on repeat all over different stations.

I had a quick Christmas dinner with my family today that I actually enjoyed. After dinner, my mom seemed genuinely interested in the fact that Chase and I were a couple. She asked me about his life and football, she asked about CeCe and my role with her. Ultimately, my role is to love her. I can do that as Chase's girlfriend or even just as his friend. No matter what happens down the road between us, she'll always know that. But I left my parents tonight feeling fulfilled, for the first time in a while, actually. It made me feel excited to eventually come back.

I rub my eyes as I'm walking down the hall to my apartment. It's barely nine o'clock, but I'm completely spent. I ate so much food and then, of course, couldn't leave without taking some leftovers home with me. Holiday leftovers are just different, sometimes they're even better the next day.

When I walk into my apartment, I immediately laugh at my delusion. It smells like Chase and makes my head shake in annoyance at how quickly my mind wants to believe he's here. I inhale deeply through my nose, laughing to myself again at how insane I probably look right now thinking I smell my boyfriend's scent.

My overnight bag lands on my counter and I do a double take seeing a fresh bouquet of flowers with a note and a small bracelet next to it.

Bright red, pink, and purple flowers stick out of the vase and I walk closer, reaching for the letter. My chest instantly constricts.

> *Kincaid,*
>
> *CeCe thought you'd like these flowers best. We miss you. I miss you. Let me know when you're home safe so we can talk.*
>
> *C*

My eyes feel watery as I stare down at the note in his horrible handwriting. Next to the vase is a bracelet that CeCe must've made with the kit I bought her for Christmas. It has pink and yellow beads on it and then three letters together on the string. CSC. The tears that were pooling from his note bubble over onto the counter as I hold the bracelet in my hand and then slip it over my wrist.

I quickly tear through my purse to find my cell phone and head into my bedroom so I can text him. But something else in the living room catches my eye. A drawing of three stick people sits on the coffee table. Two girls with yellow hair and a man with brown hair. That's really all I can make out with everything else around it looking like giant blobs or just colored circles, but it's my favorite drawing ever. I bring the piece of paper to my chest and notice two more as I'm walking to my bedroom. Both are pictures of unicorns that she colored. My hands feel like they're shaking, but my breath nearly stops when I open my bedroom door and notice my nightstand.

Just in case you get home late and you're tired.

The note is on top of my scrubs for tomorrow with some snacks sitting right beside it. I don't waste another second before sending him a quick text.

Chase

CHASE
Are you home yet?

I can't believe you did all of this.

CHASE
I'm on my way.

My hands cover my face as I stand there for a moment feeling so overwhelmed. I grab the water bottle from the nightstand to bring it to the refrigerator and when I open the door and see the groceries perfectly lined up I can't help but laugh and then nearly cry again. I check my pantry and notice the labels are all forward facing on everything, too.

My head hangs in sheer disbelief that there's someone who would take the time and effort to do something like this for me.

Chase didn't have to do any of this. Hell, he probably shouldn't have, considering I'm sure he's still not supposed to be putting too much weight on his knee.

I can't help but reminisce on how I got here. How I somehow went from being this girl who could never get it right. I was somehow always too much but also not enough for people. I wasn't the girl that guys went the extra mile for. Not really, anyway. Most of the men I've dated in my adult life have gone on to find their wife after they broke up with me. Like I was a stepping stone. The fun before the commitment. I never in my wildest dreams thought I'd ever get a chance to show Chase that we could be more than friends. We got closer as we became adults. Life kept us in each other's circle and circumstances kept him as a constant person in my life. But it was always like the confidence I had with men didn't translate with Chase. Over the course of the last month I feel like that's changed. He'd never *seen* me before. He never looked my way when I walked into a room or stared just as long, if not longer, than me.

I know he doesn't want half ass people in CeCe's life. He doesn't want to have to question people's loyalty or motives or whether or not they'll let her down. I know for as long as he can he'll want to protect her from all the bad stuff that life can bring. I know that trust and reliance are things that Chase struggles with still. But there isn't a person in this world who can love either of them better than me. I'm sure of it.

There's a soft knock at my door, stirring me out of my thoughts and I nearly trip over my own two feet to open it.

When I pull the door open, Chase is standing there in a dark green t-shirt with a backward baseball hat perfectly placed on his head. His soft brown eyes are glued to me the second he sees me and his lips curve into the sweetest smile.

"Hi." His chest exhales as he stands in the hallway.

I suck in a jagged breath. "Hi."

We both stand there for a moment, stuck in a pause.

"Can I come in?" His jaw twitches as I nod my head and he pulls me gently toward his body. His arms wrap around me tightly as he steps into my apartment and I kick the door closed with my foot.

He doesn't say anything as he hugs me, and usually that would prompt me to fill the silence. Say something to encourage a conversation. But all I need right now is to be in his arms. I squeeze him tightly, pulling his chest closer to mine until I hear the rumble of his chest and he pulls away slightly.

"God, I fucking missed that."

My head tilts slightly before resting back on his chest as we still stand barely ten feet in my apartment. "Missed what?"

"Hugging you. Being hugged by you. It's…" He stops himself, shaking his head, but I urge him to go on with a wide eye.

"What?" A childlike giggle leaving my chest.

"You hugged me before I left for college like you thought you'd never see me again." He hums, pulling a piece of my hair between his fingers. "You do that. You hug people like it's the last time you'll get to hold them. Every tense feeling I have disappears when you hug me, Summer. Any stress or frustration, annoyance even. It's like you fucking squeeze every bit of it out of me." He laughs, slowly walking with his arm around me to the couch.

"Oh, the Chase hug." I pull a pillow onto my lap as we both take a seat.

"What?"

"That's how I hug *you*."

His forehead creases as he stretches an arm over the back of the couch.

"You're going to think it's silly…but—" I sigh, taking a deep breath. "You've always been so out of reach. You were always around, but never quite close enough. We saw each other almost daily. And we talked often, but it was never… I don't know, Chase. It was never enough for me. I always wanted more. A five second hug is all I could get and I took every second of it."

"God, I'm sorry." His eyes meet mine, shining like gold as he holds contact.

"There's nothing to be sorry for. Honestly. I was a kid; you didn't look at me as anything other than that. I can't fault you for that."

"Then at least let me apologize for the other day. I was a dick and didn't need to be. I was pissed about fucking up my knee. I tried to tell myself that if I would have done more recovery on it and better workouts instead of spending time with you that it wouldn't have happened. But that isn't true. You were trying to help and I—"

"I forgive you," I cut him off. I can see in his body language, in his eyes, how much this is bothering him. Even when I've made it clear that I'm not upset about it. "You know, we're not so different, Chase." I motion my fingers between us.

"Kincaid, we're the definition of opposites." He stretches his leg and lightly rubs his knee.

"On paper, sure. You're boring and I'm a delight," I joke, earning a laugh. "You think you're a burden if you ask for help. You think that as long as the people around you are happy and fulfilled, that you don't need to be. You show up looking like an absolute beast on the field, dripping in confidence, but when you're one on one you show tenderness and vulnerability. I know Kristen made you feel like her leaving was your fault. I know you feel responsible in a way that CeCe is growing up without her. You're lonely, but you don't want anyone to know. You think you've become too hardened for someone to love you. You don't want to let people in—and not just romantically, but in general—because people leave. And people die. And that part of life really sucks." My eyes well up as I try to get the last bit out. "I'm a lot like you, Chase. I've known it for years. But you just started getting to know me."

"Not noticing you sooner is one of my biggest regrets. I promise you that."

I wipe a lone tear that trickles down my cheek at the same time his hand reaches for my face, cupping my cheek in his warm hand.

"And I annoy you, I challenge you… I know that. I'm all over the place."

"Then annoy me." He moves closer. "Challenge me. Take me with you wherever you go, Kincaid. Because this—" He moves his hand down my cheek, toward my neck and onto my chest, stopping over my heart. "This is right. This is where I want to be."

His lips press against mine in a soft, slow motion and warmth spreads through my body as I take his face in my hands.

"You love my daughter," he says when he pulls away. "You've loved her since the moment she was born. All I've ever wanted is for her to be around people who love her. People who protect her. That she can rely on. People... *women* she can admire. For a long time, I thought what I was giving her was enough. But she always needed more. She needed you, Summer. And I need you. We both need you," he says, grazing his fingers over the bracelet on my wrist. "I love you, Summer Rose." His hand tucks a piece of hair behind my ear and he touches the tattoo on my skin there. "We both love you."

"You have no idea how long I've wondered if I'd ever hear you say that," I whisper with my face inches from his. "I've loved you since I was sixteen, Chase. I never stopped." He pulls me toward him, planting a kiss on my lips and breathing life back into my chest. With each sweep of his tongue I can feel my heart growing ten sizes.

When we break apart, I run my hand over his thigh, gently feathering near his knee.

"How is it?" I ask.

"Doesn't hurt enough to stop me from doing this," he says, pulling me onto his lap. My knees hit either side of the couch as I straddle him, my arms wrapping around the back of his neck.

"Who would've thought?" I laugh.

"What?"

"It just goes to show... if you're really patient and wait, like, a decade, anyone can get the chance with the love of their life."

His lips spread into a smile and his head falls onto my chest as he holds my body against his.

"By the way, my jersey you wore the other night... I'm going to need to see you in it again." He runs his tongue over his bottom lip and I shake my head, laughing against him. "And to think, I was sure I had it all figured out," he says with a shake of his head.

"Did I mess with your little playbook?" My smirk matches his.

"You kinda did, Kincaid." His hands roam down my back before he steadies them on my thighs. "Worth it," he whispers against my lips just before he kisses me.

I think somewhere between a late night kiss during a storm and finding the perfect Christmas tree, Chase started to see the good in people again. It only took him over a decade to notice me, but I'd have waited even longer if I had to.

Previous relationships made me wonder if I'd have to change things about myself to find something real and true.

Maybe I shouldn't be so loud.

Or maybe I should just keep my opinions to myself.

I could try just going with the flow instead of being so bold.

But in reality, I don't know how to be less than I am and dimming pieces of myself to fit into a mold of what someone else wants would only hurt me in the long run. I've been so conditioned to think I'm hard to love, but Chase makes it seem so easy.

EPILOGUE

CHASE

"It's really not that big of a deal, Chase." Summer's hands press on my shoulder blades as she finishes giving me a much needed massage.

"I fucking hate doing media. Coach even said he didn't want to do it, but since we haven't been featured at all in the last ten or so years, we were basically forced to participate."

Every off-season for the last couple of decades, a camera crew will choose a team to follow around for training camp leading up to the next season.

Fans love it, I'll admit it. But as a player it feels distracting.

We've been able to skirt by it on multiple occasions for numerous reasons, but this season our backs were against a wall. And even though Coach Aarons tried to have the film team go in a different direction, his swaying wasn't successful.

"Come on." Summer runs her nails in my hair as she moves off of me.

"Oh, but we were just getting to the good part," I pout, watching the strap of her nightgown hang from her shoulder.

She stares at me with those crystal blue eyes, a temptation I've been having a hard time ignoring for too many slow mornings now. Having Summer in my life and CeCe's life has been the biggest blessing we could've hoped for. She treats CeCe as her own and we make a damn good team when it comes to handling work and life balance, plus having a toddler. I know CeCe isn't her daughter, she knows that too. But damn, if she doesn't treat her like she is.

Summer doesn't miss a single gymnastics practice or meet. She makes CeCe's favorite breakfast when she's off from the hospital, takes her shopping, they even went and had her first nail appointment the other day. CeCe couldn't wait to show me her glittery pink fingers when she came barreling into the kitchen when they got home.

"We have forever for all the good parts," she whispers against my lips before pressing her lips to mine in a slow, steady kiss.

I study her body as she moves from the bed and into the bathroom. The swell of Summer's hips still sends my pulse into a frenzy and watching her move across my bedroom floor almost daily is a reminder that I never want her to leave. She leaves the bathroom door slightly ajar as she undresses to hop in the shower, but before she gets in, she looks back at me over her shoulder with a smile that has my heart aching in my chest. Praying that mornings like this, and nights like the last, never come to an end.

Summer doesn't live with CeCe and I yet, but it's something I'm hoping will change soon. This apartment has served us well. It's been our safe space, a space of comfort and familiarity. But I want more for CeCe. Maybe a big yard where she can have a swing set and kick around a soccer ball. With some space for a dog to run, because ever since my sister and Ford expanded their family by four legs when they adopted their puppy, Thor, she's been begging me for one. I knew that would happen, though. The first words from her mouth after she spent exactly three seconds with him were "*I want one.*" I made sure to thank Ford and Abby for that. They're still waiting for their time as parents to arrive and I think the addition of a dog was a long time coming and a needed companion for my sister.

As I pull myself from the bed, I can hear the faint sound of CeCe's voice coming from across the hall. Her sound machine automatically turns off at nine in the morning, making her morning solo singing sessions very clear.

Tapping my knuckle on the door, I call out to her.

"Is this a private concert for your stuffed animals or can I come in?" I ask, peeking my head in the door frame.

"Come in." She giggles, pulling her comforter from her and reaching for a stuffed animal before she hops out of bed.

"Should we make pancakes?"

Her head bobs up and down enthusiastically, and I ruffle the already tangled hair on her head as we head down the hall.

My calendar pops up when I walk into the kitchen and tap the screen, showing the team meeting I have this afternoon that will inevitably go over what is expected of us for this documentary series.

I turn the television on for CeCe and she plops herself on the couch, settling in as I pull out the ingredients to whip up some breakfast quickly. As I'm stirring the batter, Summer makes her way down the hall. She's wearing one of my old t-shirts that she made into a crop top and a pair of bright red leggings.

"Where are you going dressed so bright?" I tease.

"I was thinking we'd have a girls day at the zoo." She shifts her eyes to CeCe, who of course perks up immediately.

"Yes! Please!" She jumps from the couch and hugs Summer's leg before she runs back down the hall into her bedroom.

"You're going to melt. It's supposed to be over ninety today with a "feels like" temp of over one hundred and five."

"Lucky for me, I'm okay with getting a little sweaty." Her fingertips feather my forearm as she leans up toward me, kissing my bicep and looking down at the bowl of pancake batter filled with sprinkles and chocolate chips.

"Careful, Kincaid." I warn.

Turning to face her, I run my hand down her backside, spreading my hand out firmly against the curve of her ass.

"Not uh." She waves her index finger in my face. "Your growly warning tone isn't going to work on me right now."

"No?" My hand squeezes and she quietly gasps. "I'm betting if I checked, you'd be wet."

"Then I guess it's a good thing for me that you can't check." Her hand skims the outside of my shorts and she smirks when she feels how hard I am before she backs away.

For years Summer didn't phase me. Years went by where she could walk into a room, or touch me and nothing would happen. Nothing would ignite in me. But then we kissed and we spent time together. *Real* time. Just the two of us. And fuck if my entire world didn't flip upside down.

"Can I wear this?" CeCe shouts from down the hall before we both see her finally emerge from the hallway.

She's in a bright pink princess dress with one of her purses hanging from her shoulder and a pair of sandals in her hand before she drops them in front of her feet.

"Is that what you want to wear? Are you comfortable?" I ask.

She nods and takes a seat at the island in front of me and I glance over to Summer who is proudly staring at CeCe with a smile on her face.

"Well, I love it." Summer pulls a chair up next to her and starts taking last night's scrunchie from her hair. "Let's put this in a ponytail, eat some pancakes and go see some zebras!"

I quietly chuckle to myself as I flip the last few pancakes on the blackstone and plate them. Both of my girls are seated at the kitchen island as I inhale one myself in a handful of quick bites before heading back down the hall to get ready to gear up for another season.

A season I wasn't sure I'd be doing if you asked me at this time last year. I wasn't sure how much more time my body had in me or how I'd manage another season away from CeCe and having to find someone to watch her. But thankfully with the right recovery, my knees have felt great. Missing the playoffs last season blew, but my body fucking needed the break. And having Summer help out last year was something I didn't know I needed. *She's* someone I didn't know I needed.

"I have the stroller in my trunk," Summer says as I walk out of the bedroom and down the hall. "And I'll text you updates. Penguins, Parrots, all the birds of course." She elbows me as I walk by to grab my keys from the dish on the counter.

"Looking forward to it," I say, wrapping my arm around her chest from behind and kissing her cheek before I bend down and kiss CeCe goodbye, too.

"Have fun," I say. "Be good."

Summer's light laugh follows me as she walks with me toward the door.

"No promises on that last part," she whispers, giving me a wink as the door shuts behind me and I shake my head as I walk down the hall.

It was easy as a kid to look the other way when it came to Summer's crush on me. But when I look back now, there were so many moments I really did miss. Things that just went right over my head. I've never been someone who's had constant people in my life. Sure, my family. But when it came to friends, I made them based on my circumstances. Where I was going to school or what team I was playing for. I don't even talk to anyone from high school anymore and it's rare that I talk to any of my college buddies anymore. But Summer was always there. I know she's my sister's best friend, and regardless of what happens down the line with us, I know that'll never change between them.

But she's become mine, too.

I've known her over half my life and I only recently started *getting* to know her. I feel like I missed out on so much time with her, so many memories that could've been made. But if I would've done *one* thing differently, I wouldn't have CeCe. And even though I wish I would've noticed Summer sooner– I have to be glad that I didn't. Because having CeCe– being a dad, it's the greatest thing to ever happen to me. Summer simply amplifies my life. She makes everything I already have brighter, better. She's it– for both of us.

———

"What's got you in such a good mood this morning? I thought you also didn't want to do this bullshit?" I ask Liam.

He's already seated in the auditorium with a giant smile spread across his face, but he doesn't answer me.

Nate and Ford both walk in and take a seat in the front row next to Liam and I.

"Looks like we have an audience today," Ford says as he leans back in the seat beside me, pointing to the media staff against the far west wall.

Media is never in team meetings, but considering we're their next "team to highlight" for the off-season film, I'd expect nothing less.

"That explains why this one is so happy." I nudge Liam's arm as I glance to the double doors, seeing a familiar face about to walk in.

"I have no idea what you're talking about." Liam sits himself up straighter in the chair as our coaches all walk in, followed by a tall brunette.

"Morning, Gentlemen," Demi Sanchez says as she walks by the four of us and toward the media staff.

I'd say I'm surprised she's here, given everything she's been publicly going through over the last six months, but she's a professional. And at the end of the day she's one of the best sports reporters out there.

Her heels click against the auditorium floor as she strides past us, walking tall and confident toward her crew.

"Morning, Demi." The four of us reply almost in unison.

I glance at Liam from the corner of my eye and can already see the smirk lined on his lips.

Here we go.

ACKNOWLEDGMENTS

To the readers who have been asking for Chase and Summer's story since Line of Scrimmage was released, I hope they lived up to your expectations. Thank you for your passion and love for these characters.

To my family and friends, as always you've shown me a level of support that I can only describe as magical. There isn't a moment I'm not thankful for you.

To Ambar Cordova and Amanda Chaperon, my colleagues and friends, I'm grateful to have had you both read this story. It's an amazing thing when we work together and I'm so lucky to have your support.

My alpha/beta team: Wren, Mackenzie, Ada, Kate, Allanah, Ashley, Maggie, Tabitha, Sarah and Caitlin, you were all the fuel that kept me going with this story. There were so many times that this story had me wanting to pull my hair out, but your comments and suggestions were always so helpful and I can't thank you enough for the way you all helped shaped this story.

To the girls who have helped me behind the scenes, whether that be through taking admin tasks off my plate or helping with content creation, you have no idea how much your efforts helped me focus more on writing than trying to keep up with everything on my own. it takes a village. @cassiescreative_, @readingwithkenzz, @mads_forbooks, @be.thearchetype

Caroline at Love and Edits, thank you for being such a cheerleader always! I couldn't ask for a better editor and friend.

Format by CC, Cathryn, as always thank you for the time you take to format my work.

Mel D. Designs, Melissa, three books down, three gorgeous and fun covers for people to display on their shelves. Thank you!

Bookstagram/Booktok, you are all some of the most passionate and supportive people I have ever had the pleasure of knowing. You shout loudly for the books and authors you love and believe that there's space in this community for everyone. Readers are some of the kindest and most open minded people I've ever (virtually) met and I hope one day I get to hug each and every one of you. Thank you for letting me tell these stories. Love you big time!

COMING SOON

Follow me on social media for more information on book four of the *Out of Bounds* series—Liam and Demi's story. You can find me on Instagram and TikTok @erinmackenzie.author.

ABOUT THE AUTHOR

Erin Mackenzie is from a small town in central Florida where she lives with her husband and daughter. Her love for reading started at a young age and then was rediscovered after she became a mom and wanted something that was just for her. When she isn't reading or writing, you can find her trying out new recipes to cook or bake, spending time outdoors or rooting on her favorite sports teams.

www.ingramcontent.com/pod-product-compliance
Lightning Source LLC
Chambersburg PA
CBHW022102310726
48972CB00007B/1852